Chasing
June

SHANNEN CRANE CAMP

Published by Sugar Coated Press

ISBN: 1484191269
ISBN-13: 978-1484191262

Cover design by Jackie Hicken
Edited and typeset by Jackie Hicken

DEDICATION

I don't know why I bother putting a dedication page. We all know I write these books for The Husband.

ALSO BY SHANNEN CRANE CAMP

Finding June (The June Series #1)

The Breakup Artist

Pwned

Sugar Coated (The Sugar Coated Trilogy #1)

Chasing June

CHAPTER 1

A rusty old VW Bus can mean a lot of different things to a lot of different people. Okay . . . so maybe that's not true and a bit overly dramatic. To most people it probably just meant, "Hey, that person can't afford a car with more paint on it than rust." But to me, standing on the front lawn of the house I grew up in, it meant freedom. Or, at least, it meant I was starting a new and scary chapter in my life.

It had been more than two years since I first landed that life-changing role on *Forensic Faculty* and launched myself into the world of some of the sleaziest Hollywood people and some of the most wonderful Hollywood people. I'd been kept on the show for more than my original allotment of four episodes. Apparently the focus group liked the dynamic that Imogen Gentry brought to the show, and so I'd stayed on through my junior and senior years of high school, becoming known to everyone in my school as "That one girl on *Forensic Faculty.*"

It wasn't so bad though. Joseph helped get me through the wrath of the online *Forensic Faculty* fandom, which was full of girls who hated me simply because my character was Lukas Leighton's love interest.

I wished I could have told them to take him. I definitely didn't want anything to do with the womanizing scumbag, and it was bad enough that I had to pretend to like him on camera.

Really though, I hadn't realized when I'd first started on the show just how crazy people would get about a fictional character. What Imogen had done on each episode the night before would greatly impact how people at school treated me the next day. It was completely insane just how invested people were.

And so Joseph and I stuck to keeping our group of friends limited. At school it was us, a few theatre kids, and Xani (who, even though she could admit I belonged with Joseph, wouldn't stop herself from shamelessly flirting with him every chance she got). Out of school it was Ryan, Benjamin, and Candice who were my only real friends on set.

I looked around my front lawn at my very small— but perfect—group of friends and family who were seeing Joseph and me off for our big departure to college in Utah, and couldn't help but smile.

Ryan, Benjamin, and Candice stood in a small circle looking at Benjamin's phone and laughing about something. Well, technically Ryan and

Benjamin were laughing. Candice looked mildly repulsed by the mere fact that the two boys existed.

Joseph and my dad (who had come home from his constant work-related traveling to see me off) struggled to shove one of my bags into the back of the VW Bus. Gran stood and talked with Joseph's parents, looking misty-eyed and sentimental. I idly wondered if Gran would actually start taking acting jobs again now that she didn't have my budding career to focus on.

After a few episodes of *Forensic Faculty* aired, I started getting offers for other parts. Most of them were smaller TV roles, although a few were supporting roles in bigger movies. But as much as I had wanted to break even farther into the acting world (Gran was practically salivating over the roles I was being offered), there was always a reason I just couldn't do it. It seemed that every role I was offered had something questionable in it.

I hadn't realized that being an actress with such high moral standards was going to hurt my career as much as it seemed to be, but I gracefully turned down most of the parts I was offered, beginning to feel like the only roles that would be free of "questionable content" would be kids movies where I did a voice-over for a talking animal.

All right. That was a bit extreme again.

But I was honestly kind of grateful I couldn't find any clean roles in Hollywood, because it made the decision to go to college *much* easier. When Joseph and I both got our acceptance letters to Brigham

Young University in Provo, Utah, there wasn't a question in my mind that I was doing the right thing. Besides, maybe once I had graduated, I wouldn't keep getting offered parts in dirty teen comedies, and instead I could act in some dramas or romantic comedies. At least, that was what I told myself to help me feel better about leaving Hollywood right as my career was starting to take off.

Gran swore that if I left for school, I'd probably never be able to get my foot back in the door, but I told her I'd be okay with that, since the only door open at the moment was the kind you'd find behind the red curtain at a video rental store.

"New Girl, come here," Benjamin said, pulling me from my reflections and still using his nickname for me even though we'd been friends for more than two years now. I smiled at the three of them and walked over to watch a video of a cat holding onto a ceiling fan . . . at least, that's what it looked like from where I stood.

"Thank you for that," I said sarcastically, shaking my head at them as the video concluded.

"You're lucky you're leaving. That's the third time today he's made me watch that stupid thing," Candice stated dryly.

"I'll miss you too," I said with a big cheesy smile, pulling her into a tight hug which she didn't reciprocate at all. It was like hugging a two-by-four, though the plank of wood might have been more affectionate.

"Personal space bubble," was all she said, making

me hug her tighter for a moment before releasing her.

Candice was really my only girl friend. Xani didn't count as a girl friend because she only hung around me to get to Joseph. Candice, on the other hand, was an actual friend. We rarely hung out without Joseph, Ryan, and Benjamin, but it was nice to feel like even though I was going away to school and leaving the show, we'd still have a relationship when I got back. And of course, Joseph felt blessed to be able to actually hang out with Ryan and Benjamin, who played his favorite characters on *Forensic Faculty*.

"If you get bored with the whole school thing after a year, make sure you come right back here. We'll get Bates to bring you back on the show," Ryan said, his deep blue eyes crinkling at the edges as he smiled at me.

He was sporting a bit of a five o'clock shadow these days, making him look much more "leading man" than the "witty sidekick" his clean-shaven baby face had made him. Even though he was still on the show, he had been picking up more and more roles lately, finally getting the recognition he deserved.

"You'll be the first to know," I promised, pulling him into a hug. He held me tightly for a moment and kissed me on the cheek as we pulled apart.

"He'd better not be the first to know," I heard Gran say behind me. I turned to face my eccentric, flame-haired grandmother who smiled at me fondly, obviously resisting the urge to cry. "If anyone is hearing about your return to the great city of Hollywood, it'll be me," she said, shooting Ryan a mock threatening look.

He held up his hands in defeat. "You win, Annette," he said. "I can live with being second in line."

"Second," Candice scoffed, as if she were the obvious choice for second in line.

"Everything's all packed up and ready to go, Button," my dad said next to me. I hadn't even realized he and Joseph had managed to stuff everything into the cobalt blue and white (and rust) VW Bus.

I turned and faced my dad, trying to memorize everything about him. I already barely saw him on a regular basis because he lived in different states (and sometimes countries) most days out of the year. But now that I was going away to college, I'd see even less of him. His dark hair had gotten grayer over the years and he wore glasses now, but his brown eyes were the same as mine and our smiles were identical. I didn't think any amount of time apart would ever erase our similarities.

Joseph, who had just finished saying good bye to his parents and herd of siblings, walked over to join us and our friends.

"I love you, Dad," I said as my dad gathered me into a warm hug.

"I love you too, Button," he replied, kissing the top of my head and instantly making me feel like I was far too young to be setting out on my own.

"Keep in touch," Candice said as I hopped into the passenger seat and rolled my window down. She instantly realized that she had said something remotely friendly and corrected herself. "Ryan will probably jump off a cliff or something if you don't."

Ryan rolled his eyes at Candice.

"He didn't deny it," Benjamin pointed out.

"I'll be back for Christmas, so keep Ryan away from any high places until then," I said seriously.

"Will do, chief," Benjamin said with a salute.

Joseph and I waved our final goodbyes as his new (to him) car pulled out of the neighborhood, and then we turned to look out toward everything that lay before us.

CHAPTER 2

The drive to Utah seemed to be taking forever, and I was amazed by just how ugly five straight hours of desert could be. We had just passed through Vegas, though, and I was starting to get my hopes up that the scenery would start greening up a bit. Joseph had been to Utah a few times to visit family, but I had never gone.

I think I didn't quite believe him when he'd said it would be a long drive, and the fact that we were in an ancient VW Bus that barely made it over hills and nearly gave up and died altogether in Baker didn't really help. But Joseph loved his new car, and I had to admit that it was convenient for moving all of our stuff up to Provo.

I wore black pedal pushers and a button-up white linen collared shirt with cap sleeves. My lips were painted a deep red and I let my bare feet rest on the dashboard, my toes hitting the windshield in time to The Elected. It was perfect background driving music—mellow and catchy all at the same time.

Joseph sat in the driver's seat staring out the window with a constant grin plastered on his face. He wore old form-fitting brown pants with a white collared button-up shirt. His sleeves were rolled up to his elbows and his brown suspenders made him look like an angel right out of the '50s.

We definitely had a thing for old clothes.

Glancing over at the boy who sat next to me, I had one overwhelming feeling constantly running through my mind: I loved Joseph. A lot, actually. It had taken me long enough to figure it out, and I'd caused him quite a bit of pain for being so dim-witted, but after we had finally gotten on the same page, life was good.

Until we decided to go to the same college.

We had mutually decided to sort of "break up" after high school, because Joseph was preparing to go on an LDS mission and didn't want to date anyone seriously before he left. (And I'd say our two year relationship counted as dating seriously.) So we decided to not be "together" for the one semester he'd spend at BYU before leaving on his mission.

It was kind of weird to know that you loved someone, but were in a situation where you weren't together.

"So, this is the most depressing place I've ever seen," Joseph remarked, taking in the landscape after Vegas.

"How much longer will this torture persist?" I asked dramatically, putting the back of my hand against my forehead.

This made Joseph laugh his beautiful, musical laugh.

"We'll probably get to St. George in about two hours. It gets greener after that," he assured me, reaching over and giving my hand a squeeze.

We weren't very good at not being together, and I kind of wondered if all we had done was gotten rid of the boyfriend and girlfriend titles without actually getting rid of anything else.

"What's St. George like?" I asked, intrigued by all the new places I was about to see. Being LDS, I guess it was pretty unusual that I was visiting Utah for my first time at the age of 18. Most people probably didn't find it very exotic, but I was excited for a change of scenery.

"It's actually pretty cool," he said happily. "There's this red rock everywhere and the really super green grass makes it very . . . surreal."

I looked over at him—Joseph Cleveland, the very first friend I'd ever had—and couldn't help but smile. He looked so much more mature than he had our junior year, and it amazed me how much of a difference two years could make. It made me think about his mission and how I wouldn't see him for two whole years while he taught people in another state or country about our church. What if he changed and we didn't have anything in common when he got back?

I panicked for a moment at this thought before deciding I couldn't really imagine that happening.

After all, he was my Joseph.

His beautiful dark brown hair was still shaggy and hanging in his chocolate brown eyes as usual, and his sideways smirk made him look like he was constantly laughing at some joke no one else really got. There was no way he'd ever change enough for me to not love him.

I was sure of it.

As it turned out, Joseph was right about St. George being pretty incredible. The red and green everywhere was unlike anything I'd ever seen, but the heat was enough for me to suggest we only stop for food before continuing to trudge on to Provo. He was also right about the landscape getting greener the further away from Vegas we got, though I didn't anticipate all of the hills we had to get over. I was almost positive the car would give up before our trip was through.

"Never buy a car you can't push," Joseph would say when we reached the top of every hill. That became our little mantra every time Blue Lightning (Joseph's name for his car) sounded like it was about to explode. *Never buy a car you can't push.*

We hadn't planned the trip in a way that left us a lot of free time to get settled, since we left on the Friday right before the start of the semester. Darkness was already starting to set in when we pulled into the parking lot of our new apartment complex. I was worried about getting everything moved in before it got totally dark, but luckily we didn't have a lot of stuff to carry. Apparently student housing in Provo meant that the apartments came furnished, so I didn't have to bring couches, a bed, a desk, or any appliances. That meant most of what I brought was clothing, bedding, and school stuff.

It worked out nicely.

I was sad that we'd gotten to the apartment so late, though, since I really wanted to explore and see what Utah was like during the day. It was slightly disorienting to arrive in a new place in the dark.

Our apartment complex was just four large buildings all sitting in a row. All of the hallways to get to each individual apartment were inside, and they were sectioned off so that the boys were on one side of the building, across the breezeway, and the girls were on the opposite end. I guess that made it pretty obvious if someone was leaving an apartment later than they should be. That would be quite the walk of shame.

Joseph helped me move everything into my apartment first, and I saw, much to my horror, that my new roommate was apparently obsessed with anime. It was almost comical to see that her side of the room looked like a crayon box threw up on it, while my side was bare and waiting for me to arrive.

My two other roommates who shared the bedroom next to mine weren't home either, but I took the liberty of peeking into their room, attempting to get a read on their personalities. Try as I might, however, I couldn't really tell much from what I saw in the space. The room was messy with expensive-looking clothes thrown all over the floor and the entire place reeked of hairspray and perfume, but other than that, there weren't any telltale signs of what they might be like.

"Wow," Joseph grunted as he put my box of books down. "Looks like you're rooming with a five-year-old," he smirked, looking at the hot pink and orange bedspread on my roommate's bed.

"Yeah, I'm not sure what to do with that," I admitted, my eyes wide. I shrugged, thinking that it was all part of the college experience, meeting people who were different than you.

"Let's get *you* moved in now," I said enthusiastically, rubbing my hands together and pulling Joseph back down to the parking lot.

"I hate to break it to you, since I know you think you're pretty low maintenance," Joseph began, the glint in his eye making me nervous. "But almost everything in Blue Lightening was yours. I have two bags."

"You're such a liar," I said with narrowed eyes, opening the back of the Bus to see that, in fact, Joseph was telling the truth. "Wow . . . I am high maintenance, huh?"

"At least you're not as bad as them," Joseph whispered, nodding over my shoulder at two beautiful blonde girls who were walking into the building. Despite the fact that it was too chilly outside for my taste, the girls both wore tight skirts, short sleeved shirts, and open-toe heels.

"Wow, no kidding," I agreed, watching their retreating forms and starting to feel like a little girl next to those two models.

I continued to watch through the glass door of the building as the two girls walked down the hallway and stopped suspiciously close to my apartment door.

"Oh no," Joseph said, voicing my thoughts exactly. "June, I think they might be your roommates."

CHAPTER 3

I woke up the next morning feeling very sore from the move and very anxious about the Asian girl sleeping in the bed across from me. I hadn't even heard her come in the night before, and it seemed way too weird to suddenly wake up in a room with someone you'd never met. She snored lightly and I brought my covers up over my face so that only my brown eyes peeked out.

Somehow, I felt like an art nouveau comforter could protect me from an awkward situation.

After a moment of careful observation, it was clear to me that she was in a deep sleep and not likely to be roused by my light footsteps. I didn't exactly want to meet my new roommate with morning breath and my hair sticking up in a million directions, so I quietly slipped out of bed and into one of the two bathrooms in our apartment.

The sinks and mirror were out in our hallway, but there were two showers and two toilets in their own little rooms off to either side of the sinks, offering at least some privacy. As sad as it was to admit, it took me a whole five minutes to figure out how to adjust the shower temperature and once I did, it took another ten minutes for the water to heat up.

I showered and changed as fast as I could, feeling like I had broken into someone's house and was now trying to sneak around without getting caught. It was like being a spy, but a lot less cool. With every step I took, I hoped the flimsy floor beneath my feet wouldn't creak, and I seriously considered making up my own theme song for my attempt at sneaking around.

Our entire apartment was suspiciously quiet for ten in the morning on a Saturday. I could understand sleeping in, but it was almost too eerily quiet. I was just waiting for my new roommates to burst out of their rooms and ask me who I was and what I was doing in their apartment. The whole situation was very weird.

I hadn't seen any sign of the two blonde girls when I'd returned home the night before, and I was starting to think that maybe Joseph and I had been wrong. Maybe they weren't my roommates after all.

Keeping one eye on the door to my unknown roommate's room, I finished curling my hair in the big glossy curls Candice had finally showed me how to do and walked into the kitchen. My growling stomach informed me that I needed some sustenance, but I hadn't brought any food with me on our trip. I was planning on going grocery shopping that day, but standing there in the dark, silent kitchen, I wondered if it would be so bad to have a bowl of my roommate's cereal. After all, I could just pay them back if they really cared that much.

Opening cupboards and searching for some food, I heard the door to a room open behind me. The two blonde girls from the night before walked out, looking like they had spent hours doing their hair and makeup and were ready to breeze down the runway in their stilettos.

They must have gotten ready in their room, I surmised, since I had been using the bathroom mirror all morning and didn't see them once. They both wore their hair stick-straight (instantly making me hate my unruly curly hair) and were decked out with acrylic nails, purses that looked more like suitcases, and lots of jewelry. I wasn't really quite sure what to make of them, but my first instinct said, "*Plastic.*"

"Are you our new roommate?" the one in pink asked me. I was suddenly very aware that I had my hand on the open cupboard door.

Caught in the act.

I pulled it away quickly, smoothed the front of my red and white polka-dotted sundress and smiled the most friendly smile I could muster under my current state of "new people anxiety."

"Yeah, I'm June," I answered.

I thought about sticking out my hand for them to shake, but that seemed like it would only be appropriate if we were all eighty, so I refrained.

"Oh, you're cute," the one in blue said. She didn't say it in a mean way. It actually sounded like I was a pair of shoes on display in a store. "That's good, isn't it?" she asked the one in pink.

"No, Whitney that's not good. Competition," she responded, as if the one in blue—Whitney, apparently—was an idiot.

"Oh, right," she answered, nodding her head knowingly.

I wasn't quite sure what these two girls were talking about, so I decided to do a little detective work. I hadn't spent the last two years on *Forensic Faculty* for nothing, after all.

"Are you guys in the theatre program too?" I asked, thinking maybe they didn't want me competing for roles they were auditioning for.

"No, why?" Whitney asked.

"I meant boys," the one in pink clarified.

"Oh I already have a . . . " I paused. I didn't really have a boyfriend, but I certainly didn't plan on dating anyone here. I was going to wait for Joseph, even though he'd never ask me to in a million years because he didn't think it was fair to me. "I have a boy," I finished, sounding like a complete weirdo.

"Oh, well, that's good then," the pink one said, smiling at me finally with her very obviously bleached teeth. "I'm Tiffany," she announced before pulling a phone out of her purse and heading toward the door. Whitney quickly followed suit, waving to me over her shoulder before closing our front door.

"That was interesting," I thought aloud, scratching my head and trying to decide if these girls were my friends or not.

Just as the words left my mouth, my other roommate came bursting through the door from the back of the apartment where the bedrooms and bathrooms were. She was talking loudly on her cell phone in Japanese and didn't give me a second glance as she walked through the kitchen and out the front door.

She stopped short as she opened it, since Joseph was standing right there with his hand poised to knock. The two of them looked at each other in silence for a moment, then she instantly went back to talking on her phone and walked past him, leaving the door open.

"That was interesting," he remarked.

"That's exactly what I said!"

"Was that your roommate?" he asked, looking back over his shoulder as if she were still standing there.

"Yeah, I guess so. It was weird enough waking up in something other than my own bed for the first time, but now there are all these new people to meet and I have to try to get along with them even though we're clearly different," I said, biting my lip and trying not to let my anxiety over all of these sudden changes get the best of me.

Anxiety was what I did best.

"Well, are they nice, at least?" he asked, looking around our kitchen and living room; taking the place in properly for the first time.

"I think so. I haven't talked to . . . um . . . I don't know her name . . . "

"The Asian?" he offered helpfully.

"I'm not going to call her 'The Asian'," I said with a giggle. "Can you imagine if we called Candice 'The Asian'? She'd probably poison my makeup!"

"I don't see anything wrong with it."

"Anyway, it's like my roommates are all walking stereotypes. I've got Whitney and Tiffany who look like over-processed Plastics and the girl who is of Asian descent—"

"The Asian."

"Ugh, yes, The Asian," I sighed, giving in. "I've got her with her anime and bright colors all over the room. Am I just being a bad person, or are they really all that stereotypical?" I asked, wondering how I could be stereotyping people after having grown up somewhere as diverse as California.

"Honestly, I think you just happened to get roommates who fit into certain molds," he said, making me feel better.

"How are your roommates?" I asked.

"I don't think I'll be hanging out with them much. They're nice and all, but they've all been friends since elementary school, so they're pretty close already."

"That's what I'm here for," I said with a smile, stepping closer to Joseph and wrapping my arms around his neck.

I brought my lips to his and kissed him deeply,

amazed that I still got butterflies in my stomach every time we kissed. He put his arms around my waist but I could feel that he was hesitant, which I'd never encountered with Joseph. At least, not since we had put it all out there and finally admitted we loved each other. I could feel his heart beating against my chest and smiled at the fact that we still made each other as nervous as when we were just kissing because our script told us to.

After a few minutes, Joseph pulled away from me. He looked intently into my eyes, a troubled look on his face.

"June, we can't do that," he said, though I did notice that he still held me tightly against him, not looking like he was going to let go any time soon. I gazed back at him and this time it was my turn to look troubled.

"Can't do what?" I asked, although I had a pretty good idea of what he was talking about.

"It's different now," he said with a shake of his head. "We're out here on our own and I'm going on a mission soon. I mean, think about it. We're alone in your very own apartment right now. Alone. Everything's more serious now. It's so much easier for us to mess up now that we don't have adults constantly breathing down our necks."

I still held onto Joseph but was suddenly aware of just how intimately close we were to each other. Looking around the kitchen and darkened living room, I had to admit that he had a point.

When we were in high school we were always

either at my house with Gran constantly popping into the living room unannounced, or at Joseph's house with his billions of brothers and sisters running around. It wasn't exactly the kind of environment where we were likely to do something stupid. But standing in my new apartment, knowing that we were completely alone and likely to be for a few hours, the mood suddenly seemed heavier.

"I guess I see your point," I said sadly, still letting my fingers play with his hair. Joseph could see the slight hurt on my face and tried to explain himself.

"It's not you at all!" he added quickly. "It's me. I'm sure you wouldn't be tempted to do something stupid. I just wish I could say the same for myself."

"I wouldn't say that," I admitted sheepishly. This new living arrangement was going to present a challenge. I hadn't even considered any of this when Joseph and I had decided to live in the same apartment complex.

"Well, then, that's all the more reason to be careful," he said logically, finally releasing me so that we weren't holding each other anymore. "Besides, didn't you say you wanted to explore today? We can't very well do that in here." He was trying his best to lighten the serious mood that had just fallen over us.

"Yeah, I did say that," I answered glumly.

It was suddenly obvious to me that we were quickly running out of time to just have fun together before things got serious. Soon every decision we made could potentially impact the course of our lives in a big way.

Growing up sucked some times.

"Hey," Joseph said, lifting my chin with his finger so that our brown eyes met. "It's not going to be *that* different. We just have to be smarter about things now," he explained, smiling warmly at me and melting my heart with his sincerity.

"I know. I just kind of forgot that we're grown-ups now. When did that happen?" I asked, giving him a little laugh to show I wasn't going to act hurt anymore.

"We may be growing up, but I'd hardly call us 'grown-ups'," he said, kissing my nose lightly and giving me that winning Joseph smile. "That being said, I'll race you to Blue Lightning!"

With that, he took off out of my apartment at break-neck speed, reminding me of just why I loved him so much—and why everything was suddenly so different.

Our drive around Provo was a good way to get over the awkward situation Joseph and I had just been in, and the more I checked the city out, the more I decided it wasn't as exotic as I thought it would be. It wasn't as busy as California, and I was pretty sure the mountains were way too big and were going to fall on me at any moment, but things weren't as jarringly different as I had expected.

I did notice that people seemed to never use their signals when changing lanes and there was a severe lack of racial diversity, but it was still exciting to be somewhere I'd never been before.

"So, I think the auditions for *Tartuffe* are right away. Like, a few days after school starts," Joseph said suddenly as we were driving back to the apartment.

"Wow. I didn't realize they were that soon," I replied, slightly shocked by this revelation. "I haven't even thought about what piece I'll audition with."

"Like you have anything to worry about—you were on a successful TV show for two years. You had paparazzi following you around Rodeo Drive. You're a shoe-in! I, on the other hand, can only claim that I was in theatre in high school," he answered, sounding genuinely distraught.

He really wanted to be Tartuffe because he loved funny roles. He basically lived for them. I, on the other hand, didn't want to try out to be Elmire, who Tartuffe very clumsily tries to seduce; I preferred to try out for Dorine, the maid. She had better, witty lines, even if she wasn't a main character.

"Joseph, you'll be fine. The only reason you didn't do commercials or anything is because you didn't have Gran constantly on your back to try out for every little part available. You would have been in tons of stuff if you had tried out," I reassured him as we parked Blue Lightening.

"Thanks June," he said, though he didn't really sound like he believed me.

Joseph was always so hard on himself. He didn't realize how talented, smart, and attractive he was. He would always just assume he wasn't good enough for anything. It broke my heart to see how little he thought of himself sometimes.

We walked into my apartment once more after finally giving Joseph's car the rest it needed, and while I didn't expect my roommates to still be gone, I was shocked to see a large group of people in our kitchen. Whitney and Tiffany stood in the center of a bunch of boys I had never seen before, chatting, laughing, and flipping their beautiful straight hair.

They all turned when we walked in and I could see them subtly looking us over. We had to be kind of an odd sight in our old-fashioned clothes and with our deer-in-the-headlights look. I suddenly felt like I was five years old again, surrounded by these people who dressed so differently than I did and who looked much older than me (although in Whitney and Tiffany's case it was because of all the makeup). It reminded me of my first table read for *Forensic Faculty*. Being surrounded by beautiful celebrities had definitely humbled me quickly.

"Hey, are you going to the ward meet-and-greet thing?" Whitney asked, being the first to remember that just standing around staring at each other is a really awkward thing to do.

"What ward meet-and-greet?" I asked. I hadn't heard about anything going on, but I had also only been there for less than twenty-four hours, so it wasn't too surprising.

"There's a ward get-together tonight down at the pool," she explained, making me feel like this was an obvious thing I shouldn't have had to ask about.

"Wait, the whole ward is coming to our apartment complex?" I asked, not quite understanding how that was going to work . . . or why they'd do that in the first place. I was sure some of them had nice houses we could meet at instead of a dirty old apartment complex.

Whitney, Tiffany, and the group of boys who resembled a rugby team all looked at me for a moment as if I were completely dense.

"This apartment building *is* our ward," Tiffany said, her voice not exactly rude, but definitely not the warmest thing I had ever heard. "And this must be your boyfriend," she said, suddenly turning her dazzling white smile on Joseph.

"Friend, actually," he corrected, sending a little pang of hurt through me.

Tiffany looked him over again after hearing he was (apparently) available and I could tell she thought he was attractive. I mean, who wouldn't? He was Joseph. She didn't exactly do much to hide her approval, and I couldn't say I blamed her, although that didn't stop me from wanting to rip her perfect blonde hair out.

"Well, you guys should come with us. We're heading down right now," she said, batting her heavily mascaraed eyelashes.

As we followed at the back of the group walking toward the pool, I leaned over to Joseph and whispered in his ear, "Looks like we might have another Xani situation on our hands."

The ward party actually turned out to be a lot of fun. It was nice to go to a pool party where I wasn't the only person in a one-piece, and I was beginning to like the wholesome atmosphere around Provo.

Our ward bishop turned out to be the nicest man alive, and I felt like I just wanted to give him a hug every time he talked to me. It was a good feeling knowing that even though I was so far away from home, I still had an actual adult I could talk to if I had any problems.

Everyone in the ward seemed pretty nice, too. There were quite a few marriage-hungry girls on the prowl, but even they were nice enough once they figured out you weren't trying to encroach on their territory. The worst of the bunch seemed to be Tiffany and Whitney.

Go figure.

I had a few people ask me if I was the girl from *Forensic Faculty*, which made me feel like I might actually have something interesting and exotic to boast about after all. I may not have been as perfect looking as Tiffany, but I did have the best after school job anyone could ask for back in high school.

All in all, by the time I got back to my room that night, I was glad Joseph and I had gone to meet everyone. Being able to see familiar faces in the hallway would make me feel less alone once Joseph left on his mission in a few months.

When I entered my room, I saw my roommate

(her name was Umeko—I'd found out by checking out the mail on her desk; another point for my fake *Forensic Faculty* training) talking on the phone.

I really wanted to go to bed, but didn't know how to politely ask her to either get off the phone or leave, so I just smiled at her and walked past, pulling some cotton pajamas from my drawer and hoping she'd get the hint.

She stopped talking for a moment and looked over at me.

"You're on *Forensic Faculty*, right?" she asked in perfect English, her accent barely detectable. It threw me off for a moment when she spoke because so far I had only heard her speak in Japanese. I hadn't even been sure she knew English.

In my dumbstruck state, I simply nodded, not sure what else to say. She walked over to me, held her phone out in front of us and snapped a picture, giving me only half a second to smile once I realized what she was doing.

"Thanks," she said over her shoulder as she left the room, going back to talking on her phone.

I stared at the door for a while, trying to understand what had just happened, but was too tired to try to interpret my roommate's odd behavior. With a shrug, then, I changed and slipped into my new bed, wondering if everyone's college experience started off so weird, or if I was just one of the lucky ones.

CHAPTER 4

My first class on Monday (or I guess I should say *our* first class, since Joseph and I had decided to take all the same classes . . . not a great way to get used to being apart, by the way) wasn't until noon, so I relished the fact that I got to sleep in late.

College was the best.

I took extra time getting ready, knowing I was about to meet a lot of people I'd be around for the next four years in my Theatre Arts Studies major. I definitely wanted to make a good first impression.

For my first day, I pinned my hair up in the back and let a few small curls frame my face, pinning a thick 1920s headband to my dark curls. I wore a long pale pink top with black lace stripes and some black stretch pants. I was pretty sure the top was meant to be a dress but I couldn't really think of anyone who'd think it was long enough, except for maybe Joann Hoozer on *Forensic Faculty*, who had been my self-proclaimed nemesis. I pulled the whole thing together with black heels and a ridiculously long strand of pearls with a knot in it.

"Missing your '20s clothes from *Forensic Faculty*?" Joseph asked with a raised eyebrow as we walked to class.

"Is it that obvious?" I asked, looking down at my outfit and suddenly feeling self-conscious.

"Only to me," he replied with a perfect little smile.

Our first class was physical science, which turned out to be awful planning for our first-ever encounter with college classes. By the time we left and were heading to our intro to film class, I felt like my brain was going to explode.

"I thought they were supposed to go easy on you your first day," Joseph said, rubbing his eyes from the two hours of sitting in a semi-dark classroom staring at a projector screen.

"Apparently not," I answered, feeling as worried as he sounded.

"What did we get ourselves into?" he asked, looking dazed as we fought our way across the crowded campus. It was amazing how empty campus was while class was in session, but that ten-minute time period between classes was like Black Friday at a Wal-Mart.

Not very easy to navigate in heels, let me tell you.

"Did a boy just ride by on a unicycle?" I asked in disbelief, stopping amidst the sea of humans to look for the person who I was one hundred percent positive had escaped from the circus.

"Should I just start studying for the midterm now?" Joseph asked no one in particular, ignoring me and apparently oblivious to the chaos around him.

"I'm pretty sure I just saw people sword fighting on the lawn over there," I remarked, now fully aware that I was just talking to myself with Joseph still stressing over the only class we'd had so far. "I'm not joking," I added, trying to turn his attention to the people near the library in full Renaissance garb, fighting with wooden swords. "I swear we're in *The Twilight Zone.*"

"And then there's all the papers we'll have to write," Joseph said, his eyes wild and his brow furrowed. "And the rehearsals for *Tartuffe* . . . assuming I get a role at all," he went on.

I grabbed him by the arm, determined to stopped his anxiety-induced tirade before it could really take off.

"Joseph, listen to me," I said, spinning him around so that he faced me.

Stopping in the middle of the huge migration of students was enough to earn us some dirty looks, but I ignored them. "It's going to be fine. The first class always seems overwhelming because they tell you about all of the work you'll be doing for the whole semester in one class period. It doesn't mean you have to do all of that work at once. You're smart, you'll be fine."

He looked at me for a moment, searching my eyes for something. Finally he nodded as if coming to an agreement with me, and then turned to continue walking. I followed beside him quietly, looking over every few seconds to make sure the crazy, distracted, stressed Joseph look had vanished.

"We can do this," he said quietly, sounding more like he was giving himself a pep talk rather than confirming the fact with me.

"Yes, we can," I answered, whether he was talking to me or not.

The first few days of school went by in a blur and as Joseph and I worked on our homework together every night, I had to fight the sneaking suspicion that he was becoming a closet stresser. His pen caps were chewed down to tiny mangled nubs and his hair was constantly standing on end from the way he kept running his fingers through it.

By the time Joseph and I walked through the doors of the Harris Fine Arts Center (HFAC, for the theatre students who might as well pay rent to that building) on Thursday night for the *Tartuffe* auditions, though, the stress of classes had been usurped by the stress of being at an audition. Walking through the building, I could already feel the all-too-familiar panic rising within me at the thought of looking like an idiot in front of a casting director.

Something I had noticed about Utah in the short time I had been there was that everyone seemed to be talented. Gran insisted that in order to be a well-rounded actress, I had to be able to sing, dance, and act. She called it the triple threat, and in California I was quite the catch talent-wise because of my extensive lessons.

Joseph and I had been in every ward talent show since we were five, with him playing guitar and me singing along to "Dream a Little Dream of Me." But for some unknown reason, in Utah most people knew how to play at least one instrument and *everyone* knew how to sing. It was like going from the top of the class to finding out you've been studying from the wrong textbook the whole time.

Joseph had been acting a bit out of character all week with our roles reversed—usually I was the one who was always worried about something and Joseph would cheer me up or de-stress me. It had been kind of nice to repay the favor for the first few days of classes, but now, suddenly things looked like they were going back to normal.

He and I sat on the floor of that crazy HFAC building, which was laid out enough like a maze that I didn't even know which level I was on or where the nearest staircase was. The whole place seemed like it was built to confuse me, and that didn't help my nerves.

"June, are you okay?" Joseph asked hesitantly, his eyes trained on me. "You have your anxious face on."

"Does this building seem weird to you?" I asked, realizing I sounded like a crazy person. "It seems weird to me."

"The layout doesn't make sense, but I think we'll get used to it since most of our classes are in here," he responded carefully, gauging my reaction, I guessed.

"Why does the staircase on one side of the building go down to the bottom floor, but it doesn't on the other side? It just stops at the second level."

"Is this about the audition?" Joseph asked knowingly. "I already told you you'll do great."

"How is a crappy floor plan related to the audition?" I asked in slight disbelief.

"Because where there's stress, there's June," he answered sagely.

I didn't respond, but nodded my head in agreement. Whether I liked to admit it or not, I was kind of a constant ball of stress when it came to auditions. Or boys. Or school. Or life in general. I sort of had an anxiety problem.

"Who are you?" a girl asked, walking up and stationing herself in front of us. She had deep olive skin, green eyes, and dark brown hair curled into large ringlets that ended at her chin. She sounded French, but since I had only heard her say three words, I wasn't going to trust my horrible sense of pinpointing accents. "I've never seen you around before."

I was about to answer the question but I noticed that this girl was very pointedly looking at Joseph and not me, her berry colored lips curving into a curious smile.

"I'm Joseph and this is June," he said by way of

an answer. Apparently he wasn't aware that this girl was giving him "the look." "We just started here, so that's probably why you don't know us."

"That's wonderful! It's always nice to have new talent in the major," she said in a rich voice that sounded like it had been dipped in honey. "Who will you be auditioning for?" she asked, and I noticed that this time she included me in her question.

"I'm trying out for Dorine," I said, since Joseph had suddenly become self-conscious about the fact that he was a freshman trying out for the lead role. "And Joseph will be trying out for Tartuffe."

"Perfect," the French girl exclaimed, clapping her hands together excitedly. "I'll be trying out for Elmire. I guess we'll need to get better acquainted."

I glanced at Joseph to see if he had caught that subtle pick-up line, but he seemed to be oblivious and only slightly aware that this girl was throwing herself at him. Maybe Joseph had become immune to any flirtation that wasn't sitting on his lap after years of dealing with Xani practically nibbling his ear every chance she got.

"Definitely," he answered with a warm smile that was usually directed at me. Since when had I become so overprotective of Joseph? It wasn't like we were dating, so I wasn't really allowed to be mad at him for talking to another girl. However, that didn't mean it had to suck any less.

"How many hipsters does it take to screw in a light bulb?" a tall lanky boy with black hair, blue eyes, and pale skin said beside me suddenly. He had almost slid across the shiny concrete floor so that he was now sitting against the wall with Joseph and me. He also had an accent, but I wasn't even going to try to place it since my track record wasn't the best.

Poor Rafe.

"How many?" I asked, politely obliging his set-up while trying not to look over at Joseph and the French girl, who were now engulfed in a conversation that didn't include me.

"It's a really small number. You've probably never heard of it," he replied, his face breaking into a wide, proud grin before he shot back to his feet and made his way to another group of people—probably to tell them the same joke.

"Is it just me, or is this place really weird?" I asked Joseph, who had apparently not seen the interaction at all. He was still talking to the French girl about the play.

This had been the weirdest week ever. Not only were there a ton of changes to get used to with moving away to college, but Joseph and I hadn't really been on the same page since school started. Normally we were perfectly in synch, but lately it seemed like we were trying to use baby monitors as walkie talkies.

One-way communication is definitely never a good thing.

"Good luck on your audition, June," the French girl said as she walked away, pulling me from my little pity party.

"You too," I mumbled unhappily. This got

Joseph's attention. Finally.

"What's wrong?" he asked, genuinely not knowing what was upsetting me. When had he suddenly become so oblivious? He knew *everything* about me and could read my moods as well as if he had studied a June Laurie handbook for years, but suddenly he couldn't tell when I was bothered that another girl was flirting with him?

"Nothing, I'm just stressed about the audition," I lied. It was done quite convincingly I think. I was an actress, after all.

"June, you're going to be fine, all right?" he said once more. "It's me we have to worry about. I'm pretty sure auditioning for the lead role as a freshman is enough to get me laughed out of the major."

"You go right ahead and think that all you want, but you'll see that I was right all along when you land the role," I answered with a smile, trying not to let Joseph see the jealousy that I was trying to keep at bay as his gaze wandered over to the girl he had just been talking with.

The girl who wasn't me.

CHAPTER 5

It was absolutely no surprise to me that Joseph landed the role of Tartuffe. I was more surprised that I had gotten Dorine. For some reason, even though I had been on a pretty big TV show for two years, I still worried about my acting ability. There was also always the fact that stage acting and screen acting were definitely not the same thing. I was used to the subtle hints of emotion that a camera demanded, while the "no gestures below your shoulders" rule for stage acting was a very big, dramatic difference.

Our first rehearsal for the play was only a week after the auditions, which took Joseph and me by surprise. They were really trying to crank this thing out fast.

The cast met in a little room right off of a huge and seemingly random tunnel in the HFAC. The longer I stayed in the building, the less it seemed to make sense. The huge tunnel did remind me of the soundstage for *Forensic Faculty*, though, and I had heard a rumor that there actually was a soundstage somewhere in the building. It wouldn't surprise me one bit that they could effectively hide something as huge as that in the crazy backwards building I was already practically living in.

At our first rehearsal, the cast all sat around on the wooden floor of the little room and talked for a while, with our director encouraging us to get to know each other better so that our chemistry on stage would really show through.

Joseph and Jade (which was apparently the French girl's name) didn't waste any time seeking each other out and launching into an involved discussion on how talented Joseph must be to land such a big role after only his first audition in college. Joseph modestly tried to deflect Jade's praise, but I could tell he liked it. Of course, when I tried to tell him the exact same thing, he completely disregarded my opinion.

Not that I was bitter.

I sat a good distance away from Joseph and Jade, fuming and trying not to look like I wanted to send Jade back to France with her charming accent and perfect hair and beautiful olive skin. It was maddening, to say the least.

"Well, here's Imogen Gentry, looking like she wants to create a dead body for her friends on *Forensic Faculty* to find," said the tall lanky boy who had sat by me for all of ten seconds last week to tell me his joke. He was sitting by me once more, and I couldn't understand how he was so good at suddenly appearing by my side.

"Excuse me?" I asked, not really needing clarification of what he had said. Mostly I just needed to stall to collect myself so that I didn't look like an enraged rhino ready to charge.

"You played Imogen Gentry, didn't you?" he asked, talking a little slower now, as though I might not understand him otherwise. He raised an eyebrow at me, waiting for my response.

"Oh yeah. Sorry. I played Imogen. Are you a fan of the show?" I asked, trying to make small talk so that I could sound interested while still focusing all of my attention on Joseph and Jade. I had to keep an eye on the situation. He had told me only days ago that he didn't want a girlfriend because he was getting ready to go on his mission, but here he was, chatting up the cute French girl.

Men.

"Apparently not as much as you like *that* show," he replied, following my line of sight to where Joseph and Jade were mooning over each other. I looked over at the boy with the odd accent, slightly embarrassed that I was being so obvious with my dislike. "Is that your boyfriend or something?"

"Who, Joseph? No he's not . . . he's leaving on a mission soon, so he's not going to date anyone." I answered, trying to convince myself more than this boy.

He smirked at me, his light blue eyes reminding me of Ryan's deep blue ones for a moment and giving me a pang of homesickness. I missed the warm makeup trailer on the set of *Forensic Faculty* and the not-so-warm sound of Candice scolding Benjamin for one thing or another.

"But you want him to be your boyfriend, I gather?"

"Well . . . no . . . it's complicated. We were dating before . . . now we're taking a break," I said, sounding like I had made the whole story up and was actually just a delusional stalker.

"I'll take that as a yes," he replied, completely ignoring what I had just told him.

"But I said no."

"But you meant yes," he insisted, trying to imitate my voice.

I couldn't tell if he was being playful or just annoying. "Anyway, don't worry about Jade. She dates fifteen boys at a time, so even if she likes your boyfriend, she's not going to be serious about him."

"Speaking from experience, are we?" I asked, deciding I could give this boy a run for his money and be just as snarky as him.

"Lots and lots of experience," he replied slowly, giving me a devilish wink.

"You're disgusting," I answered with a laugh. It was actually kind of nice to have a distraction from the current Joseph situation.

"Actually, I'm Declan," he said, grabbing my hand and shaking it forcefully. "Or I guess for the purposes of the play, I'm Orgon."

"Oh, I see. So you're attached to my little

problem over there then?" I asked, nodding at Joseph and Jade.

"Which one? The one playing my wife or the one seducing my wife? They both present a problem."

"Pick one," I said, shooting him a sideways look and scrunching my nose up.

"I think I'll stick with you for now. It looks like you could use the company," he pointed out.

I looked around and saw all of the other cast members talking in groups (with the exception of Jade and Joseph, and I guess now Declan and I). Since when had I become so unapproachable? I hadn't even noticed that I was sitting alone until Declan pointed it out.

"Do you think people don't want to talk to me because of the show?" I asked, wondering if maybe they thought I'd be a snob because I had been on a popular TV show.

"Wow. We certainly think a lot of ourself, now don't we?" Declan answered with a chuckle. "Nobody talk to Imogen Gentry over here. She was on a big famous TV show," he said loudly enough for a few people to turn and look at me for a moment, including Joseph. I blushed a deep red and tried to look like I was suddenly very interested in the laces on my saddle shoes.

"Would you shut up?" I whispered harshly once the cast had turned away once more.

"You take yourself way too seriously," he said with a shake of his head. "You really need to lighten up a bit."

"Or I just need to stop associating with crazy Irish boys," I replied, finally able to pin his accent. To most people it would probably be pretty obvious that he was Irish, but like I said, I was never good with the whole accent thing.

"Crazy Irish boys are the best people to be associating with," he answered seriously. "We help uppity stressed Hollywood types relax a little."

"Well, thank you for that. Should I pay now, or will you just bill me later for your services?" I asked, now turning to face him fully so that I couldn't obsessively watch Joseph and Jade anymore. It wasn't good for my blood pressure.

"I'll get in touch with you and we can figure out payment over dinner or something," he said smoothly before standing up and walking over to another group of cast members standing nearby.

I sat silently for a moment, a small smile playing on my lips. He had just asked me out without me even realizing it.

I would have to watch out for this one.

He was good.

As rehearsals for *Tartuffe* became more and more frequent, I found myself becoming more comfortable with the cast. Granted, I still mostly talked to Joseph, Declan, and Jade (unfortunately), but I had gotten to know quite a few people in the major. Most of them thought it was really impressive that I had been in *Forensic Faculty* and didn't seem to think I was an "uppity, stressed, Hollywood type" as Declan so nicely put it on more than one occasion.

I had also started to become relatively good friends with Zoe, who played the other maid Flipote. Since most of our scenes were together, we had a lot of time to talk between run-throughs.

I learned that she was from Seattle, Washington, and had been acting since junior high. She was Hispanic, but told me that I probably knew more Spanish than her. And she was nice, which was all I really needed to know.

It felt good to have someone who was like a friend, because I felt like I was becoming more and more isolated between my roommates who didn't talk to me, a cast who sort of talked to me, and Joseph, who was too busy "rehearsing" with Jade most nights after class.

I never actually brought the whole Jade thing up to Joseph, so I couldn't *really* blame him for being oblivious. After all, I couldn't expect him to read my mind. But I still found it insulting that he was so intent on not dating anyone before his mission and there he was, spending all of his free time over at Jade's apartment. Maybe I was being overly dramatic, but that sounded like dating to me.

"So, do you not want Joseph to go on a mission?" Zoe asked one day as we were standing on the stage waiting for Mr. Winter, the director, to finish blocking something.

Her question caught me off guard and I looked around to make sure no one was listening. I didn't want people thinking I was Joseph's cast-off angry ex-girlfriend . . . even though I kind of was, on days that I let my emotions get the better of me . . . which was every day.

"I definitely want him to go," I answered as the tech guys up in the booth turned on a bright set of lights to test them out, blinding everyone on stage in the process.

"Striking," they mumbled over the speakers, warning us a little too late about the fact that we were all about to be seeing spots for weeks.

"Are you sure? Because every time you talk about his mission, it sounds more like it's a burden to you than anything," she said, rubbing her eyes and making me take a mental step back.

As much as I hated to admit it, she had a point. Any time I thought of Joseph going on a mission, I didn't think of how great the experience would be for him or how many lives he could touch. Instead, I just thought of my own impatience with getting our life together started.

What kind of a friend did that make me? Probably not a very good one.

Joseph was always happy for me when I got exciting parts, even if he wasn't included in the excitement. Why couldn't I be happy for his coming adventure?

"I do kind of do that, don't I?" I asked guiltily, glad that she had put me in my place.

One thing I liked about Zoe was that she was brutally honest, and didn't spend a whole lot of time beating around the bush. That was also the reason we weren't exactly what I'd call *close* friends. While someone like Candice was blunt and sarcastic, Zoe was a bit tactless sometimes and my self-consciousness couldn't take that brutal honesty on a constant basis. If someone looked at me wrong I thought they hated me. I was nothing if not a people pleaser.

"I don't mean to make it sound like a mission's a bad thing," I said with a deep sigh. "I'd be mad at Joseph if he didn't go when I know how important it is to him. I guess sometimes it's hard to be a grown-up and do what's best rather than what's easiest."

"Yeah, I'm not a fan of the growing up thing," Zoe agreed. "And I know Declan already told you, but don't worry about Jade. She's like that with every boy in the world. The only reason she's so focused on Joseph right now is because he's causing such a stink being a freshman in the leading role."

I thought this over for a moment, watching Mr. Winter block out a scene between Joseph and Jade. It made me feel a little better thinking that Jade wasn't as in love with Joseph as she was acting, but did Joseph know that? Was he going to get his feelings hurt when he found out she was just into him because he was the shiny new toy?

After rehearsal, Declan walked up to me purposefully, almost looking as if he weren't about to crack a joke, which was unusual.

"Hey, can you call my cell phone for me? I think I lost it," he said.

"Sure, what's your number?" I asked, pulling my own phone out.

"So forward," he said, shaking his head in mock disapproval.

I rolled my eyes in an attempt to suppress a laugh and typed in the number he gave me. Right as I pushed the send button I heard his ringtone sounding loud and clear from his front pants pocket. He pulled it out, looked up at me with a wink, then turned to walk away without a word.

He had done it again.

Already this boy had asked me on a date and gotten my phone number without me ever realizing what was going on. How did he even manage to do that? If I wasn't careful, we'd be married with two kids by next year, with me having no memory of agreeing to marry him in the first place.

"He likes you," Joseph said next to me. Apparently Jade had already left, since I couldn't sense her perfection anywhere near me.

"He does not," I answered, shaking my head even though I knew full well he did.

"It's okay, June. I can't blame him," Joseph said, nudging my shoulder with his and giving me a little smile.

If he couldn't blame him, then why wasn't he acting like Declan? Why was he so crazy over someone else?

"Maybe we can go on a double date," I joked mirthlessly, thinking that that had to be the worst idea I had ever voiced. "Or maybe not," I amended.

"Yeah, I think we should avoid that scenario for now, but I am glad that we talked about everything before we came up here so that things don't get weird," he remarked as we began walking back to our apartment complex together.

I wasn't quite sure which "talk" he was referring to, but I was pretty sure whatever we had said before wasn't making any of this less complicated. Joseph and I still weren't dating, we still liked each other, and we still had to see each other with someone else. Not that Declan and I were together by any means—on the best of days I found him mildly amusing, but mostly frustrating. This whole situation was just a big mess.

We walked in silence the rest of the way to the complex and when we reached my door, Joseph flashed me a melancholy little smile. I pulled him into a hug and he squeezed me tightly for a moment before releasing me and saying a quick, "Good night June."

I watched him walk away and sighed deeply.

Yeah. Growing up was the worst.

CHAPTER 6

On September third, I woke up to my phone buzzing noisily on my old, wooden bedside table. Umeko was already gone even though it was only seven in the morning. She had classes at normal early morning times, rather than my very lazy school schedule. I couldn't quite see the caller ID with my eyes still blurred from sleep, but I decided to pick up anyway.

"Hello?" I asked in a groggy, sleep-filled tone.

"Happy birthday June!" exclaimed a familiar voice on the other end.

"Ryan," I answered with a smile. I closed my eyes and let my head fall back on the pillow.

"I didn't really realize until you answered that you're probably still asleep . . . sorry about that," he said sheepishly. I could just imagine the "oops" face he was making as he said it. "You get to sleep in however late you want to now that you don't have an early-morning call time."

"Yeah, you know, one of the perks of being in college," I bragged happily, rubbing my eyes and trying not to yawn loudly into the phone.

"So, how is school going? No—how is life going? Have you gotten bored and changed your mind about the whole thing? I'm pretty sure Bates would take you back in a heartbeat."

I paused for a moment, not acknowledging his joke and instead wondering if he'd like the real answer to his inquiry or the "Oh, it's fine" answer. I decided he was a good enough friend for the real answer.

"School is fine. It's not as hard as I thought it would be at first. Everything else kind of sucks," I answered with a deep sigh that turned into a yawn.

"That's definitely not good. What's wrong?" he asked, obvious concern in his voice. He was such a good guy.

"It's just a bunch of dumb little things, I guess. Joseph told me he didn't want to date before his mission, but now he's pretty much dating this other girl. I don't see him unless we're in class or at rehearsal together. My roommates don't really talk to me much, and I don't know anyone else up here. I guess I just feel kind of alone right now," I said all in one breath, the frustration of keeping these feelings inside suddenly weighing on me.

I felt my throat tighten up slightly as if I were about to cry. That was dumb. Why would I cry? It wasn't *that* bad, after all. There were worse things than being alone.

Ryan paused on the other end of the phone for a moment and I wondered if my overly emotional response had caught him off guard.

I was being a bit dramatic, really. I wouldn't blame him if he just hung up.

"I know it's hard to be in a new place and start your life over from scratch, but just think of it as an opportunity to meet new people and get even more friends. Besides, even if you feel like it, you're definitely not alone. I know Benjamin and Candice and I aren't right there, but we're only a phone call away," Ryan said warmly, making me tear up even more. My throat ached with the effort of keeping tears back and I honestly couldn't figure out when I had gotten so emotional. I didn't even think this whole thing bothered me that much until now.

"June?" Ryan said, which was perfectly logical, since I had been focusing so much on trying not to cry that I hadn't answered him.

"Sorry," I answered, my voice cracking pitifully.

"June! I didn't know you were that upset," he said, obviously trying to stop the deluge of tears he thought was coming.

I pulled myself together, swallowing back all of the crazy pent up emotions I didn't even know were there so that I didn't scare him away. He was being unusually sweet, after all. I mean, Ryan had always been a nice guy, but he was usually more of the funny guy and less of the serious, "let me try to help you with your problems" guy.

"It's really not a big deal. I think it's just nice to

talk to someone about it," I confessed. "Sorry to turn your very thoughtful happy birthday call into a therapy session."

"That's what I'm here for," he answered, still sounding worried about me. I couldn't blame him. I would be worried about me too with my ridiculous outbursts of emotion. When had I become such a whiny girl?

"Thanks Ryan, that means a lot," I told him honestly.

"Well, try to hang in there just a bit longer, okay? And it's your birthday! Go do something fun."

"Just for you, I will," I lied, knowing I didn't have someone to do something fun with, but wanting to end the call on a good note. "Thank you Ryan."

Joseph didn't walk with me to school that day. He had texted me right after I got off the phone with Ryan to let me know he was feeling sick and wasn't going to class.

This didn't do anything to lift my spirits since I was not only walking to class alone, but he hadn't even remembered that it was my birthday. Now, I'm not one of those people who go all crazy diva on you if you forget my birthday, but Joseph was my best friend. How could he not remember?

Gran had called me on my way out the door, followed by a call from my dad. Even Candice had managed a half-hearted text that she claimed counted for both her and Benjamin. I should have been reasonable enough to realize that I had a lot of loving family and friends around me, but all of the nice thoughts were somehow outdone by Joseph's lack of recognition.

This was getting pathetic. I had to do something about the fact that I had taken a serious turn for the worse ever since coming to college. Yes, it had been a big change to suddenly be on my own. Yes, I had gone from having close friends all around me to having no one to talk to. And yes, Joseph was acting weird, but that didn't give me permission to start being dramatic about every aspect of my life. I just needed to calm the heck down.

The world wasn't ending.

Still, a little support could do me some good and so (against my better judgment), I called Candice.

"I already texted you," she said dryly by way of greeting.

"What?" I asked, slow on the uptake.

"About your birthday. I didn't forget."

I wasn't sure if she wanted some brownie points for this or if she was simply wondering why on earth I'd be calling her when she'd already reached her communication quota for the day.

"I know . . . I mean, thank you?" I asked, knowing that Candice was difficult enough to understand in person, which meant phone conversations were sure to be completely baffling. "I just wanted to get your opinion on something."

"Hold on, I'm putting you on speaker," she said quickly, switching over before I could protest.

"Hi June!" Ryan and Benjamin said in unison, like a classroom full of children addressing their teacher.

"Hi guys," I said back, wondering if Ryan still thought I was emotionally unstable.

"I still can't find my scissors," an unfamiliar voice said over the phone.

"I already told you Jerry, I don't have your stupid scissors. Unlike the grip department, the makeup department can keep track of its things," Candice said with an annoyed sigh.

"Just asking," the man said before apparently leaving. It was a bit difficult to tell over the phone.

"Except that we definitely do have his scissors," Benjamin said with a laugh, sounding proud of himself.

He thoroughly enjoyed giving the grip department a hard time.

"Get those out of my makeup room. I don't want contraband in here," Candice ordered.

"Fun sucker," Benjamin replied.

"Candice?" I asked, trying to reign her back in amidst the chaos that always seemed to surround the makeup room.

"Oh, sorry. You wanted to ask me something, right?" she asked, almost sounding concerned. "It's not like I have an entire makeup department to run and two overgrown children to keep under control."

"Only one overgrown child," Ryan said, sounding very close to the phone now. "Benjamin left with his scissors."

"They weren't his," Candice pointed out.

"Point taken."

"Candice, can you take me off speaker phone? It's kind of a personal matter," I said, getting closer to my class and wondering if I could really get any useful advice in the small amount of time I had to explain everything to her.

"Okay, what do you want?" she asked, her voice sounding much clearer now that she was talking into the phone.

"I have a Joseph issue."

"Don't you always?" she asked in exasperation.

"He said he doesn't want to date anyone before his mission, but now he's dating some other girl and he forgot my birthday and he's completely ignoring me most days and I don't know what to do," I said quickly, wanting to get it all out before she could cut me off with a snarky comment.

"Date someone else," she said matter-of-factly. "If he's going to be all weird and give you mixed signals, then forget about him and do whatever you want."

"But I don't want to date someone else. That's the problem," I emphasized.

"Listen June, you and Joseph were really good together, but if he's going to turn into a jerk-wad the second you go to college, then you're too good for him and you need to move on," she stated. "Now, I'd love to give you more relationship advice because that's my favorite topic of conversation, but I have to make Ryan look pretty and it's a daunting task."

"Hey!" Ryan's muffled voice chimed in.

"Okay," I answered glumly, feeling like the conversation hadn't helped at all.

"Try to stop obsessing over it. Maybe it's not what you think, okay?" she added, realizing that maybe she'd been a little harsh.

"Maybe it's not," I agreed, giving a little smile that she couldn't see. "Thanks Candice."

"Yeah," she answered before hanging up.

She was abrupt, but I loved her.

Sitting through my classes, I replayed my conversation with Candice over in my head. I could see that I was being overly dramatic about the whole thing and I resolved to lighten up a bit and not let it bug me that Joseph was being so different. He was a human being after all. He was allowed to change.

At the end of my last class my phone buzzed, indicating that I'd gotten a text.

Sorry I couldn't walk with you today. I'm in the parking lot to give you a ride home. Hope this makes up for it!

Despite my attempt at newfound self-control, the corners of my mouth pulled up into a smile as I read the text. So what if he had forgotten my birthday? He was still the same thoughtful Joseph . . . just a less available version. I could live with that, right?

The familiar rusty, cobalt blue VW Bus sat in the school parking lot by the Wilkinson Center. I yanked as hard as I could to open the passenger door and climbed in to see Joseph giving me his perfect smile.

"Sorry you had to walk to school alone," he said guiltily as he pulled out of the parking lot and began driving.

"It's not a big deal. I'd much rather walk alone and have you feel better," I said, knowing that in spite of my dramatic emotions from earlier, I was being honest. "How are you feeling?"

"Much better," he answered with a small sideways smile.

"I seriously need to get my own car," I told him with a laugh.

"Don't you dare do it, June Laurie," Joseph answered seriously. "You need to hold out until Annette gives you that beautiful old red car."

"Yeah right, she loves that thing," I told him. "The only way she'll give that to me is if I win an Oscar or something."

"I predict it'll be your wedding present," he said sagely. "Best present ever."

I tried not to read into what he had just said, wondering if he meant that it would be the best present *he* had ever gotten because he'd be marrying me, or if he was simply making a comment and I was a complete psychopath for thinking everything he said had some deep hidden meaning.

"So, are you and your girlfriend going to hang out tonight?" I asked, trying desperately to be subtle but failing miserably.

The fact that I called Jade his girlfriend instead of Jade probably revealed my less than friendly feelings toward her.

Joseph was silent for a moment and I wondered if he was mad at me or suddenly feeling guilty. He was so difficult to read sometimes.

"She's not my girlfriend, June. Not really," he said matter-of-factly. "She's dating like, five boys. Apparently that's normal here to date a bunch of guys but not call any of them your boyfriend."

"What better way to figure out which one you're going to marry?" I said sarcastically, finding that the topic of Jade was quickly turning my mood sour once more and breaking my resolve to stop being dramatic.

"Yeah, I guess," Joseph said, shooting me an odd look as if he couldn't figure out why I didn't like talking about Jade. "Are you okay, June? You seem a little upset."

I bit my lip painfully, trying to keep myself from freaking out at Joseph about how he had forgotten that it was my birthday, and how he was dating this perfect little French girl when he said he didn't want to be with anyone. But instead I just said, "I think I'm a little tired."

I could hear Joseph sigh deeply next to me but he didn't say anything, apparently aware that he wasn't going to get any other information out of me. I set my face in a grim expression and turned to look out the window to stop myself from staring at Joseph like a crazy person, only to notice that we were far from our apartment complex.

"Where are we?" I asked as we drove into the mouth of a canyon.

Joseph didn't say anything, but continued to drive on the windy canyon road until he pulled off on a small street bearing the sign "Bridal Veil Falls."

"Where are we?" I asked again, hoping that this time I'd get a response.

He drove along until we reached a little parking lot. Backing his car into one of the spots, he pushed down the brake, turned off the engine, and undid his seatbelt.

"Come back here with me," he instructed as he climbed into the large, empty back of the bus.

"Goodness Joseph Cleveland, you're so forward," I joked nervously, unsure of what was going on.

Joseph motioned for me to sit on the carpeted floor as he threw open the two back doors of the bus, revealing a river, the sheer mountainside, and a large waterfall cascading down the rock.

"It's huge!" I exclaimed, though I wasn't a very good judge of waterfall size since this was my first time seeing one. "How did you find this?" I asked, suddenly forgetting that I was mad at all.

"Not important," he said with a wave of his hand which probably meant, "Jade told me about it." "What *is* important is that you, June Laurie, thought I forgot your birthday."

"Didn't you?" I asked, suddenly feeling very bad that I'd thought so many mean things about Joseph that day.

"June, I've known you for . . . well . . . I guess now it's nineteen years today. Do you really think I'd forget your birthday?"

I looked down sheepishly. "I guess not," I mumbled, trying hard to hide my relieved smile.

"I've been getting everything ready for you all

day," he said with obvious pride, making me feel even worse by the second. "I even cooked, which almost never happens."

Joseph pulled a Tupperware container and a glass bottle of sparkling grape juice over to where he sat on the carpeted floor, I quickly scooted next to him, excited by such an unexpected surprise.

"You cooked?" I asked, quite impressed.

"Well . . . let's not get crazy. It was just spaghetti," he said modestly as he opened the steaming Tupperware container and pulled two plastic forks from the grocery bag everything had been stored in. "Only the best," he joked as he handed me a plastic fork.

"I love this," I said, looking around at the spread as I took a drink straight from the sparkling juice bottle and handed it over to him. He took a drink and then grinned at me.

"Happy birthday," he said, leaning over and kissing my cheek.

The gesture sent a very welcome tingly sensation down my body and I quickly turned my head so that our lips met. I could feel Joseph balk for a moment, obviously taken aback by my unexpected reaction, but much to my surprise, he didn't pull away.

I wasn't quite sure what had come over me. I was the last person who would be considered "forward," but this whole first month at school had felt like I was being forced to watch the person I loved be with someone else, and I was tired of it. Besides, if he and Jade weren't actually dating, why couldn't I try to win him back?

"June," he said warningly, his lips still brushing mine as he spoke. He tasted like sparkling grape juice and I smiled with my eyes closed, breathing in the moment. "I don't think this—" I silenced his protest—which I'm sure would have been very convincing—with another kiss.

This time he brought his hand up to my cheek and I thought he'd push me away, but instead he pulled me closer. I kissed him for a moment longer before pulling away and looking sadly into his eyes. Feeling this closeness made me realize just how disconnected we had been lately.

I desperately wanted to ask him why he didn't want to be with me, but decided that would just prove how pathetically in love with him I was, so instead I just rested my head silently on his shoulder and watched as the sunset turned the waterfall cascading down the mountain a deep orange, like liquid gold running over the rocks.

It was beautiful and just out of my reach.

CHAPTER 7

Joseph and I didn't talk about our kiss at all after that night. It felt so much like it did back in high school when we'd kissed during rehearsals and refused to mention it. I had to wonder if we'd progressed in our relationship at all. Now the roles were reversed, though, because I was the one secretly pining away while Joseph worked on his blossoming romance with someone else.

I had to hand it to him—now that I was in his position, I could see how well he had handled the whole thing two years ago.

I wasn't doing nearly as well.

In all honesty, I had it a lot easier. He wasn't constantly falling asleep on my shoulder or hugging me or wanting to cuddle on the couch while we watched a movie, like I had done to him. Who knew I had been so unintentionally cruel?

"So, this may come off as creepy, but I can't help but notice that you don't prance around in lingerie all the time," came an all too familiar voice beside me at rehearsal almost a month after I had my little moment with Joseph.

"Yes, Declan, that definitely comes off as creepy," I said in exasperation, upset at having my "obsessively watching Joseph and Jade" time interrupted. "Why would I prance around in lingerie?"

Declan gave an easy shrug and ruffled his shaggy black hair a few times. "That just seemed to be your outfit of choice on *Forensic Faculty*," he remarked, following my line of sight to the other side of the stage where Jade and Joseph were giggling about the scene they were blocking.

Jade's character Elmire was supposed to be letting Tartuffe seduce her to prove to her husband that he was a fake. This, of course, meant that the entire scene made me want to break one of the Victorian vases that littered the stage.

Why had we thought doing this play would be a good idea?

I felt heat rush into my cheeks, partially because Declan had caught me staring at Joseph and Jade again and partially because he was right about my costumes on the show.

"That wasn't my fault!" I said, coming to my own defense. "They made me wear that stuff. I hated it. And they weren't all that bad after I talked to the costume department after that first episode." I gave a theatrical shudder at the memory of how immodestly they'd tried to make Imogen dress.

I felt a little guilty now that it had taken me wearing a few bad costumes to finally stand up for myself, but I knew that I had definitely made up for it with all of the big movie opportunities I'd turned down because of their questionable content.

"I don't know, I thought they added a lot of depth to your character," he joked, giving me a cheeky smile.

"Shouldn't you be hiding under that table over there while Joseph seduces Jade?" I asked, making it obvious that I was trying to get rid of him.

"You mean while Tartuffe seduces Elmire?" he corrected, a glint in his eye as he watched my reaction carefully.

"It's pretty much the same thing," I answered, rolling my eyes and smiling in an attempt to not let the situation bother me.

It definitely wasn't getting easier to watch Joseph and Jade, but a small part of me just kept thinking that it was going to be okay. Nothing too serious was going to happen between them because he still had his mission to go on. That thought was helping me make light of the situation more and more as rehearsals got progressively more awkward. But we'd perform the play in only two months at the beginning of December, and then I wouldn't have to sit and watch Joseph using his quirky charm on someone that wasn't me.

"Well, just know that I'm always here if you need a shoulder to cry on or . . . you know . . . *anything* else," he said with a devilish grin.

Even as I shook my head at him in disapproval, I had to laugh. Declan was always trying to make a big point of acting like a bad boy when I knew for a fact that he was actually just an innocent little Irish boy from a small town in the middle of nowhere.

Honestly, that was the only thing that kept me from slapping him every time he made an inappropriate comment. I knew he didn't mean it.

"I'll keep that in mind, thanks" I replied in a dry monotone, giving me a small pang of homesickness for Candice and her constant sarcasm.

Declan waved goodbye as he returned to the place he *should* have been standing near Joseph and Jade. Joseph caught my eye for a moment and gave me a quick wink before returning his attention to the task at hand. I sighed deeply and tried to stop being so dramatic. It wasn't something easy for a theatre major to do.

"Oh my heck, Umeko, do you seriously not own any black clothing?" Tiffany whispered harshly to my roommate, who wore a bright pink Hello Kitty sweater as we all crouched behind a bush in the freezing cold night air.

Our Family Home Evening group had decided to play capture the flag that night, which meant I had to spend a lot more time with my roommates then I ever wanted to. Plus, Utah nights in October were probably colder than the dead of winter in California. I was pretty sure I was going to freeze to death at any moment.

I pulled my black jacket tighter around me and hoped we could just lose the stupid game quickly so I wouldn't be forced to be around Tiffany any longer than necessary.

"Don't talk to me, princess," Umeko retorted in the perfect English that always threw me off.

Every time I saw her she was speaking in Japanese and the fact that we never spoke made it easy to forget that she spoke English flawlessly.

"This is so lame," Tiffany whined. "We're going to lose to apartment 304 just because *you* guys can't be stealthy."

Losing to apartment 304 was apparently the end of the world because it was an apartment full of boys and Tiffany wanted . . . well . . . any one of them she could get really.

She wasn't picky.

It also happened to be Joseph's apartment and that meant there was no way I'd be of any help. He knew me too well. There wasn't a single thing I could do in this game that would surprise him.

"You did a really good job of being stealthy," Whitney said reassuringly, trying to console her friend.

Tiffany was wearing tight black pants, a black coat, her hair in a ponytail, thick black eyeliner, and black stiletto heels.

Yeah.

She wore stilettos to play capture the flag in a freezing cold park.

The girl was just asking for a broken ankle.

"You kind of look like a spy," I remarked over my shoulder, shivering and keeping a lookout for the boys.

"Maybe we should dangle her from a wire," Umeko joked, making us all laugh for probably the first time since we'd met each other.

Maybe they weren't so bad.

"Crud!" Tiffany exclaimed, reminding me that there was no end to her arsenal of Mormon curse words. I tried to suppress a laugh at the thought of what Candice would say about these fake swear words, but quickly refocused when I saw the object of her distress.

The boys were silently creeping through the playground nearby, looking like they thought they were Navy Seals. It was obvious that they hadn't spotted us yet, but as they inched closer, we knew it was only a matter of time.

"Umeko is the flag hidden?" Whitney asked quietly.

"I buried it under the bush," she said crisply.

The whole thing felt like a bad action movie.

"Uh, I don't think you're allowed to bury it," I pointed out.

"There's still a corner of it sticking out," she responded with a shrug, as if this cleared up the debate.

"That works for me," Tiffany said, taking charge once more. "We need to sneak around the bushes and past the playground. I'm pretty sure they hid their flag near the water fountains."

"And then we win and we can leave?" I asked hopefully, rubbing my hands together and wishing California hadn't turned me into such a baby when it came to cold weather.

"Holy crap on a cracker, June," Tiffany began.

"Holy what?" I asked.

"We're not going to win this thing with that attitude. Be a team player!"

"Sorry," I said quickly, more because I had no idea what "holy crap on a cracker" meant and because Tiffany could be a little scary sometimes.

She didn't respond, but placed her gloved finger over her glossed lips, indicating that we should shut up and follow her. We all snuck around the park, trying to be as stealthy as possible as the frost crunched under our feet. It was hard to sneak when you were so crunchy.

Even though I hadn't really become friends with my roommates, it was nice to spend an evening hanging out with girls my age rather than obsessively wondering what Joseph was doing and missing my friends back home.

As we rounded the playground I saw a red square of material, flapping in the light breeze near the drinking fountains.

"Amateurs," Tiffany said with a smile as she ran forward to grab the flag.

"Hold it right there, ladies," Joseph's roommate Scott said, wielding what appeared to be a bright pink gun.

I felt a plastic object prod me in the back and turned around quickly to see Joseph behind me, wearing the smirk of someone who had just won the lottery. He also held a plastic gun and winked at me as he forced my roommates and me to abandon our cover and walk out in the open.

"It was a valiant effort, Tiffany," Scott continued, now aiming the gun at her. "But we're just too good."

"Nice pink gun," she scoffed. I could see her cheeks turning red and I didn't think it had anything to do with the cold. She definitely had a thing for him. "Very manly."

"Any last words, girls?" Joseph asked, raising a mischievous eyebrow at me.

"Joseph," I warned, finally understanding what was about to happen. "Joseph Cleveland, don't you dare!" I shouted, just as a deluge of icy water hit me in the stomach.

"You're dead!" I yelled over the squeals of my roommates who were now being soaked by the other boys from apartment 304.

I ran straight at Joseph as Scott hoisted Tiffany over his shoulder and took a victory lap around the playground while she pounded his back with her small, perfect fists.

"Stop or I'll shoot," Joseph warned just before I tackled him, sending him sprawling on the ground as I sat on top of him and forcefully took the gun out of his hands.

"Not so tough now, are you?" I asked, soaking his

shirt mercilessly and laughing like a maniac.

"I surrender!" he shouted between bouts of laugher.

"Of course you do," I said, "Say I'm the best."

"Never," he responded dramatically. "I'll die first."

"Don't be a hero, Joseph. Just say it," I warned, placing my finger on the trigger of the water gun and aiming at his forehead.

"Do what you want, but I'll never give in. I'll never say it!"

"Your funeral," I proclaimed as I let the thick stream of water hit him right in the face for a few seconds.

He sputtered and thrashed beneath me theatrically for a moment before going limp, his eyes slowly closing.

"Tell my mother," he began, his voice sounding weak and shaky, "Tell her I fought valiantly."

And with that, he let out one final groan and closed his eyes.

"You guys are so weird," Tiffany said as she walked by, holding hands with Scott and looking like the world was a perfect place. I had to admit—she might have been right.

With Joseph joking around with me once more and roommates who I might actually get along with, things were starting to look up.

One Saturday morning in the middle of October I

woke to very loud knocking on our front door. I looked at the clock, which verified that it was indeed only eight in the morning and not a time I should be awake on a Saturday.

Umeko wasn't in her bed and I started to wonder if maybe she didn't actually live here anymore, since I hardly ever saw her. We'd had a good time together playing capture the flag, but that hadn't exactly led to us braiding each other's hair and sharing all our secrets.

I rolled over in bed and pulled my pillow over my head. There was no way the door was for me since I didn't have thousands of friends trying to come visit me all of the time, and Joseph had already told me that he had plans with Jade this weekend. I figured it was probably one of Whitney's boyfriends wondering why they didn't want to spend every waking minute together.

Or maybe it was Scott.

Tiffany and Scott had been practically inseparable since our little Family Home Evening game. It would have actually been cute to watch if it didn't remind me of how much I was lacking in the relationship department at that particular moment.

"Whitney," I yelled across the hallway, figuring I'd ask the nicer of my two plastic roommates to answer the door.

A moment later I heard the door to their room open and saw a very bedraggled Whitney stumbling through the darkened hallway. Her perfect blonde hair was actually standing on end, which I didn't think was possible. For once in her life she didn't look like a model.

"Who the fetch is knocking on our door so early?" she asked grumpily, tripping over a bump in the carpet.

"Fetch?" I repeated, not quite sure how that word fit into the sentence she'd just constructed. I really needed to brush up on my Mormon cursing.

"Ugh, California people," she replied with a grumble, making her way to the front door in shorts that I was pretty sure weren't exactly in line with the BYU honor code. Frankly, though, she could be naked and answering the door for all I cared. I just wanted to get back to sleep.

Snuggling into my warm comforter against the chill October air that came through my open window, I started to drift back to sleep when I was, once again, interrupted.

"Oh. My. Gosh." Whitney said from somewhere in the kitchen. "You're Rich and John," she squealed. "And I'm totally in my pajamas."

My head popped off the pillow for a moment, trying to make sense of what Whitney had just said. I had an idea of what her words meant, but it just didn't make sense. Rich and John were Ryan and Benjamin's characters on *Forensic Faculty*, but they definitely couldn't be here.

"June, you're so totally dead," she shouted down the hall as she went running into her room, slamming the door behind her.

"Why?" I yelled back to her, still trying to

understand what was going on.

"This is cozy," Candice said, suddenly appearing in my doorway with Ryan and Benjamin in tow. At least, I assumed it was Candice. I couldn't really see her underneath the layers of scarves and coats she had on, but all of the layers in the world couldn't cover up her signature sarcasm.

I sat straight up in bed, my dark hair sticking to my face like a mad woman. A wide and unbelieving grin broke across my mouth as I tried to reassure myself I wasn't still asleep.

"New Girl, this place is the size of the makeup trailer. How do you live here? And with three other people to boot?" Benjamin said, surveying my room disapprovingly. "And it looks like your roommate is a kindergartener."

"Glad to see you wear more to bed than Imogen," Ryan remarked with a laugh, and I was suddenly self-conscious of the yoga pants I always wore to bed and my baggy v-neck T-shirt that was hanging loosely off my shoulder.

"Ryan kept saying we should call first to make sure you were decent, but I told him that would ruin the surprise," Candice said proudly.

"This is honestly the best surprise ever," I exclaimed, jumping out of bed and running over to my three friends to give them each a hug. "What are you doing here?"

"Freezing to death, mostly," Candice said dryly, pulling some of her scarves off. "What's wrong with this state? And why do you have your window open?

You're ridiculous!"

"You get used to it," I said with a shrug. "Apparently this is nothing. Soon there's supposed to be actual snow on the ground. Not the kind we make in the studio."

"I'll believe it when I see it," Benjamin said.

"How long will you guys be here?" I asked, not wanting them to leave now that I finally had people to talk to.

"Just a few days," Ryan said with a frown. "We filmed an episode out in Monument Valley, which looks like Mars, by the way, and we just kind of figured that since we were so close, we might as well come and visit our little college student. Get a taste of the wild college life."

"You've come to the wrong place," I replied with a laugh. "We're not exactly a wild bunch here."

"Yeah, everyone's really polite," Candice said suspiciously. "It's starting to freak me out."

"I'll try to be extra rude to you to make you feel more at home," I promised, giving her another hug which she tried to wriggle away from.

"See, you say that, but I know you won't follow through," she replied, obviously disappointed that I wouldn't be rude to her.

"Well, let's get on it, New Girl! We don't have all day. You need to give us the full Utah experience," Benjamin said snapping his fingers to hurry me up.

"Okay, you guys go wait in the kitchen and I'll get dressed. Strictly speaking, you're not even supposed to be in my room right now, boys. Honor Code," I said, waving my finger at them accusingly.

"This place is so backward," I heard Benjamin whisper to Ryan as they left my room.

"Just think of it like Catholic school," he replied.

I smiled and shook my head. It was good to have my friends back.

CHAPTER 8

I was only partially surprised by the fact that Whitney and Tiffany had gotten ready faster than me and made their way out to the kitchen to harass Ryan and Benjamin. Determined to rescue the boys, I tried to quickly pin up my wild brown curls so they were in a pile at the back of my head. A few loose curls escaped and framed my face as they always did, but I ignored them, pulling on my black skinny jeans and grey tunic top before I grabbed my black jacket on my way out the door.

"So, how long will you boys be here?" I heard Tiffany ask as I walked into the kitchen to find a very awkward scene.

Tiffany was practically in Ryan's lap (so much for Scott), which gave me a small twinge of unexpected jealousy, while Whitney was staring at Benjamin with what she must have thought was a seductive grin. I just thought she looked like she needed to go to the bathroom.

Candice sat at the opposite end of the table staring at Benjamin and looking surprisingly mad. I would have thought Candice would be filming this experience to use against the boys later on, but instead she looked as though she wanted to murder Whitney.

"They're leaving right now, actually," I said abruptly, which wasn't technically lying. "We have to go. Sorry girls," I apologized, not really feeling very sorry.

Tiffany would thank me later when she and Scott got married. I could imagine the speech now, "Thank you to June Laurie—that girl I sort of knew for one semester who didn't let me fall for the Hollywood guy so I could see my true love Scott, standing right in front of me."

As we stood to leave, I saw Tiffany give Ryan the "call me" gesture and I tried not to glare at her. That girl seriously needed to calm down with her boy drama. Not that I was really one to talk about boy drama, but at least my boy drama was almost justified, since it was only one boy and not every single boy I'd ever met.

"Your roommates are . . . friendly," Ryan said as we walked through the parking lot to a car I assumed they had rented. He cleared his throat uncomfortably and I couldn't help but laugh.

"Mr. Big Shot Hollywood Star can't handle being flirted with by a little Mormon girl?" I teased.

"How did you know Ryan felt that way about you?" Benjamin asked in mock shock. Ryan's cheeks turned an adorable shade of red as he rolled his eyes at his friend.

"June, I'm not a big fan of your roommates," Candice finally said.

She hopped into the front seat of the black SUV they'd rented, which I thought was odd, since I just assumed she'd sit in the back with me like she always did. The entire car was drenched with the smell of coffee and even though it wasn't a smell I was particularly fond of, it did pull me right back to our many tired mornings in the makeup trailer.

"I thought they were nice," Benjamin remarked with a sideways smirk at Candice.

"You would," she muttered darkly as she stared out the side window.

"Don't worry, they're like that with everyone," I assured her.

"Ouch, June," Ryan said with a playful grin in my direction.

"Keep it under control back there. I need directions," Benjamin instructed from the driver's seat, taking charge.

"Okay, well how long do we have for this little sightseeing expedition?" I asked.

"I need to be back by six," Candice said quickly. "I have a conference call with the costume department tonight."

"Yeah, I need to be back by six too," Benjamin added. "I've got some phone calls I need to make."

Ryan looked at me and raised his eyebrows, but I couldn't figure out what he was trying to tell me.

"All right," I said slowly, wondering what was going on. "Maybe we should stick around Utah Valley for today so we make sure you guys get back for your very important phone calls."

We ended up pretty far from Utah Valley for most of the day, as it turned out. I ran out of things to show them in Provo, so we drove through Provo Canyon and spent the day in Heber, exploring the cute little town. I had actually never been there before and it was fun to see it for the first time with my friends.

The expedition made me realize just how little of Utah I'd seen since we'd moved there. I really needed to work on getting out more, although not having a car of my own had a lot to do with my recent status as a bitter shut-in. If only Gran would give me her old red car . . . or I could buy the cute green moped I had seen for sale. There were options.

After our little adventure, we got back to the hotel right behind my apartment complex off of University Avenue. We arrived just before six, which turned out to be a good thing since Candice and Benjamin were serious about getting back on time. They both hurried out of the car and left the keys with Ryan as they disappeared through the hotel lobby.

"Okay, so what was all of that about?" I asked Ryan as he got on the freeway heading to Salt Lake

City so we could continue our sightseeing.

"They're together, June! I swear they are. They haven't said anything, but it's been weird like this for the past two months," Ryan said excitedly, obviously as happy to be talking to someone as I was. "Every time I try to hint to them that I know, they get all cryptic and stop talking about it."

"Some people are weird about that kind of stuff," I said with a shrug.

"It's the worst when Candice is doing my makeup for the show and I see them staring at each other in the mirror and smiling. It's kind of creepy."

"Yeah, I think seeing Candice smile would be a little . . . unsettling," I replied with a laugh.

"You have no idea," Ryan said with a shake of his head. "So where in Salt Lake City are we going?"

"I heard there's this outdoor ice skating rink there, right in the middle of the city. I thought it might be fun," I told him. Ryan looked over at me and smiled.

"I like that plan."

We only got lost a few times trying to find the outdoor ice skating rink, but once we finally made it there, we had our skates on and were out on the ice in no time. I was a little more graceful than Ryan as we attempted to keep from falling on our butts, but that wasn't saying much since it took all of my concentration to stay on my feet. He grabbed my hand to steady himself on one particularly bad fall and ended up bringing me down with him. I threw my head back and laughed as other skaters swerved to avoid running over us.

"I'm totally trying out for the Olympics," Ryan said seriously.

"You're so bad at this," I laughed, trying to get up without slipping again.

Once I was upright, Ryan kept hold of my hand as we skated and eventually gained some semblance of confidence on the ice. We skated in silence for a while before he finally spoke, sounding as if he was giving himself a pep talk to get out what he said next.

"So, I had some Mormon missionaries come over to my apartment," he said with a quick glance in my direction.

I looked over at him in surprise, now feeling like I was the one who was a little unsteady on my feet. I had only ever really talked to Ryan about the church a few times, and even then it wasn't a very in-depth discussion. He hadn't ever seemed interested, and I hadn't wanted to be pushy.

"Oh?" I said noncommittally, not wanting to scare him off of the topic.

"This is probably going to sound really cheesy, but after you left I really noticed how much warmth is always surrounding you, and I kind of wondered if it might have something to do with your religion," he explained. I had to try to hide a happy smile at his words.

"That's not cheesy at all," I assured him. "So, what did you think?"

"Some of the stuff they said is a little too hard for

me to believe," he admitted, though it wasn't in a way that put me on the defense. "But I liked their overall message. I like the way they live and how they treat others." He gave a little shrug and I could tell he was uncomfortable talking about religion so openly.

"That's really cool that you tried to find out more on your own rather than judging us Mormons based on what you've heard from other people," I said, giving his hand a little squeeze. He looked over at me with a warm smile that made my stomach do a little unexpected flip.

"There's something special about you and I wanted to figure out what it is," he admitted, still smiling at me.

"I want to show you something," I said suddenly, feeling like this would be the perfect time to bring him to Temple Square and show him just how beautiful and peaceful it was there.

We brought our skates back and hopped on the city light rail system to travel over to the temple in relative silence. I was hoping Ryan wasn't regretting telling me about his interest in the church. I didn't want him to think that because he'd said something I would suddenly become pushy about it. Mostly I just wanted him to feel the peace in Temple Square. I thought he'd like it.

As we walked through the front gates, he took my hand. I didn't pull away like I would have a few months ago. Instead, I pulled him closer to my side and linked my arm through his so that we were arm in arm as we walked through the crisp October air.

"Isn't it beautiful?" I asked as we stood in front of the Salt Lake Temple, which was lit up like a nightlight in the chilly darkness.

"It looks like it's glowing," he replied, staring up at the striking building that reminded me of a castle.

"I've only been up here once since I moved to Utah, but I just love it."

"The whole place is calm," he said in wonder. "Even in the middle of the city." He sounded impressed and I smiled over at him.

"That's why I love it. All of it. The temple, the church, my religion. It makes me feel calm in the middle of all the craziness," I said.

We began to walk once more, skipping the light rail ride this time for a lazy amble down the street.

"I admire that you turned down so many movie parts just to stand up for what you believe in," he said as we walked back toward the car.

"You might be one of the only ones," I admitted. "Most people think I'm committing career suicide."

"I don't think I'm the only one. Maybe a lot of people will think you're being crazy, but some people notice more than you assume they do."

"Like you?" I asked.

"Exactly."

We walked in silence for a little while before Ryan began speaking once more.

"I've been in negotiations for a movie role," he said suddenly, with an unexpected change of topic.

"What kind of movie? What's your role?" I asked,

interested to see if Ryan was finally starting to get the leading roles he deserved.

"It's kind of a Jane Austen knock-off, but told from the man's perspective," he said, instantly grabbing my interest.

"Are you going to wear those breeches with the high boots?" I asked, giving him a wicked grin.

"Oh, so that's what does it for you?" he said with a laugh. "And all this time I've been trying to dress more 1950s when I should have been going 1800s."

"It's not just me," I said seriously, "Ask almost any woman and they'll tell you, it's all about the breeches and high boots."

"So when guys want girls to look sexy they wear less clothing, but when girls want guys to look sexy they put more on?" he asked, crinkling his nose up at my apparently backwards logic as we got into the car and headed back toward Provo.

"That's the trick," I told him with a playful wink.

"Well, in that case, yes I will be wearing breeches and high boots."

"If only I were there to see it," I said wistfully. Half joking.

"Well, here's the thing . . . " he began but soon stopped, as if trying to figure out how to voice his thoughts. "There's this part in the film for a female lead. They've been talking about a few different actresses and your name came up."

I looked over at Ryan, my breath catching in my throat as he spoke. I had turned down so many roles before I left for school but the truth was, I was itching to get back into screen acting. I tried not to get too excited and nodded for him to go on.

"I told the director I'd really like to work with you on this film, but that he'd have to make a few changes to the script. There was one scene that was a bit . . . racy," he remarked.

"In a Regency Era film?" I asked, trying to imagine how racy a period piece could possibly be.

The most Jane Austen characters ever did was look longingly at one another. I guess those looks could be pretty smoldering.

"Well, it's not exactly historically accurate," he explained. "Think *Marie Antoinette*."

"Oh," I said emphatically with a sudden understanding. "And you asked them to take it out of the script for me?" I asked, touched by his thoughtfulness.

It wasn't like he was a hugely famous actor like Lukas Leighton. To make a request like that on his first big role was pretty risky, but he'd done it so that I could have a shot at the female lead. He did it for me.

"I knew you wouldn't even audition if they kept that scene in, and they agreed that, if they decided to go with you for the part, they'd take it out."

I turned this thought over in my head for a moment. It sounded like they'd be having auditions soon, which meant they'd be filming the movie during winter semester. I didn't feel like it would be smart to take a semester off when I'd just started college, but at the same time, this was the exact reason I'd left for school rather than staying in Hollywood—I couldn't find any roles that fit my standards, but here was a perfect role, just waiting for me to audition for it.

"Are they definitely going to contact me about it? I just want to know how excited I should let myself be right now," I said with a grin so big that it hurt my face.

"Wait, so you'd actually want to do it?" Ryan asked, looking over happily. "I thought maybe because of school you'd say no."

"If they're willing to give me the part, I'll definitely do it," I answered with a little giddy laugh. It was nice to feel like all of the roles I'd turned down maybe hadn't been for nothing.

"I'll let them know," he said, turning his attention back to the road as he exited the freeway toward my apartment. "I'm so glad you want to do it. I really didn't think you would."

"Trust me, I still love acting more than ever. I just turned down those other movies because they wanted me to be something I'm not."

"You'll love this script. It's really clever how they took a typical Regency movie and implemented some modern touches," Ryan said, excitement lining his words.

He pulled into the parking lot of my apartment complex and quickly ran around to my side of the SUV to open my door. Always the gentleman. Even Hollywood couldn't beat that out of him.

We walked to my front door quietly, my head full

of the possibility that I'd actually get to be in a big movie. I hadn't realized just how much I missed Hollywood until the possibility of going back was standing in front of me.

I definitely wasn't expecting to be presented with a possible movie role when Ryan had shown up at my apartment that morning, but that was the best surprise I could have ever asked for.

I turned to thank him for the thousandth time since he'd mentioned the role, but was instantly silenced by the look in his eye. He was intently staring at me. I wasn't quite computing what was happening until he leaned in to me, ever so slowly.

His kiss was restrained, as if he wanted it to be much deeper but was using his willpower to keep it toned down. I was much more shocked than I guess I should have been, given the fact that Ryan and I had always joked about liking each other. Still, it caught me completely off guard.

Still timid, he began pulling away and looked into my eyes, trying to gauge whether or not he'd made a big mistake or possibly to see if I was mad at him. He was hard to read.

"You have no idea how long I've wanted to do that," he admitted sheepishly, sounding scared that I'd blow up at him for wanting to kiss me.

As I looked at him, I wished that I did want to blow up and yell and scream about how I loved Joseph and how dare he kiss me . . . but all I did was stare in silence. His deep blue eyes began to fill with worry as my silence stretched on thanks to the internal debate brewing within me.

Ryan was sweet. He was kind, caring, and a complete gentleman, and he had never been anything but nice to me. But I loved Joseph. Didn't I?

"I'm really sorry June," he said quickly, deciding that maybe I hadn't wanted to kiss him back.

The tricky thing was, as I stood there in dumbfounded silence, that I really did want to kiss him back. And that made me feel like an awful person. How could I say I loved Joseph when I really wanted Ryan to kiss me again? I knew Joseph and I were no longer in a relationship, but people couldn't just go from loving one person to suddenly having feelings for another, could they?

I mean, unless they were Whitney and Tiffany. Which I definitely was *not*.

"Should I go?" he asked quietly, disappointment evident as he continued to study my face. "I know that was really stupid of me. I just thought, maybe with you and Joseph not being together anymore that you might . . . I don't know . . . " his words trailed off, his voice growing small as I continued to watch him try to apologize for doing something I had wanted him to do in the first place.

I know the fact that I wanted nothing more than to grab Ryan by his hair and pull him into another kiss made me a despicable person, but my eyes just couldn't help trailing down to his lips that had been pressed against mine only moments before.

I'm sure I also should have been concerned by the

fact that I was pinned up against the door with Ryan in such close proximity while in the apartment complex hallway, but I was naturally distracted by what had just happened. Besides, it wasn't like there were a bunch of paparazzi to worry about in Provo, Utah.

As I continued to stare at him, trying desperately to form a sentence from the slush of confusion in my brain, I felt the doorknob turn against my back—my first clue that something bad was about to happen.

Ryan and I toppled over onto the floor of my kitchen as Umeko opened the front door. She looked down at us for a whole half a second before leaving the apartment and closing the door behind her, engulfing us in darkness. I was just lucky she hadn't recognized Ryan or she would have snapped a picture and posted it all over the Internet just waiting for Gran and Joseph to see.

That would have been a fun one to explain.

We lay on the ground in silence for a moment, me still trying to figure out how I felt about everything that had just happened when a wide smile spread over Ryan's previously worried face. Seeing his smile, I couldn't help but return it, beginning to laugh at how bad the situation would have looked to an outsider.

I slapped my hand over Ryan's mouth to try to quiet his soft laughter so he wouldn't wake up Whitney and Tiffany, but found that most of the noise was coming from me.

"Shhhh," he said, trying to quiet me even as he was shaking with the effort of being silent.

"She just walked away like nothing weird happened," I whispered between giggles as I sat up on the linoleum floor.

Ryan sat up with me and took a few deep breaths to stop his amusement and regain his composure. He tucked a stray curl behind my ear, gazing at me fondly.

"I've missed you June," he said.

"I've missed you too," I whispered back.

"I'm really sorry if that wasn't okay what I did. Please just tell me and I won't do it again," Ryan quickly added.

I was silent again for a moment, studying his kind face and trying to make sense of the feelings I was attempting to suppress.

"It's okay that you kissed me," I said, partly because I didn't want to make him feel bad for doing it, and partly because I had really wanted him to.

"I'm guessing I'm not supposed to be in your apartment at night?" he asked, glancing around at the dark, empty space.

"Not after midnight," I affirmed, hoping he didn't think I was making that rule up to get rid of him.

"Well, I guess I'd better go," he decided.

"Sorry."

And I was sorry. Sorry that I couldn't just tell him that he didn't need to feel bad about anything. And sorry that I wasn't brave enough to kiss him right then and there just to prove how okay I was with it.

"What time should we come over tomorrow?" he asked, his voice barely above a whisper, trying to talk about anything but the kiss we had just shared. It was weird how much you noticed the things that *weren't* being said in a conversation.

"I get out of church at noon," I told him.

"I'll let the troops know."

He smiled slowly and got to his feet, helping me up as well. He opened the front door, and the light streaming in from the outside hallway was almost blinding after our having sat in the darkness for so long.

Before Ryan left, he turned back to me, his cheeks slightly red from embarrassment and said, "Don't tell Benjamin and Candice."

CHAPTER 9

Joseph was a little upset with me when he found out that Ryan, Benjamin, and Candice were in town and I hadn't told him, but I used the defense that he was with Jade, which silenced his anger pretty fast. He came over to my apartment right after church, looking like a puppy waiting for its owner to come home.

"I didn't think you'd be so excited to see them," I remarked with a bobby pin in my mouth, trying to tame my curls as usual.

"Of course I'm excited to see them!" he exclaimed with an adorable smile that made his eyes crinkle in the corners. "You may be the big shot celebrity who works with them, but they're my friends too," he said playfully.

"Actually, at BYU it's *you* who's the big shot celebrity, Mr. Tartuffe," I shot back with a smile.

I tried not to think about Ryan's kiss from the night before, but the very thought of the kiss, combined with the possibility that I might land a big movie role, were the only things that had been running through my mind all day.

I hadn't told Joseph about the film yet, mostly because nothing was set in stone. And I definitely hadn't told him about the kiss. That was a topic I wasn't anxious to discuss with him at great length.

As Joseph sat at my kitchen table flipping through a very girly fashion magazine that I was sure he wasn't at all interested in, I got a text.

"Oh, it's from Candice!" I told Joseph, thinking she'd let me know how close they were to getting there.

What did you do to Ryan yesterday? He hasn't stopped grinning like an idiot all morning!

"What does it say?" Joseph asked, obviously excited to see his friends.

I closed the phone quickly, hoping Joseph hadn't seen the text. I hadn't even thought about all of us being together today. It wasn't like Ryan and I were suddenly dating just because we had kissed . . . but the dynamic between us had definitely changed, and even though Joseph and I were far from together, I still didn't want him to know. Somehow it almost felt like cheating.

"Um . . . they should be close . . . is what she said," I lied hurriedly—and quite badly, I might add.

Some actress I was.

"That's good, isn't it?" Joseph asked, obviously a bit surprised by my reaction.

"Oh yeah. It's great," I said through gritted teeth,

trying to look like I was smiling. "Yay!"

Joseph gave me an odd look but was still smiling from his excitement at seeing our friends. He had always loved Ryan and Benjamin's characters on the show, and once we had all started hanging out, it was like a dream come true for him. He loved how they constantly bounced jokes off of each other and sometimes I got the feeling that he was jealous they were such good friends.

He didn't really have a close guy friend until they came along. Just me. I think he was starting to crave guy company.

I was about to text Candice back and tell her nothing had happened when a knock came at the door and my stomach sank. I stared at my front door with wide eyes, not making any move to open it.

"Uh . . . June?" Joseph said in a puzzled voice. "Do you want me to get it?"

"No!" I said a bit too fast, not sure why I thought it was such a big deal if he answered the door or not. He was with Jade and he didn't mind me knowing it. I wasn't even *with* Ryan, so what was the problem? "I'll get it," I quickly amended with a smile that came way too late to be natural.

When I opened the door I was met with a five-foot-nothing Asian pillar of suspicion. Candice gave me a searching look before making her way into the kitchen. I stepped back and let the other two boys in. Benjamin looked as if he suspected something but was making a point of not looking at me, probably to make things intentionally awkward.

Next to enter the apartment was Ryan, who wore a tentative grin that faded when he saw Joseph sitting at the kitchen table. The instantaneous change in his face would have been funny, if it wasn't such an awkward situation for me.

"Joseph," Ryan said, sounding like he was slightly confused at being caught stealing cookies from the cookie jar.

I was the cookie in this scenario.

"I can't believe you guys didn't tell me you were here!" Joseph said with a laugh as he stood up and gave them each a hug, oblivious to the extreme discomfort Ryan was feeling at the moment.

Ryan shot me a quick look as if asking me what he should do. I hadn't realized how intimidated he apparently was by Joseph. It must have been pretty bad if he couldn't fall back on his sense of humor. It was the one thing he always defaulted to.

We all stood in the tiny kitchen in silence, Candice searching my face for a tell of what had happened last night, Benjamin looking pointedly at the floor with a grin, Ryan tapping his thumb against his pants anxiously, me taking a breath to start a sentence that didn't seem to be coming, and Joseph looking thrilled to have his friends there with no idea of the many thoughts flying around the room.

"So, I thought we could maybe go up to Temple Square," Joseph finally offered.

I saw Ryan's eyes grow wide at the suggestion even as he stared at the floor. Apparently he hadn't told Candice and Benjamin anything about last night.

I wondered how he explained the hours he'd spent with me.

"Sure. We've never been, so that could be fun. Besides, New Girl didn't do a very good job of showing us all of the city stuff here . . . just the small town stuff," Benjamin said, since no one else seemed to want to speak.

"Great, let's go," I stated hurriedly, wanting to get out of the confines of the small kitchen.

Silly me.

Had I known I would be riding up to Salt Lake squished between Ryan and Joseph in the back seat, I think I would have taken the kitchen any day. I kept my hands neutrally in my lap, careful to not let my shoulders touch either boy as I stared straight ahead out of the window. I could see Candice texting madly from the front seat and I'd feel my phone buzz every few minutes, but I pointedly ignored it.

"June, I think your phone is going off," Joseph said, nudging my elbow with his own.

"I'm with my friends, I don't need to look at my stupid phone," I said with a laugh that sounded unnatural. Candice scoffed from the front seat, confirming my fear that it was her texting me.

"Suit yourself," he said with a raise of his eyebrows. "At least sit like a normal person. You're making me nervous sitting like that. It looks like you're about to jump out of the car."

"Tuck and roll," Benjamin said from the front seat, making Joseph laugh and Ryan shift uncomfortably beside me.

I sat back in my seat and tried to relax between the two boys, very aware of every part of me that was touching either of them. It was amazing how much people touched when they sat together. Suddenly I wasn't a huge fan of the middle seat.

A car cut Benjamin off, causing him to swerve slightly as we were entering the freeway, and Ryan grabbed my hand instinctively. He only held it for a moment, which would have been fine, except that he lingered there just a bit longer than he normally would have before pulling away again. At any other time I would have gotten butterflies at this gesture, but as Joseph looked down at my hand and then quickly back out the window, I felt nothing but nerves.

Why was this such a big deal? I hadn't declared my love for Ryan or anything. Even if I had, Joseph and I weren't a couple anymore. (Not that I was going to declare my love for Ryan—I loved Joseph.)

The rest of the car ride up to Salt Lake was spent with me trying desperately to keep steady on every corner we took so that I didn't lean toward either Ryan or Joseph, and Benjamin joking with Joseph, who was now only half-heartedly returning his witty banter. Candice had given up trying to text me and now sat staring silently out the window like a child throwing a temper tantrum.

It was ridiculous how the smallest things had suddenly turned into a huge choice for me. After we parked, Joseph and Ryan both got out of the car, holding their doors open for me to climb out.

How difficult was it to pick a side of the car to exit? Apparently it was a monumental decision, because I kept looking back and forth between them like an idiot. In the end I got out on Joseph's side, mostly because it was getting uncomfortable sitting there trying to make a decision and also because my purse had fallen to his side of the car anyway.

As we walked through the temple grounds, I could see Candice trying to let the boys get ahead of us so she could talk to me, but I very purposefully kept pace with them, not wanting another difficult situation on my hands. Eventually she gave up and joined Benjamin at the head of our group.

"So Joseph, I hear you've got a girlfriend up here," Ryan said.

I could hear in his voice that he was trying to be subtle, but I knew what he was doing. He wanted to figure out just how much of a threat Joseph was to him. I put my hands awkwardly in my coat pockets, trying to ignore the gnawing guilt growing within me. As much as I wanted to dislike Ryan, I couldn't. He wasn't a monster. He and Joseph both happened to be wonderful guys who were unfailingly sweet to me (although Joseph hadn't exactly been sweet lately).

Life would be so much simpler if Joseph and Ryan were one person.

"She's not my girlfriend. We're just kind of dating," Joseph answered carefully, glancing over at Ryan as if he were sizing him up. Since when did these two boys look at each other like that? They'd always gotten along so well back in California.

"You should have brought her with us," Ryan responded as he walked. "I would have liked to meet her."

It was obvious that Candice and Benjamin had stopped talking ahead of us and were now listening to the exchange between the two boys very carefully. I walked at the back of the group and chewed on my lip, hoping that neither of them suddenly became bold enough to come right out and say what they were thinking.

Luckily I was blessed with two boys who were complete cowards in the "expressing their feelings" department. At least I had that going for me.

"So, what did June show you guys yesterday?" Joseph asked the group, although he was looking directly at Ryan.

I did notice that he had ignored Ryan's last remark.

"We went to this little town that I've honestly already forgotten the name of," Benjamin answered in a lighthearted tone.

He was never very good at dealing with tense situations. He would automatically turn into "likable Benjamin" as soon as a situation became too awkward for him. It was like a defense mechanism— ostriches stuck their heads in the stand, Benjamin became funny.

"It was Heber," I put in from the back of the group. Everyone turned to look at me for a moment as if they had forgotten I was there. "In case you were wondering," I mumbled.

"What time did you guys get back?" Joseph asked when the many pairs of eyes had drifted off of me.

Why had he suddenly turned our nice friendly stroll into an interrogation?

Ryan looked back at me, a questioning look in his eyes. I firmly kept my mouth closed, refusing to be the one to give us away. If Candice or Benjamin spilled the beans that we'd gone out alone, I'd cross that bridge when I came to it, but it wasn't going to be my fault.

"Ryan and June dropped us off at six. I'm not sure what they did after that," Candice said in a pointedly stubborn voice.

Apparently that bridge was a lot closer than I was hoping.

"Oh?" Joseph said innocently.

I was guessing he was proud of himself for his deductive skills.

"Yeah, Candice and Benjamin sounded like they were going to be pretty busy," Ryan said with a glare at Candice, who quickly looked at the ground as if she had been put in her place. "So June took me up here to show me the Gallivan Center," Ryan finished with a shrug, as if that were no big deal. Which, of course, was completely true, even though everything suddenly felt like a big deal. "I got to go ice skating for the first time."

"Was it everything you hoped it would be?" Joseph asked sarcastically, being quite bold for someone who avoided being confrontational like it was the plague. His statement was clearly not referring to Ryan's expectations for ice-skating.

"Definitely," Ryan answered with a small grin, easily picking up on what Joseph was hinting at.

This was becoming uncomfortable.

No, in fact, I was positive we'd passed uncomfortable miles ago. "Uncomfortable" is being forced to partner up with the only uncoordinated boy in your ballroom dance class. This was quickly passing into "finding out your roommate has been drinking your milk straight from the carton all semester" horrible. (Which Umeko had been doing, by the way.)

A heavy silence fell over the group as we walked, Joseph looking moodily at the ground and Ryan looking like he felt really bad, despite his attempt at matching Joseph's rude comments.

"So Temple Square is pretty beautiful, don't you think?" I asked, trying desperately to change the subject.

"If you like big beautiful buildings and nice people," Benjamin said in an odd voice that told me he was just as intent as I was on steering clear of the awkward turn our trip had taken.

I still walked at the back of the group, even though Ryan and Joseph were walking far enough away from each other that I could squeeze between them. Somehow, I just knew that would open up a whole new possibility for snarky comments between the two boys, so I let myself trail behind.

"Is there a bathroom in that big building? I need to pee," Candice remarked dryly, nodding her head toward the Salt Lake Temple.

I balked for a moment at her question, before remembering that she didn't quite understand that the building she was talking about in such a cavalier manner was, in fact, very sacred.

"There's one in the South Visitors' Center," I told her, turning to lead our little angsty tour group in the right direction.

As we passed into the building, Candice grabbed me forcibly by the arm and pulled me into the bathroom with her. I gave Ryan a fleetingly nervous look over my shoulder and saw him shaking his head at me with his eyes wide. The others were looking at him, so I was pretty sure this gesture was much more of a giveaway than anything I could have told Candice, but who was I to judge? The poor boy was a wreck with all of the tension that was building up.

"What did you do to him?" Candice asked loudly.

"Shhh," I said with a finger over my lips. It wasn't like we were actually in the temple, but I didn't think the missionaries working in the visitor's center would appreciate Candice's less than reverent volume.

"I'll be quiet if you tell me what you did to him," she said, folding her arms in front of her chest and giving me a death glare.

I'd never been on the receiving end of one of Candice's infamous glares, but I had to say, at this moment, I feared for my life a little.

"N-nothing happened," I stuttered, surprised by just how intimidating little Candice could be.

"Ryan is fragile, June. The boy is pretty much in love with you, but I know it's not going to work out, so you need to just keep your distance from him," she warned.

It didn't sound as if she were particularly mad at me—more like she was worried about her friend.

"I was fine with his obsessing over you when you were with Joseph because he didn't stand a chance, but now that you're all hurt and confused, you're using him as a rebound and that's not okay. You may be my friend, but so is he, and you can bounce back much faster than him."

I was touched that Candice was so willing to stand up for Ryan, but her accusations were way off base. I wasn't using Ryan as a rebound for Joseph. I had always liked Ryan. But I had also always liked Joseph too. Was it possible to have two good choices and not be sure which was the right one?

"Candice, we aren't together or anything. We live in two different states," I said reasonably.

"Unless you get that movie part. Then you'll be around each other *all* the time," she countered.

How did she know about that? She must have read my confused expression because she immediately said, "Ryan told me."

"Why don't you think it will work out?" I asked her, fully aware that I was changing the course of the conversation pretty abruptly. I didn't really care though. I was curious.

"Because this thing with Joseph is just a little blip. It'll pass and then you guys will be just how you were before, and Ryan will be devastated. If you and Joseph are together, it's fine, because Ryan can feel like he's got this innocent crush on a girl he can't have. But if he's with you for a while and then loses you, he's not suddenly going to go back to being okay with it," she explained, her tone finally softening so that I didn't feel like I was being attacked. "He's kind of a sensitive little guy."

"I don't know what to do," I told her, placing a hand on my cheek and rubbing my temple. "If this had happened a few months ago I would have known what to do right away. But I've seen a different side of Joseph lately . . . and a different side of Ryan, for that matter. Now things aren't as clear."

Candice glanced over at me for a moment. She looked as if she was deciding whether or not she was going to believe me.

"So you're not just planning to hook up with Ryan until Joseph is available again?" she asked.

"Candice, how long have you known me? I wouldn't have let Ryan kiss me last night if I was planning on getting back together with Joseph," I assured her.

"He kissed you?" she asked. "I knew it!"

My eyes grew wide as I realized I had done exactly what Ryan had asked me not to do.

"You can't say anything! I promised Ryan I wouldn't tell," I told her, suddenly feeling like a five-year-old for being so secretive about one little kiss.

That happened to be amazing.

But that was beside the point.

"Yeah, sure. Like Ryan really thought he would be able to hide it from me for more than a day. He's been practically vibrating the paint off the walls with his stupid smile all morning. It's sickening," she said with a shudder, though she was grinning. "Did he say he loves you?"

"What? No! It was only a kiss," I said quickly.

"Whatever, he loves you," she answered matter-of-factly.

Apparently I wasn't the enemy anymore since she had turned off her glare and was now checking her bright red lipstick in the mirror, her perfect long black hair falling over her shoulder as she leaned in close to her reflection. "Sorry I yelled at you," she offered in her usual monotone.

"That's fine. It's nice to know you care about Ryan so much," I said truthfully.

"It's not just Ryan. I care about you too June. I just had to take the side of the weaker party here. Though don't tell Ryan I called him the 'weaker party.' Poor guy has some major confidence issues."

"Duly noted," I answered with a smile, glad to have a friend as fiercely loyal as Candice.

"So . . . Joseph is being pretty rude," she said after we had stood in awkward silence in the bathroom for a moment.

"Oh, gosh. I don't even know what to do about that whole situation. I've never seen him like that."

"It's the testosterone. They can't help it. We'll just

have to separate them like children," she said with a shrug as we headed back for the door.

"What's going on with you and Benjamin?" I asked, wondering if our moment of honesty could get her to confess her own little love affair.

"So, I'll distract the other two and you make sure Ryan is okay. I'm pretty sure he's about to have a heart attack," she said, blatantly ignoring my question.

I let her get away with it this time.

"Okay," I said slowly, wishing I could ease Ryan's mind by giving him a more concrete sentiment than "Sorry I'm really confused right now and don't know how I feel."

When we left the bathroom I could see the three boys looking at a display of the temple in a large glass case. It was a pity that an attempt at injecting some inspiration into my friends had turned into such a dramatic outing. I doubted anyone was feeling the Spirit at that moment.

"Joseph, I want to see that building with the round roof. Can you show me?" Candice asked, pointedly grabbing Benjamin by the arm to show that he had to come with them.

Even though Benjamin was being oddly quiet, I could tell that he was taking in the whole situation. He knew as well as Candice what had happened between Ryan and me, and he wanted to be supportive of his friend. I definitely didn't want Joseph being cast as the bad guy, though, because I knew he wasn't. He was acting a bit jerky today, but

I had been rude to him several times during rehearsals when I saw him with Jade, so I could relate.

"Sure," he said, looking over at me for a moment with an unreadable expression before exiting through the automatic doors with Candice and Benjamin.

I grabbed Ryan by the elbow as he began to follow them and pulled him in the direction of the opposite end of the building, glad to get him alone and away from the craziness of the evening.

"Run while you still can," I joked.

Well . . . I half joked.

CHAPTER 10

The street running along Temple Square was incredibly noisy, so I led Ryan over to the reflection pool so that we could walk in a more peaceful area.

"I'm sorry everything's been so weird today," I told him as we walked. "Joseph normally isn't that rude."

"It's my fault," he said automatically. "I should have asked you before I kissed you. I don't know what's going on with you and Joseph and I probably just complicated things."

"I think I'm glad you did it," I admitted, keeping my eyes trained straight ahead and wishing I hadn't said "I think" at the beginning of that sentence. Weren't the butterflies in my stomach a pretty good indication that I was *definitely* glad he'd done it?

"Really?" he asked.

"Really," I told him, stopping our walk in front of the reflection pool and turning to face him.

His breath came out in little puffs in the crisp

October air and his stubbly cheeks were slightly pink. His eyes were the most amazing shade of blue. They weren't light blue like Lukas's or Declan's—they were the same color as a straight blue crayon.

Deep and rich.

I hadn't even thought that eye color existed.

As I looked at him with his pink cheeks and blue eyes, I realized that I meant what I had just said, as much as I didn't want to.

"I don't want you to feel like I'm forcing you into some big decision. I know these last few months have been hard, so don't think of this as another stressful situation you have to figure out. It's just an option that will be waiting for you if you decide to pursue it," he said.

His words were casual—or at least I'm sure he hoped they sounded casual.

"Ryan, you're not a backup plan. You're a wonderful person who's always been a better friend than I could have asked for."

"Friend," he interjected with an overly dramatized shake of his head. Always the comedian.

"I just need some time to figure out exactly what I'm doing," I said, going on without acknowledging his interruption.

"I know. That's why I don't want you to make any solid decision about things right now. This," he said, motioning between the two of us, "doesn't have to have a label or be a huge decision. It can just be . . . whatever, until you decide if you want to solidify it."

He almost sounded like he was being serious; like he might not crack a joke at any moment.

"It's not even really a *thing*. I just happen to be a completely smooth famous Hollywood actor who practically declared his love for you but, you know, no rush," he finished, sounding much more like his old self.

I had been wondering where my friend had gone these past few days with all the drama. "Serious Ryan" was about as normal for me to see as "Non-Jerky Lukas Leighton."

"I don't know if you know this, but I'm kind of over the whole 'famous Hollywood actor' thing," I said, wrinkling up my nose at him.

"So the Lukas Leighton approach isn't working? I'll have to check that off the list of tactics," he said, making a check mark in the air and pretending to stroke his chin. "I'll have to return that motorcycle, which is kind of a pain. What about the wounded artsy type? Should I go buy a bowtie, maybe? Or dye my hair black?"

"Wow, you read me like a book," I said sarcastically. "Please go buy an acoustic guitar, grow a mustache, and wear thick black glasses that you don't really need."

"Consider it done," he answered with a big cheesy grin. "The things I do for you, woman," he said, pulling me into a quick hug that felt toasty warm in the freezing night air.

"Practically selling your soul," I agreed with a somber nod against his chest.

We were silent for a moment and I wondered what it would be like to actually date Ryan rather than just joking about it like we had been for years. Then I reminded myself that I was in no mental state to make any boy-related decisions in the near future, since my separation from Joseph had left me slightly—oh, what was the word?

Pathetic.

That was it. The word I was looking for.

"Oh, and by the way, Candice knows." I said guiltily, pulling away from him and putting on my best "what could I do?" face.

"Yeah, I figured. If she gets you alone with *that* look on her face, you don't really stand a chance. Our scandalous barely-a-peck kiss will be the talk of the tabloids, I'm sure."

"You should probably tell Benjamin what happened or he'll be really mad when he reads about it in *People Magazine*," I advised, half joking and half serious. I was serious about Benjamin being upset that he was the last person in on a piece of gossip. Not the *People Magazine* part. I doubted I'd ever be famous enough for magazines to care what I did.

"He's been winking at me all day. It's creepy, but I think that means he knows," Ryan said with a laugh. "He'll keep raising his eyebrows at me and nodding like this." Ryan did his best Benjamin imitation, which I had to admit was pretty good.

"Well, at least you guys will have something new to talk about in the makeup trailer, huh?" I said with a short giggle, looking up into Ryan's deep blue eyes.

"Exactly," he agreed, looking at me and making me shiver slightly at his proximity. I ignored the fact that I had been hoping he'd kiss me again and cleared my throat awkwardly.

"We should probably be getting back," he said after a moment, his voice deeper and more serious than it had been a moment before.

It was strange to see how quickly he could shift between the normal, joking boy I was used to, and someone who could give me a smoldering look that would melt an ice sculpture in two seconds flat. Had he always looked at me like that? It was unsettling and made me want to kiss him all at the same time. It was a thought I buried so deeply in my mind that I could never access it again.

Horrible, horrible June—thinking I liked two boys at once. So shameless.

"Probably," I said.

As we walked to the Tabernacle to meet up with the others, our hands brushed, although neither of us were bold enough to let our fingers lace together. I looked down at our very obvious non-hand-holding situation but was quickly brought back to the here-and-now when the door to the Tabernacle opened and Candice, Benjamin, and Joseph left the building.

I saw Benjamin give Ryan the exact same look he had found so creepy and tried not to smile at the gesture. Joseph didn't exactly look happy, but he didn't look like he wanted to kill anyone either, so that was definitely an improvement.

Any improvement was a good improvement, right?

"Were you a good tour guide?" I asked Joseph with a smile.

He seemed a bit taken aback that I was addressing him directly and I realized that I hadn't said anything to him since the whole awkward trip had started. I guess I couldn't really be upset with him for being a bad friend when I was being a pretty awful friend too.

"I did my best," he replied, his tone holding much less ice than it had before. He even let his mouth twitch slightly in the corners as if he might smile.

Benjamin was apparently ready to jump all over this small ease in the tension.

"So, New Girl, how come when we said 'show us around Utah,' you took us to some lame little town when this whole big city was waiting for us?" Benjamin asked, giving me an accusatory stare.

"She didn't want to scare you away by the fact that there are actual normal people in this state," Ryan answered with a grin, acting exactly how he and Benjamin always did on the show.

I swear, they couldn't help automatically falling into their roles when they were around each other.

"If by normal you mean rude, dirty, and scary, then yes, that's exactly what I was trying to avoid," I joked, shooting Joseph a tentative smile that he actually returned.

"I'm glad we came. I would have never come back to this state if I thought it was only full of people who hold doors open for you and say polite things," Candice added in a way that made me think she might be serious.

Joseph and I attempted to show our three friends a few more things on Temple Square, but the cold was quickly setting in and none of us had brought big enough coats to keep us warm, so we soon retreated to the car.

I actually allowed myself sit like a normal person for the car ride back home, letting my shoulder rest against Ryan's in a way that I hoped was subtle. I still kept my hands in my lap, though.

"I heard you're starring in *Tartuffe*," Ryan said suddenly in the silent car.

While I was glad that Joseph was being much more civil, I wondered if he was really ready to start talking to Ryan like there was nothing weird going on between them. But I had to give Ryan some credit for trying to make things okay. Honestly, I didn't understand what Joseph's deal was. *He* was the one who broke up with *me*, after all.

"Yeah, I got the part," Joseph said in an unreadable tone.

"That's great, man," Ryan answered sincerely, and I could see Joseph smile a little at this approval.

He may not like Ryan at the moment, but he had always looked up to him, and I knew Ryan's approval as an actor was a big thing to Joseph.

"After years of waiting, you finally get to break out of your dramatic cage and be funny," Benjamin said from the driver's seat.

"It's about time, right?" Joseph said emphatically. "It'll be the last time I act for two years, so I would've been pretty mad if BYU had decided to do *Hamlet* or something."

"I love *Hamlet*," I said with a pout in Joseph's direction.

"No, you love Ophelia. That's the only reason you even like that play, you weirdo," he replied with a grin.

"There's nothing weird about it. Ophelia is awesome."

"Except that she kills herself just because her boyfriend doesn't like her anymore," Joseph pointed out.

"Whoa. Talk about desperate," Candice mumbled from the passenger's seat.

"I stand by what I said," I stated resolutely.

"New Girl, aren't you in the play too?" Benjamin asked.

"Yeah, but I have a pretty small part. I'm just Dorine, the maid," I answered with a modest shrug.

"The maid?" Benjamin asked, suddenly interested. "What does your costume look like?"

Candice hit Benjamin on the arm so hard that I was surprised the car didn't swerve.

"Watch it," she threatened, inadvertently reminding me that I'd have to find out what was going on between the two of them.

If she was allowed to get information out of me, why couldn't I do the same thing to her? Unfortunately, I was infinitely less scary than her, so intimidation was out of the question.

"I'm pretty sure my costume for this play will be nothing compared to what you guys have already seen me in on *Forensic Faculty*." I said with a shake of my head.

I glanced over at Ryan, who was grinning as he stared out the window. I opened my mouth wide at his blatant display of typical "boy" behavior and gave him a shove with my shoulder.

"I didn't think there was anything wrong with those costumes," he said with a laugh.

"Boys," I lamented, rolling my eyes up toward the ceiling.

We ended up heading back to the hotel room shared by Benjamin and Ryan (Candice was in her own room) to talk, despite the fact that it was getting pretty late and they had an early flight the next morning. Somehow, none of us wanted to end the night.

Even though she would never willingly admit to it, I think even Candice had missed us and was enjoying our time together.

"Do you remember when Joann Hoozer stood too close to that light on set and singed her hair?" Benjamin asked as he sat on the floor of the hotel room, his thumbs swiping across the screen of his phone like they always were.

"I still dream about her shrieking how she would get the lighting guys fired," Candice replied with the dry monotone that told me how much she hated Joann and what a diva she thought the actress was.

"I remember it because she had just gotten done telling me that maybe acting wasn't my thing," I said in annoyance.

Joann and I had never really gotten along. Since day one, she had been throwing me death glares and flipping her perfect honey blonde hair in my face like she thought I wasn't good enough to be on the same set as her.

"She said that?" Joseph asked, indignant on my behalf. "What a witch."

"There's another word for it," Candice sing-songed from her position on the bed where she lay on her stomach popping miniature peanut butter cups into her mouth.

"At least she wasn't as bad as Will Trofeos," I said with the mischievous grin of someone who had insider information.

"What was wrong with him?" Candice asked. "I mean, besides the fact that he's an egotistical jerk-wad?"

"He was always hitting on me. It was creepy," I answered with a shudder.

Will Trofeos had been the star of the show and was definitely much too old to be hitting on a seventeen-year-old girl. But that hadn't stopped him, unfortunately, and his thinly-veiled pick-up lines were always enough to make me cringe when he walked by.

"Yeah, that's definitely not okay," Ryan agreed. "And don't get me started on Lukas Leighton."

There was a collective groan at the name, since we

all had an equal dislike of the show's "hottest" star. I had been lucky enough to start falling—but then escape from—Lukas's charms, but then I still had to endure a full two years of awkwardly playing his love interest on the show.

When the cameras were rolling he'd kiss me and act like we were completely in love, and the second they called "cut," he wouldn't even make eye contact with me. I always thought he hated me for rejecting him—something no girl had probably ever done. Candice thought that he was intimidated by me, since I actually stood up for myself. I guess we'd never know who was right.

"That guy is such a tool," Candice complained.

"Are you sure about that Candice? Because New Girl didn't seem too repulsed by him," Benjamin pointed out.

"I still can't believe you dated him," Joseph said with a shake of his head.

Since he had seen through Lukas since the beginning, he felt that it was his duty to remind me of how bad my judgment had been on that one.

"I know, I know," I said, raising my hands in surrender. "At least I saw the error of my ways."

"Took you long enough," Candice mumbled.

"Yeah, you would think it wouldn't take him parking outside of your house and trying to sleep with you in the back seat of his car for you to realize he's not the best guy ever," Benjamin stated.

I shuddered at the memory of the night I finally grasped what an awful person Lukas was. The second he realized he wasn't going to get what he wanted, he was done with me. The one silver lining was that the encounter had taught me to watch out for people in my profession. Their acting abilities weren't always reserved for the screen.

"Why are all The Tall Ones so awful?" Candice asked, using her nickname for the show's stars.

"Doesn't it make you glad that no one cares about Ryan and me?" Benjamin asked with a smirk.

"Yeah, I'm glad you guys are nobodies," she agreed.

"It's so dumb that you aren't in more movies. You're easily the best actors on that show," Joseph said, kicking off the same argument he'd gone over with me many times.

He did have a soft spot for Ryan and Benjamin on the show, so his biased may have had something to do with the fact that he loved their funny characters. But I completely agreed with him—they deserved more parts.

"I've been picking up more roles lately," Benjamin said modestly. "And Ryan's becoming quite the heartthrob."

"Oh, yeah, I'm a real heartthrob," he answered sarcastically. "The fourteen-year-old girls are just lining up around the corner to get my autograph."

"I didn't say teen heartthrob," Benjamin corrected seriously. "Do we need to go over the degrees of heartthrob-ness again? I could give you a refresher course, but fall semester is almost over, so you'll have to sign up for my winter class."

"Do I need to resend you my transcript?"

"I've already got it on file from my 'how to not look like an idiot on camera' class, so you're good," Benjamin answered.

"You probably should have signed Joann Hoozer up for that class," Ryan countered.

"Oh, you guys are so funny," Candice deadpanned from the bed.

"How is it, balancing the show with other jobs?" Joseph asked.

"It's not bad, really," Ryan shrugged. He was sitting on a chair with one ankle resting on his knee, absentmindedly playing with his shoelaces. "We have a pretty long break from the show every year, so we'll try to cram in as many roles as we can."

"Even when we're filming, some productions will try to work around that," Benjamin added. "I've got a smallish part in a movie coming up. Most of it I'm filming in our downtime from *Forensic Faculty*, but some of it is during shooting, so they're working with me."

"I've got a movie coming up, too, but it's all during the off-season of the show," Ryan said distantly, still focusing on his shoelaces and not even realizing he was alluding to my possible future role.

I watched him intently until I saw recognition cross over his face. He glanced over at me for a moment, silently questioning if I had told anyone.

I didn't say anything, but changed the subject, hoping that would be all the confirmation he needed that Joseph didn't know about the role yet.

"Well, we'll probably be seeing you guys in November for Thanksgiving," I said, not having any other topic of conversation handy to change the subject abruptly.

"I am not looking forward to making that drive again," Joseph said with a groan.

"I don't even know if your car *can* make that drive again," I teased.

"Hey, Blue Lightening has spirit. She's not intimidated by a few hills."

"That thing needs to be put out to pasture," I told him, still laughing softly.

"I thought you loved her," Joseph replied, sounding hurt.

"I do, but that doesn't change the fact that she's on her last leg."

"Never buy a car you can't push, right?" he asked, a glint in his eye as he smiled at me and brought up some confusing feelings, which I promptly ignored.

I seemed to be doing that with most feelings today.

"Wouldn't it be nicer to just fly down?" Benjamin asked, never letting his gaze wander from the phone that seemed to be attached to his hand.

"I'm saving up for a mission, so I have absolutely no extra money," Joseph said with a shrug.

I knew Joseph's mom and dad definitely wanted to help him pay for his mission, but with three younger brothers and two younger sisters, his parents were stretched a little thin in the money department.

I always wished that Joseph wasn't too proud to let me help with the money I'd made on *Forensic Faculty*. It wasn't like I was a big spender and needed the money for anything huge. BYU wasn't exactly an expensive school to attend, and Utah had some of the cheapest housing I had ever seen. But as fate would have it, Joseph was one of those people who insisted on making his own way in the world, and to him, that didn't include getting handouts from his best friend.

"What's your excuse?" Candice asked me, knowing I could afford the plane ticket to California easily.

"I'm not just going to let Joseph drive down by himself," I answered, thinking that this would be obvious.

Ryan glanced at me for a moment, a look on his face that I couldn't read, before returning his gaze to his apparently very interesting shoelaces.

"So buy him a plane ticket, Moneybags," Benjamin answered.

"I would if he'd let me," I said, nudging Joseph with my shoulder and smiling over at him.

"What can I say? I have an ego."

"The male ego is a sensitive thing," Benjamin agreed sagely.

"You've got that right," Candice added, making me wonder—not for the first time—what was going on between her and Benjamin.

"On that inspiring note, we should probably get going," Joseph said, glancing at his phone to check the time and undoubtedly thinking of calling Jade before he went to bed.

"I can drive you guys back to your apartment," Ryan offered, making my heart sink as I realized I wouldn't be seeing him for a while.

His eyes met mine, and I knew he had been thinking the exact same thing. Suddenly I really wanted him to drive us back.

"It's okay. Our apartment is literally right behind your hotel. We can just walk," Joseph insisted, standing from the floor and shrugging his coat on.

I followed suit but shot Ryan a sad look, wishing I could say goodbye to him properly before our long time apart.

I wrapped my arms awkwardly around Candice in an attempt to hug her, which she tried to wriggle out of.

"The whole reason I was lying on the bed was so you wouldn't be able to hug me," she mumbled.

"I'll miss you too, Candice," I said, giving her one last awkward squeeze before turning to Benjamin, who at least had the courtesy to stand so I could hug him.

"I know something's going on with you two," I whispered as I gave him a hug.

"You're one to talk, New Girl," he whispered back, giving me a quick wink as I let him go.

Then I turned to Ryan, who looked at me with a mixture of excitement and sadness in his eyes. I hadn't even known those two emotions could be mixed until I looked at him, wearing the combination perfectly.

I gave him a tight hug, which he returned whole-heartedly and fleetingly wondered if he would try to kiss me in front of everyone. My heart skipped a beat at the idea, but I was quickly pulled back to reality when he released me and said, "I'll miss you guys."

I guess reality always wins out in the end.

CHAPTER 11

Things seemed pretty bleak after Ryan, Benjamin, and Candice left. Joseph and I easily fell back into our old routine of not talking about anything, and he spent most of his free time with Jade while I spent most of my free time trying to figure out how I felt about that. It was true that, while Ryan and I weren't dating, his kiss had brought out some confusing feelings inside of me that I didn't want to figure out. It was too complicated.

I had had crushes on boys before—poor Joseph could attest to that. But the only boy I'd ever seriously dated was Joseph, and when we started dating, I was completely convinced that one day we'd end up married. Of course, it was a long ways in the future with our being so young and him still wanting to go on a two-year mission. Still, it had seemed like the natural path our relationship would follow.

Now, as I sat on the stage at our last rehearsal before Thanksgiving break watching Joseph shamelessly flirting with Jade, I felt doubt fill me.

Joseph was doing the one thing I had never anticipated: he was outgrowing me. I didn't know what this meant for our friendship. Joseph and I had been friends since we were born, but now that we had dated, I wasn't sure if we could go back to being just friends. He had Jade now, and I had a whole pile of confusion.

I loved Joseph, even when he was being a little jerky and despite the fact that he was oblivious to how much his relationship with Jade hurt me. I didn't really care if that made me one of those weak, pathetic girls in movies that everyone hates because they can't see how pathetic they are.

I didn't think it was so awful to love someone unconditionally when you knew they were worth loving, and Joseph was definitely someone deserving of unconditional love. He was a loyal friend and a good person and I loved him.

But I had also liked Ryan's kiss.

The guilt that I had been feeling ever since he left washed over me once more. Candice's warnings rang in my ears, and I had to seriously ask myself if I only wanted Ryan because I couldn't have Joseph. The many times I had asked myself this question over the past few weeks, the answer had always been the same. I really didn't want to like Ryan. It only confused things. But I did like him, and I also couldn't escape that fact.

Somehow, I couldn't understand how life could really be this difficult. I mean, honestly, I had so much going for me, so why was I so unhappy? Gran had called to tell me that a casting director wanted to meet with me over Thanksgiving break for a part in a Regency film. I, of course, hadn't told Gran that I'd half expected the call after speaking with Ryan about the part.

But still, here I sat, fuming that my ex-boyfriend and hopefully current friend was flirting with some perfect French girl right in front of me. Maybe that's how the ex-boyfriend thing always was? I hadn't had an ex before, so I wasn't really sure what to expect, but it seemed only logical that you would always be annoyed by your former boyfriend liking someone else.

As Joseph walked back to our apartment with me after rehearsal, I tried to quell the many feelings that were bubbling up inside of me. It was a bad time to have a mental breakdown . . . There were so many things I needed to talk to someone about and normally that someone would be Joseph, but as we walked, I didn't feel like I could share anything with him.

"So, I have an audition in California in a few days," I said suddenly, almost wanting to shock him to get back at him. What was I getting back at him for, though? Having a relationship he was totally entitled to have?

"Are you serious?" he asked, sounding genuinely excited and making me feel bad for being so angry with him over nothing in particular. "What is it for? When did you find out?"

"It's for a feature film. I heard rumors that I'd be getting a call when Candice and everyone was here, but I found out for sure a few days ago," I said, trying to keep my voice neutral.

"Why didn't you tell me right away? That's a huge deal," he said, slightly annoyed that I hadn't immediately confided in him.

"You haven't been around much," I answered shortly, keeping my eyes trained ahead and wishing I could have my friend from two years ago back.

We should had never ruined things by dating.

"What are you talking about?" he asked, genuinely confused. "I see you all the time."

"Do you? Because I haven't seen you around much lately."

"June, are you mad about something?" He was still clueless.

Apparently that was all it took to unbalance my already hormonally unbalanced mind.

"Am I mad about something?" I snapped, forgetting about my attempt to be subtle. "Joseph, I'm mad that you lied to me!"

It was a good thing that we were walking through an old deserted parking lot to get back to our apartment. I wasn't quite sure this was a conversation I wanted everyone in the school to hear now that I had lost my cool.

"When did I ever lie to you?" he asked, getting defensive at my angry tone.

"Let's see," I began, sounding much colder than I had meant to. I hated myself for being so mean, but couldn't seem to stop the words from coming out of my mouth. "You didn't have the backbone to say you don't want to date me anymore, so you made up some stupid story about how, because you're going on your mission, you don't want a girlfriend."

"How is that lying?" he asked, now raising his voice as well.

"Because you have a girlfriend now, Joseph," I shouted, wondering how he could seriously not understand my anger.

"Who? Jade?"

"Obviously."

"June, Jade isn't my girlfriend," he said, calming down a bit.

"Give it up," I scoffed. "You may not have a label on your little relationship with her, but you treat her like a girlfriend. If you were really concerned with the label, we could have stopped 'dating' but still treated each other exactly the same."

"Why do you even care, June?" he asked, starting to get angry. "You have Ryan now, so it doesn't even matter."

That one shut me up for a moment, catching me off guard, since Joseph hadn't brought up the whole Ryan thing once since they had left.

"Ryan and I aren't together," I shouted at him.

"Don't lie to me—I can read you like a book. Besides, you may be a good actress, but you're a horrible liar. You always have been."

"I'm not lying. We kissed, but we live in two different states. It's not like we can actually have a relationship that way," I explained, my face reddening. "Besides, I only kissed Ryan after you had pushed me away. I don't understand how after all of these years you couldn't just tell me you wanted to go back to being my friend. Why did you have to lie about it? Were you trying to protect my feelings? All you've done is confuse me with your constant flirting with Jade."

Joseph balked at that statement and as angry as I was with him, I could tell that he truly hadn't known how much he was hurting me. He didn't say anything for a moment. Instead, he searched my bright red face for what he should say next.

"June, I didn't," he began before stopping again and collecting his thoughts. "I didn't realize that's how you saw everything."

"I honestly don't know how else I could have seen it, Joseph."

"I never wanted to hurt you. It's just . . . it's easier for me to date Jade than it is to date you," he finished, looking like he had said something that should make me happier, even though all he had done was turned the knife.

Dramatic? Maybe.

Accurate? Completely.

I took a deep breath, telling the actor in me to not react theatrically to such a hurtful statement. I nodded in understanding and instead of screaming a dramatic monologue at him, I turned on my heel, wanting to walk the rest of the way alone.

"I'm sorry I made your life so difficult for those past two years," I called over my shoulder, wondering how everything had turned so badly so quickly.

"Thanks for driving me to the airport," I said to Declan, sitting in the passenger's seat of his roommate's car and staring out the window sullenly. I seriously needed to buy my own transportation. That cute green moped someone in our apartment complex was selling had tempted me more than once, and it would be better than nothing, right?

"I know you're desperate for a reason to hang out with me, but there are less elaborate ways, you know," he said, flashing his winning smile in my direction.

"I like a good scheme," I answered with a shrug, a smile coming to my face for the first time since my fight with Joseph.

Before our fight, I had already bought him a plane ticket back home for Thanksgiving as a surprise. Even though we hadn't spoken since he told me I was difficult to date, I slid the ticket under his door the night before the flight and hoped I could avoid sitting by him on the plane. Just because he had been a huge jerk didn't mean I would let a perfectly good non-refundable ticket go to waste.

Besides, if he tried to drive home alone, his stupid car would probably break down in Baker and he'd fry to death out in the desert. As appealing as that scenario sounded at that particular moment, I wasn't quite that cold-hearted.

"Why couldn't your boyfriend take you to the airport?" Declan asked after a long, uncomfortable silence.

"Because A) he's not my boyfriend and B) he was a giant idiot a few days ago so I'm not speaking to him."

"Very grown up of you. I commend your use of the silent treatment," Declan said with a slow clap.

"Every time I start to like you," I threatened with a playful glare.

"So now that you hate him, do I get a chance?"

"I'm sort of dating someone. A little bit," I lied. Or at least, I think it was a lie.

"How do you date someone a little bit?" he asked. Luckily his cell phone started ringing and saved me from having to answer a question I didn't even know the answer to.

"Hello?" he said into the receiver. The conversation that followed let me zone out for most of the ride to the airport, since Declan was tied up trying to calm a shouting woman over the phone.

By the time we had gotten to the terminals where he parked to let me out, he finally hung up, shooting me an almost apologetic look.

"Sorry," he said with a wince. "It was my mum."

"She sounds lovely," I joked, having just heard her shouting for the past hour.

"She suffers from Post-Partum Aggression," he

said seriously.

"Depression," I corrected.

"Trust me, it's aggression," he answered. "Well, have fun with your sort-of boyfriend and your not boyfriend! I'll just be here by myself. All alone and lonely."

"I don't buy that for a second," I told him, knowing Declan better than that. "You probably already have five dates planned just for tonight."

"Well, yeah, five dates is a dry spell for me," he answered cheekily, shooting me one more wink before driving away.

I laughed as he left, envious that he could always be so lighthearted about everything and wondering when I had turned into such a drama queen. Granted, I was an actor and a girl, so I had a right to be dramatic if I wanted to be, but still—taking Declan's approach to life didn't seem like such a bad idea right at this moment.

Maybe I could lighten up a bit?

CHAPTER 12

"Please slate for the camera, Miss Laurie," the casting director said.

I always felt like an idiot telling the camera my name and acting agency but today, it was doubly embarrassing because on top of the normal table of people watching me audition, I also had Ryan standing right beside me. He had been grinning from ear to ear since I walked through the door. We hadn't talked since he left Utah, so I wasn't quite sure where we stood in our relationship/friendship, which was giving me mild panic attacks.

Why did relationships have to be so awful when you were trying to figure them out?

Uncomfortably, I turned to the camera and put on the brightest smile I could muster under such overwhelmingly awkward circumstances.

"Hi, my name is June Laurie and I'm with the Annette Adams Agency," I said, trying to sound personable and not like I thought this was idiotic.

It wasn't like the casting director didn't know who I was. *They* had asked *me* to come, after all, and I was pretty sure they'd recognize my face later when they went through the audition tapes to make their final decision. Mostly I just hated having to go from "normal person" to "super perky slating actress" in two seconds flat. It was always odd.

"All right, June, have you had a chance to read over the side we sent your agent?" the casting director asked, talking to me like an animal who might scare if he spoke too loudly.

Actors are sensitive creatures, I guess. I think I had even read a book on directing telling future directors this very thing.

"I've looked over the side," I assured them, holding the script they spoke of in my hand and trying to keep calm.

I had been to my share of auditions in my life, but with the exception of *Forensic Faculty*, I hadn't wanted any part as much as this one. Having the opportunity to be in a big movie that I didn't have to turn down to maintain my moral high ground was exactly what I had been hoping for after leaving Hollywood to go to school in Utah.

The fact that Joseph hadn't brought me happy and sad ice cream to eat later that night or called to wish me luck didn't help my nerves at all. Our fighting was throwing me off balance. As much as I hated to admit it, my life didn't quite function normally without Joseph there.

"We have Ryan Hex here to read with you as he

will be playing the male lead. We just want to get a sense of your on-screen chemistry," the casting director informed me, as if this fact weren't obvious.

Perhaps they thought that because I had left the Hollywood scene I had suddenly forgotten all of my acting knowledge.

"So, if you'll just read from the top of the page to the end of the scene."

"Who should I read to?" I asked, before realizing what a stupid question that was. No wonder they were treating me like an idiot.

Normally I'd be auditioning by myself and I'd need to know if they wanted me to read to the camera or to one of the people sitting at the table. When they bring in the lead actor specifically to read with you, I guess it should be pretty obvious who you're supposed to direct lines to.

"Hello Miss Laurie, I'll be reading lines with you today," Ryan said, trying hard to keep from laughing at me.

I wanted to slap him but knew that the camera was rolling, so I just narrowed my eyes at him, subtly letting him know he'd be in trouble later.

"Thank you, Mr. Hex. I appreciate that," I replied with veiled sarcasm.

"Whenever you're ready," the casting director said, bringing me back to reality and reminding me that while I thought our little game was cute, the room full of people watching us were probably just tired and wanting to get on with things.

I glanced down at my script one last time to make

sure I remembered my lines before looking back up at Ryan, falling instantly into character. I let my expression grow somber as I tilted my head toward the floor to look up at him through my eyelashes.

"I can't see you again after today," I told him, trying to sound like my character didn't care, even though she totally did. "My father says that I shouldn't spend so much time in the company of a gentleman I don't intend to marry."

Ryan let concern wash over his face. The genuine emotion there instantly gave me a flashback to how much trouble I had almost gotten into the last time I trusted a famous actor. It was so difficult wanting to believe someone's intentions are true when you know they could easily fake emotion better than a normal person can express genuine feelings.

Ryan's concern quickly melted into an easy smirk that was very out of character for him. It was roguish, a little devilish, and completely leading man material. I had never been more proud of him.

"Who says I don't intend to marry you?" he asked, taking a step toward me and making me back away from him, startled by the sudden movement.

I hadn't intended to do it, but the completely un-Ryan-like person who stood before me had startled me for a moment. Luckily for me, it just looked like I was a good actor, since that was probably how my character would have reacted to this very situation. I frequently found that a lot of "good" things I did at auditions were accidental. Oops!

"You already know I can't marry you," I replied,

placing my hand on his chest to keep him from coming any closer to me. I could feel his heart pounding rapidly, although it didn't make sense to me that he would be nervous about an audition for a movie where he'd already landed the main role.

Of course, looking at him, you'd never know his heart was racing. The boy was seriously an amazing actor.

"And why is that?" he asked, still keeping the mischievous grin on his face and taking a step closer to me despite my best efforts to keep him at bay.

"Because I have to marry someone respectable; someone . . . different than you," I said, trying to look conflicted when all I wanted to do was find out where Ryan and I stood. I guess in a way I was conflicted, so that was perfect.

"I have money," he said matter-of-factly.

"That you spend on lavish and frivolous things."

"I have a good family name."

"A name you've dragged through the mud with your various conquests," I pointed out, sounding like I was trying to convince myself of his awfulness.

"I believe you already know what you want from me. Why don't you go ahead and tell me?" he finally said after a long pause. "It will make the process of giving you what you desire much easier."

"I want you to be the kind of person I want to marry," I told him, letting my voice crack a little. "I don't care about your money or your family name. I care about your actions that speak volumes about the kind of man you really are."

"You've known me all my life. If my actions are so undesirable, why do you still see me at all?"

"Because you act differently around me than you do around everyone else," I told him, bringing a hand up to his cheek and stepping closer to him. I looked up into his blue eyes and tried not to smile.

I didn't want to count my chickens before they hatched, but from what I was feeling, we had definitely nailed it.

"Thank you Miss Laurie," the casting director said, breaking the spell I had fallen into. "We'll be in touch."

I wanted desperately to see Ryan after the audition, but he had to stay behind to read with a few other actresses the casting director had called in. Because we hadn't spoken since he'd left Utah, I had slipped into a bit of an avoidance cycle that I was determined to break. Though my confusing feelings did make talking to Ryan a bit pointless, since I didn't even know what I'd say to him.

I guessed our conversation would go something like, "Oh, hey Ryan! So you're still wondering why I haven't spoken to you for almost a month after you kissed me? Oh yeah, I'm wondering that too. I guess I'm just a horrible person who can't make up her mind about what she wants. Who knew, right?"

Somehow in the course of leaving for college to become an "adult," I had become nothing but needy when it came to relationships. Honestly, it was a little disgusting and I planned to toss the undesirable trait out the window the first second I got.

That meant, of course, going to talk to Joseph to establish that we could, in fact, remain friends even if we weren't dating.

I had planned an entire speech to deliver to him the day before Thanksgiving, but lost my nerve (surprise, surprise) and decided that the best time to have the conversation would be back in Utah where I could overcome my neediness by facing it head-on.

"Bliss, you seem conflicted," I heard Gran say from my doorway.

I wasn't sure how long she had been leaning like a supermodel against the frame, her short, curly red hair framing a quizzical expression. "Is there something you want to talk about?"

I didn't say anything for a moment, but just looked up at the ceiling and wondered how so much had changed in only a few short months. How could I take everything I was feeling and put it into words?

"There are a lot of things I want to talk about. I just don't even know where to start," I told her honestly, rolling over onto my stomach so I could get a better look at her.

"I find that one thing at a time works best. Otherwise you get overwhelmed by everything."

She sat at my vanity and crossed one long leg over the other, looking more like my agent and less like my grandmother, although the concerned expression she wore trumped her professional side by a long shot.

"The audition today went really well," I began tentatively.

I could imagine Joseph cracking a joke about how hard it must be for me to constantly have perfect auditions, but he wasn't here. Instead, Gran silently watched me, wordlessly asking me to continue.

"If I get the part, they would be filming during winter semester at school."

"And now you're wondering if you should take the part and take a break from school, or if you should turn it down to continue your education?" she asked, hitting the nail perfectly on the head.

"Pretty much," I sighed, draping my arm over my eyes to block out the world.

"What do you think would be the best thing to do?"

"I guess getting an education is always the right answer, isn't it?" I asked, honestly not sure anymore.

"Always is a dangerous word to use, Bliss. It's very rare for something to be *always* right."

I dropped my arm from my face and looked up in surprise at my grandmother, who had practically just told me it was okay to drop out of college to act. I watched her face with narrowed eyes, trying to see if this was some sort of test or joke. After all, what grown-up would tell a teenager that maybe staying in college wasn't such a great idea? I guessed, weighing the evidence, that a grandmother/agent who knew her granddaughter/client could get more work if she were in Hollywood rather than in Utah—that kind of grown-up.

"You wouldn't be mad if I took a break from school for now?" I asked, still suspicious of this implausible conversation.

"The way I see it, you went to school for two reasons. The first was to gain an education in the art of acting, am I right?"

I nodded my head in affirmation of this first fact. I had, indeed, wanted to learn more about theatre and stage acting.

"You're already a successful actress, Bliss. Hollywood has been desperate to place you in roles, despite your efforts to turn them away. That almost never happens."

I didn't point out the fact that the roles Hollywood had been offering were sleazy and crude, because I could sense Gran's momentum building and didn't want to interrupt.

"The second reason you left for school was to get away from the Hollywood scene—grow up a little so that you could take on more mature roles with less crude teenage humor in them."

I guess I had been wrong; she did acknowledge the fact that most of the roles I was getting were less than appealing. At least I had known better than to stop Gran when she was on a roll.

"You've now been offered a chance at a role that has everything you want. It's tasteful, serious, and will earn you a respected spot in the acting world," she said, ticking each point off on her fingers.

"That's true," I conceded, knowing already that I wanted to take a break from school after this semester, but feeling infinitely better hearing from someone else that my logic was sound.

"Either way, I want you to do what you feel is best, and know that I stand behind you all the way," she finished with one of the soft smiles that made me forget she had been an actress and model back in her youth. Instead, she just looked like my loving grandmother.

"Thanks Gran, that really helps," I told her, glad that we had talked even though I had been reluctant to disclose my feelings.

"What else is bothering you?"

At this question, I paused for a moment, unsure of if I wanted to tell her about Joseph and risk sounding like a jealous ex-girlfriend. Going on and on about our current predicament also wasn't the best way for me to stop whining. If anything, it would open the door to more neediness, and after my newly-made resolution to stop being such a drama queen, I really didn't want to fall back into my old ways.

"Out with it," she prompted, when I didn't speak.

Heaving a great sigh, I relented.

"Things with Joseph have been weird lately," I said, being as vague as I could be so that I didn't whine too much.

"You two aren't dating anymore, right?" she asked, although she knew very well that we had broken up right before starting college.

"Well, that's the thing. He said we had to stop dating because he didn't want to have a girlfriend to distract him before he went on his mission, but now he's dating some girl in our major," I said all in one breath, thinking that it wouldn't hurt as much if I said it really fast.

"Hmmm," was all Gran said as she thought this information through.

It was actually a little frightening seeing her lost for words. I couldn't remember a time in the past when that had happened.

"Do you want my honest opinion, Bliss?" she finally asked, making me wary.

"That doesn't sound good," I said.

"I'd give the boy a break. He has a lot of confusing feelings right now. I've seen how he's looked at you for the past nineteen years. He loves you, and I don't think some girl he just met is going to change that," she explained, sounding wise and sure of herself. "That being said, he is about to leave on a mission soon, and that's a good thing. I think the only person in the world who he would stay here for would be you."

"I'd never ask him to stay," I said indignantly.

"You wouldn't have to. I think he's worried that if he dates you, he'll *want* to stay too much, and he'll give up on his lifelong desire to serve a mission."

I turned this revelation over in my head and tried to decide if I really believed I had enough to power to make Joseph stay here. Even if I did, I wasn't sure I believed that's why he didn't want to date me anymore.

"So you don't think he suddenly stopped liking

me?" I asked, now feeling like the answer was obvious. After all, I wouldn't suddenly stop liking Joseph if he hadn't done anything wrong.

"Do I need to answer that, Bliss?"

"Well, then, I have an even bigger problem," I said, painfully aware of how whiny and dramatic I was being despite my best efforts to abandon all hormone-driven problems.

"And what's that?" Gran asked patiently, definitely acting as my grandmother now and not my agent.

"I think I like Ryan," I told her quietly, whispering the words as if they were a secret.

"Ryan Hex?" she clarified as I nodded. "The boy from *Forensic Faculty*?"

"That's him," I confirmed.

"Normally I'd tell you to avoid dating actors, but he seems like a genuinely nice boy," she said, as if that solved all my problems. If anything, that only made them worse. If he were a scumbag, my decision would be easy.

"Gran, that doesn't help," I wailed, giving in to my dramatic side just for the sake of this conversation. As soon as I was done talking to Gran, I'd get back to being mature and calm.

Or *start* being mature and calm, I guess.

"Bliss, what would keep you from dating this boy?" Gran asked, and I could tell that she was trying to lead me to a certain conclusion.

"I love Joseph, Gran. It's not possible that I can love Joseph so much and then feel butterflies when

Ryan kisses me."

"How do you feel about Ryan right now? Even compared to Joseph?" she asked, really making me think about it.

"It's hard to compare the two of them. For a while I was really mad at Joseph, so it was obvious which one I liked better. But now that he doesn't seem like such a jerk, I feel like it's comparing apples and oranges," I said, resting my chin on my bed and wishing I didn't feel like I needed to decide. "I've known Joseph my whole life, so he seems like the comfortable, obvious answer. I didn't really expect anyone else to put a question in my mind."

"But?" Gran prompted.

"But Ryan is so wonderful. I mean, we haven't even 'dated' really, but I've known him for a few years and I really like him. I wish I didn't. It feels cheap for me to decide I like him right as Joseph is leaving."

"If you like him, why don't you date him?" she asked, making me wonder if she had heard any of what I'd just said. "Going into this relationship with Ryan, do you intend to leave him right when Joseph gets back from his mission?"

"I don't *intend* to, but what if we happen to break up around that time and it looks like I left him for Joseph? Even if I didn't." I asked, hoping she'd be able to tell me what the best answer was. I obviously wasn't coming to the right conclusion fast enough.

"If that's what happens, then it happens for different reasons. It doesn't happen because that's what you planned all along. It happens because relationships end and peoples' feelings change," she explained. "I think Ryan would be going into this with the same feelings as you. He doesn't know how far the relationship will go, but he's excited by the prospect. And if you don't date him, maybe you'll be missing out on something great. You two could very well end up together."

"Yeah, I guess," I said, still feeling like no matter what I did, I was being a bad person. "So what do I do?"

"Be excited, Bliss," she said as if it were the most obvious answer in the world. "It's okay that you like Ryan. It doesn't make you a bad person. I know that you love Joseph and I honestly can't see a future where you don't love that boy, but loving someone and wanting to be with them are two different things."

"Really?" I asked, wondering if it could really be that simple.

"Do you not want to be with Ryan?" she asked, ignoring my question.

"I want to date him. I really like him, Gran," I said, remembering the way he had tried not to grin at me during the audition as I made a fool of myself.

I thought of his self-deprecating humor and his lack of confidence—a trait I'd somehow have to fix. I thought of the butterflies I got in my stomach when I was around him.

"So then, what's the problem, Bliss? Date the boy you like. Date the boy you want to be with, not the boy you feel like you *should* be with because he's been the obvious answer for so long."

"What about when I get little pangs of jealousy when I see Joseph with another girl? Does that make me a horrible person since I like Ryan?" I asked.

"I think it makes you human," she said, vocalizing what I had suspected all along. "Now stop being such a drama queen and tell that boy he'd better come over for dinner if he plans on dating my granddaughter."

CHAPTER 13

I woke up on Thanksgiving morning feeling much better about myself and my resolution to be less whiney about my relationship woes. I knew that New Year's was the time for making resolutions, but who says I couldn't make a nice Thanksgiving Day resolution? A day dedicated to stuffing ourselves with way too much food seemed as good a day as any to start making decisions and so, with that mentality, I established four Thanksgiving Day resolutions.

First, I would be friends with Joseph. Even if I got miffed when I saw him with Jade and even if I wished things hadn't ended so awkwardly between us, I'd much rather have him in my life as a friend than not have him at all.

Besides, my being so excited about possibly dating Ryan had dulled the hurt of our breakup. Joseph had always made a perfect friend and the idea of having that relationship back was exactly what I needed.

some stability in my life and someone to talk to again in Utah was just what I wanted.

The second resolution was to let myself be excited about Ryan. I had been so happy when I'd been with him in Utah, but my overactive mind had quickly squashed my happiness and replaced it with anxiety. Instead of giving in to my more dramatic side, I'd just trust my gut, which was currently telling me to go for it.

My third resolution was to do what I thought was right as far as my schooling situation went. I had called my dad the night before to get his opinion as he sat in the airport on his way back home for the holiday, and miraculously, he had told me to follow my instincts. I wasn't sure when all of the adults in my life had suddenly decided I was mature enough to make my own decisions, but it was a bit scary.

The fourth resolution was to avoid eating my weight in mashed potatoes at Thanksgiving dinner, but I had a feeling I'd be tossing that resolution out of the window the second I sat down at the table.

That, however, was the only resolution I was going to let myself drop. The rest were firmly in place, and my mood was already lighter than it had been for several months.

It didn't take long for my mood to improve even more when I woke up to the sounds of my dad and Gran arguing in the kitchen about some food item that was apparently "not traditional" enough for Thanksgiving.

With Dad being away so often for his super top-secret government job, it was always a huge deal for him to be home. I relished in the feeling of waking up to the sound of his voice in our home, and made my way down the carpeted stairs with bare feet, wearing old pajamas, and my wild dark brown curls sticking up in all directions.

"Dad!" I said excitedly when I entered the kitchen to see him smiling behind Gran's back about how worked up she got over her weird health food version of Thanksgiving. I ran over to him and threw my arms around his neck, instantly five years old again.

"Hey Button," he said as he squeezed me back. "How's my favorite college dropout?"

"So not funny, Dad," I said as I let him go, beaming from ear to ear.

Even though I hated that he was gone so much for work, I was happy that his job at least allowed him to be home during the holidays. It made me look forward to them that much more.

"When will you find out about the audition?" he asked, handing me a bowl to put real cereal in, rather than whatever actress-specific concoction Gran had dreamed up.

"It could be today or it could be a few weeks. I never really know," I told him, pouring the ultra sugary cereal he had brought me into my bowl and laughing when Gran shot me a look of disapproval. In her mind, I should always be eating weird fish and putting odd fruit masks on my face to help keep me camera-ready.

Dad had a slightly different approach.

"You know, Mom, I wouldn't mind making dinner this year," he said in an attempt to save us from another year of tofu turkey and black bean brownies.

"Don't even think about taking one step into my kitchen while I'm preparing our dinner, darling," she said in a singsong voice.

Dad raised his eyebrows at me dramatically before opening the newspaper to read while he ate.

I ate my very crunchy and very unhealthy cereal with a smile on my face, happy to have my family around me. Unlike Joseph, I didn't have a houseful of screaming siblings running around every day, and with Dad gone most of the time, it got pretty quiet around here. Today seemed perfect, with the sounds of Gran in the kitchen and my dad lazily flipping pages in the newspaper while he ate.

"Bliss, I wasn't joking when I said you need to bring that boy over for dinner if he plans to date you," Gran said, wielding a wooden spoon in my direction as if she'd use it as an implement of torture if I didn't listen to her. With her healthy cooking, she might be able to do just that.

"I will," I replied in the most noncommittal tone possible.

"Well, have you called and asked? Dinner will be ready by six," she threw over her shoulder.

"Today?" I said in disbelief. "Gran, I'm sure he has plans for Thanksgiving dinner."

"How can you know that if you haven't asked

him?" she asked logically.

"Dad," I whined, not wanting to suddenly look like a clingy stalker girl just because Ryan had barely kissed me once, over a month ago. It was one kiss that was hardly a kiss. It was more like a peck. Not calling him for a month might have squashed the idea that I was clingy, though.

"It couldn't hurt to ask, Button," he said, smiling as he read his paper.

Oh, he was enjoying this way too much.

"You guys are awful," I said, letting out a long-suffering sigh and wondering if I should just lie and say I called him when I didn't.

"You can't interrogate him if he comes over," I said warningly to my dad, placing my cereal bowl in the dishwasher. "I don't care what your top secret-government job teaches you. No methods of torture may be used!"

"I'm not making any promises, Button," he said.

"And you can't call me Button!" I cried, thinking of how embarrassing it would be for Ryan to hear all the weird pet names my family had for me. Bliss. Button. Where did the madness end?

"You love it when I call you Button," Dad said in a hurt tone, making me feel bad. Although, if we were being fair, he had brought it upon himself when he tried to force me to invite Ryan over.

"Yeah, I do, but not in front of the really cute, really famous actor who will be eating dinner with us," I pleaded.

"I'll do my best," he replied, still grinning at what

he apparently thought was a very funny situation. I thought it was the end of the world.

"And as for you," I said, pointing an accusatory finger at Gran.

"Oh, what could you possibly have to say about me?" she asked dramatically, even as she was pulling out a packet of seriously questionable green goo from the fridge.

"Do we have to do the whole 'healthy Thanksgiving' thing today?" I asked, knowing full well that I sounded spoiled rotten. But I had finally decided to let myself like Ryan; I didn't want him to run screaming from the house after seeing our rubbery tofu turkey.

"We absolutely do. No questions," was all she said, instantly ending the conversation.

I let out one more long dramatic sigh for effect before heading up to my room, accompanied by the sound of Gran saying, "Actresses are so high-maintenance," following me as I climbed the stairs.

Sitting down and waiting for my computer to boot up, I twirled my hair around my finger, wondering if I should run the decision to invite Ryan over for dinner by Candice first. She seemed knowledgeable with that sort of thing, but she also didn't seem like the type to want to talk about boys.

Instead, I logged onto Twitter, assuming that if Ryan had plans for Thanksgiving, he'd post them there and then I wouldn't have to invite him at all. I'd have a perfectly good excuse to give Gran and Dad.

I searched until I found his page and then clicked on it, not sure if I was hoping he'd have plans or wishing I could spend some time with him. Life was a little confusing right now.

Looking nervously at the last thing he'd posted, I was instantly grateful that Gran had suggested inviting him over. Only minutes ago he had posted all the confirmation I needed that he should be with us today:

@RyanHex: Off to visit some family for an hour then it's TV dinner turkey time. Jealous? #HappyThanksgiving

I couldn't help but smile at the fact that his personality showed through even on Twitter, although his message made me feel like a jerk for not knowing he'd be alone on Thanksgiving. I wondered why he didn't mention it to me before realizing that I wouldn't go around telling people something like that. It would just look like I was trying to get invited over or wanted to start a pity party.

Not wanting to seem overbearing, I avoided the actual phone call method and utilized the cowardice afforded by technology. That way if he let me down, he wouldn't have to do it over the phone.

@MsJuneLaurie: @RyanHex Why have TV dinner turkey when you can have tofu turkey over here? It's ½ step up right? #HappyThanksgiving

I clicked the send button quickly so that I couldn't

take it back before realizing that by asking him to come over on Twitter, he could possibly turn me down in front of *a lot* of people. That was worse than him doing it over the phone.

Scrambling to delete my terrible attempt at humor, I was surprised when a new tweet appeared above mine. I held my breath as I read it. Yeah, I was *that* excited to see him. I know. Pathetic.

@RyanHex: @MsJuneLaurie Should I bring my wheatgrass infused soil rich mashed potatoes? They're brown but good.

I couldn't help but laugh at his post, not only because he hadn't thought I was a complete weirdo, but because we might actually have a date. Kind of. You know . . . the kind of date with your grandma and your dad.

Awkward.

As I contemplated writing him back, my phone buzzed on the nightstand. I sprang to my feet to answer, not even bothering to look at the caller ID. I already knew who it was.

"Hello?" I asked, waiting to hear the sound of Ryan's voice on the other line.

"Hey June," I heard a very non-Ryan voice say. "It's Joseph."

"Oh," was all I managed to say, not quite ready to face my first Thanksgiving Day resolution just yet.

"How are you?" he asked after an awkward pause. Even the phone static seemed to be uncomfortable.

"I'm fine, how are you?" I asked in return, trying to be polite after having forgotten my entire apology speech.

"Fine," he answered.

Silence.

"Happy Thanksgiving," he said finally.

"Yeah, you too."

Silence.

"Listen, thanks for the plane ticket. That was really nice of you, especially considering that we had just . . . you know," he trailed off, leaving us with the awkward phone static once more.

"No problem. I didn't want you driving that beat-up old car all the way to California by yourself." I wasn't sure why I wasn't apologizing like I had planned to—it wasn't like the words were hard to form, but suddenly, I couldn't do it.

"Well, thanks again," he mumbled, apparently not quite ready to apologize yet either.

"You're welcome," I responded just as my phone beeped, indicating that I had another call waiting.

"Hey June?" Joseph said tentatively.

"Sorry, I've got another call," I told him.

"Oh. Right. Okay, well, have a good Thanksgiving," he said again.

"You too Joseph," I answered, trying to keep my voice neutral.

"Bye."

I didn't let myself think about the bizarre conversation I'd just had as I switched over to the other call that was waiting for me. I'd have to mull over what it all meant later.

"June Laurie, is it just me, or was that an invitation to come over for Thanksgiving dinner?" Ryan asked right as I picked up his call, bringing a smile to my face.

"I wasn't actually inviting you over," I said in the most serious voice I could muster.

"Oh. Wow, I feel like a huge idiot right now, then," he replied, instantly making me feel bad for teasing him.

"Ryan, I'm totally kidding. I really want you to come over today if you don't have any plans."

"Or an aversion to tofu turkey."

"That too," I said with a laugh. "So, what do you think?"

"I think that sounds way better than eating a TV dinner alone and watching reruns of your *Forensic Faculty* episodes," he joked.

"Wow, you're so creepy," I informed him.

"At least I didn't tell you about the lock of your hair I keep stashed under my pillow. Oh, oops. Did I let that slip?"

"Okay, we need to change topics before your joking does some permanent damage to our relationship," I said, before slapping a hand over my mouth.

I had said we'd had a relationship.

That could mean anything, really. It could mean our friendship, so it wasn't like it was a big deal that I'd used the "R" word right?

"Right. Our *relationship*," he said, exaggerating the word I'd hoped he hadn't heard.

He was such a punk.

"So, when do you want to come over?" I asked, shamelessly changing the subject. He laughed on the other end of the line at my attempt to be smooth, but accepted the conversation shift without question.

"I'm going to go visit my grandma today at noon. I can come over probably any time after one?"

"Sounds like a plan," I said glancing at the clock and wishing that one o'clock wasn't three hours away.

"You wouldn't want to come visit my grandma with me, would you?" he asked, which I was definitely not expecting. The joking tone had left his voice and now he was completely serious. "Never mind. That was stupid to ask. Just pretend I didn't say anything, okay?"

"I'd love to," I said quickly. I felt horrible that I had never asked Ryan about his family situation before. I had no idea if he talked to his parents or grandparents, and this would be the perfect opportunity to get to know him better.

"Wait, really?" he asked in surprise. "You do know Lukas Leighton won't be there, right?"

"Yeah, I think it would be fun," I said, shaking my head at his joke. No one was ever going to let me forget my short-lived crush on that guy, were they? "Plus, you have to put up with meeting my family today, so I should at least get to meet some of yours."

"I've met your family before, though," he pointed out, quite accurately.

"Yeah, but not as . . ." I stopped there. Not as what? Not as my boyfriend? Because technically he still wouldn't be meeting them as my boyfriend. We had only kissed once.

One peck does not a boyfriend make.

"Gotcha," he said in understanding, not forcing me to finish my sentence, for which I was very grateful.

"Also, I sort of don't have a car and have no way to get to L.A.," I said guiltily.

I honestly should have just bought a car, but Gran or Joseph had always insisted on dropping me off and picking me up from the set so I wouldn't get mugged or kidnapped or whatever they thought would happen. Having a car just didn't make any sense if I wouldn't be using it, and I was still holding out hope that one day Gran would get tired of her beautiful, red, old-fashioned car so I could take it off her hands.

"Forget it. We're done. You're way too needy," he said jokingly.

"I know, I'm like the worst non-girlfriend ever."

"My grandma is actually in West Hills, so it's right by you. I'll pick you up at about eleven thirty?" he asked.

I looked at the clock again.

"I can be presentable in an hour and a half," I said. "Maybe."

"Just remember, this is my grandma we're going to meet, so none of those costumes you wore on *Forensic Faculty*," he said in mock sternness, as if he were giving me a lecture. "We'll save those for later tonight."

"Wow. I'm hanging the phone up now," I told him, trying not to laugh.

"See you soon."

CHAPTER 14

By the time eleven thirty rolled around, I had tried on about fifteen different outfits and attempted to rip out my hair, wishing it was straight and not so difficult to manage. Why was it so hard to figure out what to wear when meeting your non-boyfriend's grandma?

I ended up in a brown tulle skirt, purple heels, a long-sleeved dark purple shirt, and a brown scarf. I looked myself over in the mirror, sighing at my long dark curls falling down my back unapologetically. Even if my hair was out of control, the rest of me looked acceptable.

I wasn't sure what I was so worried about—it wasn't like I was a bad girl, by any means. I guessed that because this was my first time ever doing the "meet the family" thing, I had a right to be a bit on-edge. I never had to meet Joseph's family; I'd pretty much been born into it.

The doorbell rang downstairs and my stomach

instantly filled with butterflies, shocking me a bit. It wasn't like I hadn't hung out with Ryan before, but this was different, for obvious reasons.

I bolted down the stairs as fast as I could, tripping down most of them in an attempt to get to the door before my dad did.

Unfortunately, that didn't happen.

I got there just in time to see him open the front door and give Ryan his best "Dad glare."

"Hello Mr. Laurie," Ryan said, sounding like the nice, respectable boy he was.

"Nice to see you again, Ryan," my dad replied—a little stiffly, if I'm being honest.

The last time Dad had met Ryan, I'd been leaving for college and there was nothing going on between us. Now that Ryan was almost dating his little girl, it was a whole new ball game, and that ball game included Dad trying to be intimidating.

"What are you and June doing today?" he asked. "Dinner will be ready at six."

"We're going visit my grandmother in her nursing home," Ryan replied.

A perfectly innocent activity that my dad couldn't have any problem with, right?

Wrong.

"Well, that shouldn't take too long. That gives you a good four hours between activities. Where are you going after you visit your grandmother?"

Seriously, Dad? Could this get any more embarrassing? What did he think we were going to do?

"Oh," was all Ryan managed to say, apparently not thinking he'd need to lay out our entire non-existent itinerary on the spot. "I don't think I understand, Sir."

"Don't you?" my dad replied, definitely utilizing his government job training now.

"Okay, thanks for getting the door, Dad," I interrupted, walking straight past the awkward scene at the door and grabbing Ryan by the hand as we walked toward his car. "We'll be back soon. Love you!"

"Bye Button," Dad called.

Oh, he was good.

I tried to ignore my bright red cheeks as I forcibly pulled Ryan to his car and let myself into the passenger's side. After he got in, he let out a deep sigh and then looked at me with raised eyebrows.

"I don't remember your dad being quite that scary," he said, looking a bit rattled.

"He thinks he has to be intimidating now that we're . . . you know . . . not quite friends."

Ryan smirked at this explanation of our relationship status, but didn't say anything.

"What does he do again?"

"I have no idea," I said honestly. "All I'm allowed to know is that he's a math genius, works for the government, and is gone all the time."

"Scary," Ryan remarked as he pulled away from my house.

"Tell me about it. You aren't the one who stays at home wondering if he's just working in an office or if he's some sort of CIA agent out in the field getting shot at all the time."

"That has to be rough."

"It's not fun, I can tell you that much," I admitted, though I was anxious to change the subject away from my dad's cryptic work. "I feel bad that we've never really talked about *your* family. What are your parents like?"

Ryan was silent for a moment and I wondered if maybe he had a bad relationship with his parents. Maybe I should have asked Candice before just coming right out with a question that might make this day awkward.

"My parents were really great," he finally said, one word showing me why he hadn't told me about his family before.

"Were?" I asked.

I had to.

You couldn't just ignore something like that.

"They died in a car accident when I was eight," he said very matter-of-factly.

Too matter-of-factly. As if he had rehearsed that answer as many times as possible so that he wouldn't get emotional when repeating it.

"Ryan, I'm so sorry," I said sincerely, wishing he wasn't driving so that I could give him a hug.

Instead, I grabbed his free hand and didn't let go. He shrugged as if it weren't a big deal, even though I knew what a big deal it was. No matter how easily I shrugged off the fact that I had never had a mother, it still hurt on days when I wanted her advice.

"I guess we have more in common than you knew," he said with a smile that was very forced, even for an actor as good as Ryan.

"Did your grandma raise you?" I asked, feeling my heart break for him. Even though I had never known my mom, since she died when I was nine months old, I at least had Gran and Dad.

"She did. You'll love her, June, she's great," he said with the warmest smile I'd ever seen. "She's in a nursing home now and sometimes her memory isn't the best, but she's really sweet."

"I can't wait to meet her," I told him, still wondering how I could have known someone for two years and never asked about their family life.

I was kind of an awful friend.

"What should I call her?" I asked as we stood outside of his grandma's door.

Ryan held a small bouquet of flowers that instantly gave him brownie points in my book. What kind of guy brought his grandmother flowers? Only good guys.

"She goes by Nana," he said, his cheeks flushing slightly at using the nickname in front of me.

"Nana," I repeated, trying it on for size. "I like it."

Giving me one last smile, Ryan opened the door to his grandmother's room and entered, with me following tentatively in his wake.

The first thing I noticed about the room was the pictures. They were everywhere!

A picture of a little boy with bright blonde hair and deep blue eyes, missing a tooth and holding up a fish in a plastic bag full of water at the fair. A picture of a teenaged Ryan in a tux standing in front of a house with a girl in a formal dress; corsage on wrist and all. A picture of Ryan as I knew him now, leaning down to be at the same level as his sitting grandmother and smiling broadly. There were even pictures of Ryan from magazines that she had apparently clipped out.

The room screamed "Proud Grandma" and I loved it.

"Ryan!" I heard a woman exclaim from an armchair in the corner of the room. Ryan's grandma was exactly as a grandma ought to be. Granted, I was probably an odd judge, since my Gran was still too young and way too outgoing for her own good, but Ryan's Nana looked like a stereotypical grandma from a hot cocoa commercial—white hair, knit sweater, and glasses.

"Hi Nana," Ryan said, giving her the flowers and leaning down to kiss her on the cheek. "Happy Thanksgiving."

"Happy Thanksgiving," she said in return. "I watched your show this week."

"Oh yeah?"

"You looked very handsome," she informed him. "I don't know why you aren't the star of that program yet."

"I'll be doing a movie soon, remember?" he asked, in the manner of someone who knew the person they spoke to didn't remember.

"That's right," she said as it dawned on her. "With that pretty girl you like?"

My cheeks reddened at this statement and I tried desperately to be silent by the doorway and ignore the fact that Ryan had called me pretty. Obviously his grandmother didn't realize I was in the room. And apparently Ryan had been talking about me to his grandma, which was pretty flattering, but probably embarrassing for him right at that moment.

"Nana, she's here right now," he said through gritted teeth as he beckoned me over. I walked to where she sat and extended my hand, trying to exude friendliness. It was obvious that Ryan's grandma meant a lot to him and I didn't want her disapproving of me.

"Hi, I'm June," I told her as we shook hands.

"My word," she said with wide eyes. "You look exactly like Lillian Gish, young lady. Did you know that?"

"I have heard that before," I said, leaving out the fact that I had heard that from just about every casting director I had ever met.

"You should take that as a compliment. She was a beautiful girl," Nana explained.

"June is a bit of an old soul," Ryan said with a smile in my direction. "She's pretty well versed in silent films."

"Is that so?" Nana asked, seeming to approve of this. "And are you dating my Ryan now?"

I balked at the question, not wanting to tell Ryan's

sweet grandma that things were a bit complicated between us, but not wanting to say we were together and freak him out either. Luckily Ryan saved me from having to answer.

"We're spending Thanksgiving together," he said simply.

"Ryan is the best boy you'll ever meet, so don't you go breaking his heart, young lady," Nana warned.

"No ma'am," I said, glancing over at Ryan, who shrugged at me.

"I am pretty great," he said, making me want to shove him or hit his arm, even though neither seemed appropriate in the current situation.

"Why don't you two have a seat?" she offered. We sat side by side on the couch and I tried to keep myself from being painfully aware of every little facial expression I made. It was ridiculous how nervous I was.

"So Ryan, have you spoken to Julia lately?" Nana asked.

A shadow passed over Ryan's face, though I couldn't understand why. He glanced over at me for a moment with a pained expression, as if he suddenly wished that I wasn't there. It didn't make any sense until I heard his response.

"Nana, Mom isn't here anymore," he said quietly, and suddenly I understood the darkness in his eyes.

"Did she and your father go on another one of their trips? I swear, if I've told them once, I've told them a hundred times that they need to spend more time at home," she said, unaware of the pain Ryan was going through.

"They're not too far; just in Carlsbad," he told her, catching me off guard.

I had been sure we were in for a long, uncomfortable explanation of the truth. Instead, Ryan had suddenly invented a vacation for his parents who were no longer alive. I guess sometimes lying is easier than telling the truth.

"Well, as much as I miss them, I'm sure they're having a good time," she said, turning her attention back to the book in her lap. "I just wish they'd visit more often."

"I miss them too, Nana," he said with a small crack in his voice that I pretended not to notice.

Lying could definitely be easier than telling the truth.

CHAPTER 15

The ride back to my house was mostly silent. I kept trying to think of something to say, but nothing would come to mind. As we pulled into my neighborhood, I remembered the look on Ryan's face as he lied to someone so important to him. Maybe that was the reason he had become an actor; he had gotten a lot of practice over the years.

"I feel bad taking you away from your grandma on Thanksgiving," I finally said as he parked the car in front of my house.

"She prefers to eat dinner with her friends at the nursing home," he said, still looking straight ahead. "Plus, on bad memory days, it's better to let her think I'm going home to dinner with my parents."

"Rather than explaining what's going on?"

Ryan looked over at me with an unreadable expression, indecision passing over his face.

"I hope you don't think I'm a horrible person for lying to her. She has days where she knows the truth and days where she doesn't. Sometimes I'll explain it to her, but those seem to be her worst days. I've found that giving her hope by keeping them alive is better for her."

"But how is it for you?" I asked, never wanting to see the hurt on his face that I had seen today again.

"It's hard," he admitted. "But it's worth it to keep her happy."

I didn't know what to say to that, having never made that kind of sacrifice for someone. I tried to imagine talking about my mom as if she were alive when all I wanted to do when people brought her up was cry.

"You're strong," I told him, taking his hand and holding his gaze.

"I don't know if it makes me strong. Most likely it means I'm a coward."

"I think it takes more bravery to put on a good face for someone you love, even when you don't want to."

"What do you have to cover with a brave face?" he asked, his gaze intense.

I thought about his question for a minute, thinking of how little I talked about my mom, about how I hated that my dad was always gone, about how hard it was to love a profession that let you down so often, and I sighed.

"A lot," I said, giving him a small laugh as if all of the disappointing things in my life were no big deal. "Aren't we supposed to talk about things we're grateful for today?" I said, realizing that my current pity party was very out of line with my Thanksgiving resolution to be less dramatic.

"I'm grateful for tofu turkey," Ryan stated as he got out of the car.

I followed suit as I said, "I'm grateful for a dad who embarrasses me by calling me Button in front of my non-boyfriend."

I linked my arm through his as we walked into the house. We still had a few hours until dinner and Gran wouldn't let me anywhere near the kitchen, so I pulled Ryan upstairs into my room.

"I'm grateful for Twitter, without which I wouldn't be here in June Laurie's room today."

"Door open, Bliss," I heard Gran call from downstairs.

"I know," I called back with a giggle. "I'm grateful for the trust of my family," I said sarcastically as I nudged my bedroom door with my foot so that the door swung halfway closed.

"I'm grateful for two-story houses," Ryan finally whispered as he leaned in and kissed me.

I'm not sure if it's some sort of built-in girl radar, but I definitely knew the kiss was coming. In fact, before Ryan had even leaned in to kiss me, I was already standing up on my tiptoes to bring my lips to his. We were like magnets.

The fact that I had expected it, though, didn't mean it wasn't the most perfect thing I could have asked for after the emotion-filled scene at the nursing home.

I wrapped my arms around Ryan's neck as his

arms around my waist pulled me closer to him. Our first kiss had been about as intense as a stage kiss performed by elementary school kids, but this was on a whole other level, and I kind of wish I hadn't enjoyed it as much as I did. Part of me was hoping that it would be awful and we could just end our relationship right then and there to avoid any complications.

But it wasn't awful. It was amazing.

His hands grasped my waist and kept me close to him as I tried to keep any coherent thought in my head; a losing battle to say the least. I let my fingers slide through his hair (messing it up I'm sure) while trying to catch my breath that had caught in my chest at this sudden intimacy we were sharing.

I smiled as he kissed me and was completely caught up in him. I had no idea how long it lasted, but I knew it was probably longer than it should have been. I also had no idea when Gran had come up the stairs and opened the door to my bedroom all the way until she cleared her throat and Ryan and I pulled apart faster than if we were on fire.

"Nice loophole, Bliss, but an open door is open, not just unlatched," Gran said with the most frightening smirk ever. I couldn't tell if she thought this situation was funny or out of line. Either way, I could feel my cheeks burning as she walked away and went back downstairs.

I looked over at Ryan, whose hair was sticking up in all different directions and face as red as mine, and bit my lip to keep from laughing. He mouthed "Wow" as he returned my gaze, his eyes wide.

"So this is my room," I said very loudly so that Gran would hear downstairs.

"It's great," he replied just as loudly.

"That was awkward," I offered in a normal voice, walking over to sit at my vanity. Ryan took a seat on the bed across from me and looked around my room, patting his hair back into place.

"Understatement," he said as he inspected the room I had grown up in. I wondered what it looked like to him, what each little knick-knack said about my personality. I had plenty of Art Nouveau decorations everywhere and more silent film DVDs than I could count, but I still wanted to know what he thought of it all.

"Your room is very . . . you," he finally said, stating the obvious. "A set dresser with a June Laurie fact sheet could have built this, it's so perfect."

"That's exactly what we did. We commissioned a set dresser to come decorate for me," I deadpanned, making Ryan laugh.

We were both silent for a moment as Ryan's eyes roamed over my lips and the small smile that crossed his face told me that he was doing the exact same thing as me: reliving the brief moment we had just had.

"Sorry about Gran," I said after another short silence.

"It's probably for the best," he said cryptically, still studying his surroundings and confusing me to no end with his words.

"I can't believe we've known each other for over two years and you've never seen my room," I began, trying to make conversation while my mind was screaming *I just kissed Ryan!*

"You've never even been to my apartment, have you?" he asked.

"I haven't," I confirmed. "We always just went out when we were all together, or we'd go back to Benjamin's place."

"You'll have to visit. Maybe I can cook you dinner before you head back to Utah?" he offered, surprising me yet again. I had no idea Ryan could cook.

"I would love that," I told him with a slow, easy smile.

"Also, I didn't want to say anything that would get your hopes up, but the casting director liked your audition."

"Wait really?" I asked, my energy level instantly picking up.

"Nothing's for sure yet, but they couldn't stop talking about you," he told me, his eyes looking up at me while his head stayed tilted toward the floor. He raised an eyebrow in a way that said he knew something I didn't, but I tried to ignore it, not wanting to jinx anything.

"So, what you're saying is that we might be spending more time together after all?"

"It is a possibility."

"I guess if I have to suffer through your company,

I will," I told him with a grin, knowing that right at that moment, there was nothing else I'd rather "suffer" through.

"What exactly is this?" I asked Gran, eyeballing the side dish that looked like that cranberry cylinder that comes out of a can except that it was green.

"Jellied artichoke hearts and spinach," she answered without missing a beat, finishing something brown and steaming on her plate.

I stole a glance at Ryan, whose mouth was twitching in the corner as if he might smile. I'd bet money he was trying to think of the best way to relay this experience to Benjamin later that night.

"Everything's wonderful, Mrs. Adams," Ryan said, earning some major black bean brownie points with Gran.

"Everyone thinks health food automatically means tasteless food," Gran began.

"Oh, I can definitely taste it," I put in quietly.

"But it doesn't," she finished loudly, purposefully drowning me out.

"You've really outdone yourself this time, Mom," Dad said beside me, though I did notice that he purposefully didn't specify whether or not she had outdone herself in a good or bad way.

"Seriously, though, thank you for keeping us healthy against our will, Gran. We'll keep looking twenty years younger than we are—just like you— because of your crazy remedies," I said, wanting her to know that we really did appreciate her cooking our entire Thanksgiving meal for us.

"Thank you, Bliss," she said as she stood to retrieve a plate of sketchy-looking brownies.

"What's that?" I asked through gritted teeth, trying to smile like I was excited about the less than appealing concoction she held on her plate.

"Black bean brownies," she said, as if those words should always be uttered in the same sentence.

"Actually, Ryan wanted to take me out to get dessert after dinner," I lied, kicking him under the table and hoping he'd play along.

"I'm really sorry Annette, I didn't realize you'd be making dessert on top of everything else you did today," he said with so much sincerity that I wondered how he hadn't won an Oscar yet.

"Oh, you couldn't have known," she answered, sounding flustered.

Was it possible that Ryan was actually smooth-talking Gran—a woman who could tell when someone was acting before they even realized they were doing it?

"We don't have to go out to get dessert," he quickly amended, making me want to kick him under the table again, although this time it would be for a very different reason.

"These brownies will keep for a long time since they don't have egg in them," she said, causing me to shudder as I wondered what they *did* have in them. "Why don't you two kids go have fun. Your father and I can clean this up ourselves."

"Lucky," Dad whispered to me as he began collecting the plates.

"Are you sure?" I asked, now feeling a little bad about my lie. Not only did we get out of clean-up duty but Ryan would be forced to buy me dessert. Okay . . . so maybe I didn't feel all that bad about that part.

"Positive. Go have fun," she insisted.

"I'm sorry you were forced to buy me dessert," I said to Ryan as I got another spoonful of the melting chocolate cake we were sharing.

"No you're not," he countered right away.

"No, I'm not," I agreed, savoring the combination of rich chocolate cake and vanilla ice cream. I closed my eyes as I ate, never ceasing to be amazed by the power of good chocolate. "This has to be the best cake I've ever had," I told him.

We had gone to a little sidewalk café in Hollywood that Ryan swore had the best desserts, and I had to admit, he wasn't wrong.

"I love that you do that," he said, breaking me out of my trance.

"Do what?" I asked, looking up at him, suddenly self-conscious.

"Close your eyes when you're eating something you really like." I wasn't sure when he had noticed something about me that I didn't even know, but it made my stomach do a little flip.

"I do that?" I asked, trying to decide if it was true

or not.

"It's really cute," he said, trying to hide a small smile as he continued to eat.

"When did you notice?" I asked, suddenly curious.

"About a week into shooting your first episodes for *Forensic Faculty*," he said as he moved some chocolate cake around on the plate with his fork. "You were eating that fancy Swiss orange chocolate Benjamin brought. While we were all talking you just sat there with your eyes closed and the smallest hint of a smile on your face. It was probably the single cutest thing I've ever seen," he finished, making me blush. Apparently I was blushing a lot that day.

"I can't believe you noticed something like that."

"Yeah, I'm pretty creepy," he joked as he took care of the bill so we could leave.

Walking back to his car, I tried to imagine what my life would be like if I got the part in the movie. I could be living here in Hollywood, spending every day just like this one. I could walk through the city with my hand in Ryan's, not worrying about perfect French girls who liked Joseph or roommates who didn't talk to me. It would be nice.

When Ryan opened my door for me to get into the car, I turned to look at him. He looked different now than he had when I'd first started on *Forensic Faculty*. His cheeks were covered with a short 5 o'clock shadow, and his deep blue eyes seemed more grown up than they had before. But despite the differences in his face that showed his transformation from the sidekick into the leading role, he was still the same sweet Ryan.

"Thank you for everything today," I told him as I stood on my toes and touched my nose to his. "It was so perfect."

And then I kissed him again, my hands grasping the collar of his coat and a smile playing on my lips.

Oh yeah. I could get used to this life.

CHAPTER 16

"Good morning Button," my dad said over his ever-present newspaper.

"Hi," I mumbled, still fighting against the call of my warm, inviting bed that really wanted me to go back to sleep. "Where's Gran?" I asked, looking around the spotless kitchen as I pulled out the sugary cereal that was pretty much contraband in this house.

"You know your grandmother—she can't resist a good excuse to go shopping."

"Black Friday?" I guessed, to which Dad just nodded.

"Did you have a good time getting dessert with Ryan last night?" Dad asked, his eyes peeking out over the top of his newspaper.

"Yeah, it was really fun," I answered, trying to hide my smile since Dad was, in fact, watching me.

"Looks like it," was all he said as he slid a piece of paper across the counter. I looked down at it in confusion, wondering what on earth he was talking about.

As I scanned the paper, my heart sank. There, on the printed sheet, a headline screamed, *"Are things heating up off the set of Forensic Faculty?"* right above a very large picture of Ryan and me kissing by his car yesterday.

I slapped a hand over my mouth, mortified. Yes, I was nineteen and Dad knew I kissed boys (honestly, since I was Mormon, he had it pretty easy, since kissing was all I was doing) but that didn't mean he had to *see* me kissing boys!

"Oh. My. Gosh. Dad, where did you get this?"

"It was the strangest thing," he said in a voice much too calm for the current situation. "I went online to check my mail and there it was, on the MSN homepage."

"It's on MSN?" I wailed, thinking this day couldn't get any worse. "I'm going to die," I shouted over my shoulder, completely abandoning my resolution to stop being melodramatic as I ran upstairs to my room and booted up my computer.

I typed wildly into the search engine, wondering if anything else would pop up when I searched Ryan Hex and June Laurie. Much to my horror, there were a few sites bearing the same picture of us kissing.

I tried to think back to when we were outside of his car. I guess there were a lot of people around and we were in Hollywood, so pretty much *everyone* had a camera, but I hadn't seen any paparazzi types lurking. Plus, I didn't think in a million years they'd be interested in Ryan and me. Ryan was hardly ever in the tabloids and no one had ever bothered taking my picture since I just had a small role on the show.

Not sure if I really wanted to, I clicked on one of the links that brought me to a fan site for Ryan. (Who knew that someone had made him a fan site, right?) The header of the site was a collage of pictures of him from *Forensic Faculty* promotions and a few candids, and right beneath that was the same article copied and pasted from MSN.

"This can't be happening," I told my computer—not that it changed reality.

At the bottom of the article was a link stating that there were comments on the post and—yet again, against my better judgment—I clicked on them.

Now, before you wonder how I could be so stupid, I have to admit that I did know better. When I was on *Forensic Faculty*, it only took one comment on a blog saying that I couldn't act to save my life to stop reading what "fans" had said about me. But when there's a giant color photo of you kissing your non-boyfriend on a busy street in Hollywood, you can bet I wanted to know what people were saying about it.

Most of the comments weren't too bad. A few even said we made a cute couple and it's about time Ryan found a nice girlfriend.

Some of them weren't so nice. A few said Ryan should be their girlfriend. A few people thought he could do better (which, honestly, he probably could). But there was only one I really chose to focus on.

Wow, is it just me or has June Laurie really let herself go since Forensic Faculty? What a fatty.

I stared at the comment with an open mouth, not sure if I had read that right. I had always been petite and even after heading off to college, I hadn't gained more than two or three pounds. As I stared at that comment, I had to wonder, though—had I let myself go?

I looked down at my legs in my tight black yoga pants. Had my thighs always touched when I sat on a chair? Suddenly I couldn't remember and I began to panic. Didn't everyone's thighs touch when they sat down? Wasn't it physically impossible for them not to?

All of a sudden I felt lightheaded. It's not that it would be the worst thing in the world if I had gained weight, it would just be the worst thing in the world if people all over the Internet were talking about it behind my back.

Suddenly I had to know. I looked through other posts with other comments and read awful sentence after awful sentence.

Hasn't she heard of a flat iron?

Aren't celebrities supposed to have nice skin?

If Ryan's so hot, why is he dating a porker like June Laurie?

Wow, she's hideous.

I would say she should go jump off a cliff but she probably couldn't lug her bulk up there to do it.

My eyes were pricking as tears filled them and I tried not to let them spill over as I stared at the hateful words on the screen. Apparently everyone thought I was fat, ugly, and a horrible actress with frizzy hair.

That was just perfect.

"Button, didn't you want to come down and finish your cereal?" my dad called up from the kitchen, not knowing how much I never wanted to eat again.

"I'm not hungry," I called back, trying to get used to the phrase I knew I'd have to utter frequently if I wanted these mean comments to stop.

About three hours and two hundred yoga positions later, I was feeling a little better about myself. I knew working out for a few hours wasn't going to suddenly make me thinner, but the fact that I wasn't sitting on the couch gorging myself on ice cream and leftover turkey somehow felt productive.

"Looks like you're having fun on our very short school break," Joseph said from my doorway, causing me to jump about five feet in the air. What was it with people sneaking up on me in my own room lately?

"What are you doing here?" I asked, panting half from the workout and half from the scare I'd just received.

Joseph looked a little hurt by my question and I instantly wanted to rephrase it to let him know I'd meant how did he get into the house and upstairs without making a sound.

"I just wanted to bring this over," he said in a deflated voice, holding out the biggest dark chocolate cookie I'd ever seen. "Tradition and all that," he mumbled.

"Oh, I totally forgot," I answered apologetically.

Despite the fact that I wasn't in any position to start eating my weight in cookies, I took it from him. I'd just give it to Dad later and let Joseph think I'd eaten it.

"If you don't want it, that's fine. I just didn't want to break tradition," he added quickly, obviously uncomfortable standing here with me.

"No I definitely want it," I lied. "You just scared me. I didn't even hear you ring the bell."

"Your dad was outside, so he just told me to walk right in," he explained with a shrug, looking out of place in a house he'd practically grown up in.

"Thanks for my Black Friday dark chocolate cookie," I said finally, remembering my Thanksgiving Day resolution to keep things between Joseph and me as normal as possible. I was determined not to hold any hard feelings over the fact that he thought dating me was difficult. "I'd hug you, but I'm all sweaty," I explained.

"I don't care," he said, still mumbling slightly and keeping his eyes trained on the ground.

"Well, then, in that case, you can have one very gross hug," I replied lightheartedly, pulling him into a hug that felt perfectly familiar. As much as I hated to admit it, I had missed him. He hugged me back tighter than he ever had, and I could tell he had missed me too. We could definitely do this friend thing.

When we pulled apart, he looked at me for the first time in ages and smiled.

"Thank you for my cookie," I said.

"It's not exactly a round-trip plane ticket, but hopefully it tastes pretty good," he answered.

"I hope that wasn't weird that I did that. I really didn't want you driving that junker of a car all by yourself."

"It wasn't weird. It was nice," he assured me, looking around my room as if he hadn't seen it in ages. "Why are you working out on Black Friday? Isn't Annette out shopping?"

"I don't only work out when she tells me to," I said a little sharply, becoming a little defensive about the topic ever since I'd read all of the mean comments online. "I work out a lot."

"Yeah, I know you do," Joseph answered with an odd glance in my direction. He was trying to read me, I could tell, but he couldn't quite decipher what was going on. That had to bug him. As he'd told me many times before, he'd been taking June 101 for nineteen years.

We were both silent for a moment—me trying to remind myself that freaking out at anyone who mentioned something remotely related to weight wasn't helping my situation at all, and Joseph . . . well . . . I wasn't quite sure what he was doing.

"I turned in my mission papers," he finally said, watching me carefully as he broke the news.

"That's great!" I exclaimed. It was, even if I didn't want him out of my life for two years.

"Thanks," he replied, because that's all he could really say when we were on such shaky ground with our friendship.

"I wish we had never dated," I accidentally blurted out, my unintentionally raised voice leaving the silence that followed that much more awkward.

I don't know why I said it—I mean, besides the fact that it was semi-true. We had been talking about mission papers! I was supposed to say something like, "where do you think you'll go?" or, "are you nervous?" not, "I wish we had never dated."

That was me: brimming with tact.

"Oh," Joseph said, breaking a very uncomfortable silence. He looked at the ground once more and I mentally kicked myself for doing the exact thing I had resolved not to do—make things weird.

"Not because I didn't enjoy it," I explained, thinking he might misunderstand me. "Just because now that we've dated, things are really weird between us and I hate it. I miss how we used to be."

"I'm glad you explained that," he answered with a small smile. "I thought you meant you hated dating me."

"No. Unlike me, you're not difficult to date," I said, yet again displaying my stunning lack of tact.

Good job June. That didn't make things awkward at all.

"June, that's not what I meant," he said, placing his hands on my shoulders and staring intently into my eyes. "I know my bad phrasing is what started this whole mess, but I want to fix that right now. Set things straight."

"I don't think your phrasing started this mess. I think deciding not to date all of a sudden started it."

"Either way, when I said it was too hard for me to date you, I didn't mean that I don't want to date you. I actually *really* want to date you. That's the problem," he explained, still making absolutely no sense to me. "No that's still not right," he added, almost to himself. "I don't want to date you."

"This isn't helping, Joseph," I told him, wondering if he, like everyone else, thought I had let myself go and that's why he'd broken up with me.

"No, June, I don't want to date you. I want to marry you," he said so matter-of-factly that I couldn't stop my mouth from falling open in shock.

"What?" was all I could think of to say.

"You heard me. I want to marry you. But I want to go on my mission first. Dating you just hit way too close to home. It was like seeing what I could have when I came back, and it scared me."

"What about that could possibly scare you?" I asked, thinking that if what he said was true, then seeing that side of our relationship would be a good thing.

"It scared me because you might not be here when I get back," he said, squeezing my shoulders as if willing me to understand him. "You might be dating someone . . . You might be married."

"Joseph, I'll only be twenty-one when you get

back. I highly doubt I'll be married."

"You say that now, but there's no doubt in my mind that some guy could come sweep you off your feet and you'd be all too happy to be with him," he said, violently reminding me of the picture of Ryan and me kissing.

I had to wonder if Joseph had seen it. All he would have had to do was log on to check his e-mail and there it would be, on the MSN homepage.

"You could have asked me to wait for you," I pointed out quietly.

"I would never ask you to do that," he said immediately. "It's not fair to you and it's not good for me. I don't want anything distracting me while I'm gone, especially if the distraction is the promise of coming back to you."

"I don't know if that makes sense," I told him.

"It's hard to explain," he agreed. "That's why I completely botched it when I tried before. The main thing I wanted you to get out of this is that I never meant to hurt your feelings. I didn't want you thinking I had hated our relationship."

I was silent for a moment, trying to understand everything he had said. Now that I knew Joseph didn't regret the time we'd been together, it made me feel even guiltier for liking Ryan. If I had never developed feelings for Ryan, I would have gladly just waited for Joseph without saying I was waiting for him. Now everything was just . . . complicated.

"Honestly, it probably would have been better to let you keep thinking I didn't want to date you. It was much easier that way," he said, making me wonder exactly what about the past few months had been easy. Apparently he hadn't been going through what I was going through. "I just couldn't stand fighting with you and being so distant."

"What about Jade?" I asked, still a little sore about her.

"We're not dating, June," he said, before going on after seeing my skeptical look. "I haven't even kissed her. She dates pretty much every boy in the theatre major and I think she likes to be around someone who doesn't want a girlfriend. It means we can just hang out and not worry about any complicated feelings between us. She's fun to be around, like you are, but I don't have to worry that I'll suddenly not want to go on a mission because all I want to do is marry her."

"I'm sure this whole confession should flatter me; I'm just still trying to understand it all," I said.

"I had to clear the air and lay everything out on the table so I wouldn't leave on my mission with you thinking I'm a huge jerk," he said, releasing my shoulders now. "But at the same time, I don't want you waiting for me. I don't want you to feel like you can't date because you've made some sort of commitment to me."

"When we were dating, I always thought we'd get married," I said quietly, like I was telling him a secret.

"Me too," he answered.

"Now everything is . . . " I let my voice trail off,

not quite sure what *everything* was.

"Different?" he offered.

"I guess."

"I was going to tell you all of this before, but then when Ryan, Candice, and Benjamin came up to visit and I could tell there was something going on with you and Ryan, I just . . . didn't. I didn't want you to think I was saying all of this to get you to break up with him."

"We're not *really* dating," I said, since I wasn't sure what Ryan and I were.

Joseph gave me a skeptical look that instantly made me re-word my statement.

"We haven't labeled it yet."

"Honestly? This is going to sound petty, but I think Ryan is the only guy I wouldn't want you to date, which is another reason I kept my mouth shut. I don't want to tell you what to do."

"Why wouldn't you want me to date him? He's a great guy."

"Exactly. He's a great guy. He's the kind of guy who would sweep you off your feet," he said, revisiting his earlier assessment. "He's not Lukas Leighton. He's not going to suddenly become a scumbag. There's nothing wrong with Ryan and the longer you date a guy like that, the more you realize you should do what you can to hold onto him."

"How do you know so much about relationships?" I asked, wondering when Joseph had leaped so far ahead of me in the wisdom department.

He shrugged. "I think everyone knows this stuff. It's just that no one says it out loud."

"That might be true," I agreed.

We were silent again.

I wasn't quite sure what I should say to him. Everything he said had, unfortunately, been true. I did like Ryan. We were dating, and Ryan was a great guy who I could see myself ending up with.

But I liked Joseph too.

And *that* was the real problem.

CHAPTER 17

Joseph and I sat in our Reading and Constructing Narratives class, half-listening to the discussion as we kept up a whispered running commentary on the class. We only had a few hours until our last performance of *Tartuffe* started, and soon we'd be almost done with our first semester of college.

"Are you nervous about tonight?" I whispered to Joseph, glad that we were finally on comfortable ground again.

I kept my laptop perched on my knees, ready to take notes on anything that actually sounded important. With the ongoing class discussion, though, important information was looking scarce.

"Not nervous, really, just sad that it'll be over soon," he answered, giving me a little pout.

"I wish they recorded shows so we could watch them again years down the road when we're feeling nostalgic," I said with a deep sigh.

"You're nothing if not nostalgic," he agreed,

before adding, "Is it just me, or do these discussions usually end up being a bit . . . cyclical?"

"Everyone just keeps saying the same thing over and over again."

"No, I think it's that people keep repeating what's already been said," he replied, giving me sideways smirk at his bad joke. "I bet it's those dang film majors' fault," Joseph remarked, eying the group of hipsters skeptically.

It was a well-known fact that there was a bit of a feud between the theatre majors and the film majors. Film majors thought we were overly dramatic and weird, and we thought the film majors were pretentious and trendy.

It was a love-hate relationship.

It probably didn't help that we very purposefully sat on two separate sides of the classroom, keeping our majors divided. On top of that, the two majors constantly battled during lectures to prove that they were the more "enlightened" bunch, endlessly trying to one-up the last person's comment.

Of course, all they really managed to do was say the exact same thing as the person before them, but in a different way. It was kind of fun to see how many ways you could rephrase the same concept.

We had just watched a clip from *The Hitchhiker's Guide to the Galaxy* and were currently discussing . . . something. Honestly, I wasn't even quite sure what the professor had asked us to talk about, since the comments were so far off-track already.

"Absurdism does not provide solutions because it

is simply trying to reveal the problem and have the audience consider the implications, rather than solve it and move on to the next problem," one boy from the film major said.

He was wearing TOMS and had the first hints of a mustache. Definitely a hipster.

"Yeah, but I think what they're really trying to do in this clip is present conflict," a girl from my theatre major said. She looked over her shoulder and raised her eyebrows at the film major, her bright red lips forming a smile, obviously feeling smug about her revelation.

"But absurdism doesn't provide the audience with an escape, because the frustration hits too close to home," the film major retorted, not realizing that they were arguing about the fact that they agreed. "We cannot escape within the confines of this story when the frustration is such an accurate reality within our lives."

I glanced over at our professor who, bless his heart, was trying to look supportive, but mostly just looked like he'd seen way too many students trying to sound deep.

Joseph reached over and typed on my keyboard, adding four words to my class notes on the screen.

Beating a dead horse!

I tried to suppress a giggle and elbowed him in the arm, placing a finger against my lips to keep him from making me laugh anymore.

As much as I couldn't understand the endless discussions in class, I had to admit that I would miss lectures. Joseph and I were just as weird and quirky as the rest of the film and theatre majors, so I couldn't really make fun of them, and somehow, the prospect of leaving Utah to go back to California actually made me a little sad.

I'd miss the unspoken feud between the two concentrations and the fun that brought with it. I'd miss walking through the HFAC and seeing someone juggling, someone singing, and someone practicing a scene all within five steps of my class.

I also couldn't ignore the fact that I had spent so much time at BYU feeling sorry for myself that I hadn't let myself get involved in anything. I could complain all day that my roommates hadn't talked to me, but I wasn't beating down their doors to get to know them either. I definitely could have done more to be involved in the "college experience."

The small pang of sadness at the prospect of leaving caught me off guard, and for the first time, I actually second-guessed my decision to leave BYU if I got the part in the period piece with Ryan. In the end, I knew leaving would be the right decision if I was even offered the part, but that didn't mean it would be easy to leave the independence behind. As much as I didn't want to admit it, I had kind of loved having roommates and my own apartment.

"Absurdism is listening to these two bicker for an hour about the same thing," Joseph whispered, catching me by surprise. I had completely tuned out the conversation between the girl with red lips and the boy with the mustache.

"Absurdism is you running into that poor stage manager last night right before you went on for your last scene," I replied.

"They wear all black! How am I supposed to see them in the dark?" he asked incredulously.

"I will miss seeing you in your ridiculous Tartuffe costume," I admitted, now fully ignoring the class discussion that only involved two people anyway. I was pretty sure I wasn't the only one who had ceased listening.

"Maybe I'll ask if I can keep it," he joked, just as the professor forcibly stopped the argument that had broken out to announce that class was over.

"Ready for the end of an era?" I asked Joseph.

"Are you ready to be Tartuffified for the last time?" he responded with a grin.

"Can't wait."

The makeup room was full of discarded wigs and hugging actors after our last performance of *Tartuffe* that night. It was late, we were all tired, and we still had to strike the show, return our makeup kits, check in wigs and costumes, and do about a million other things, but I was happy.

Finals were a few days away and soon we'd all be on our way home for Christmas. My mess of a love life was still baffling, but Joseph and I were friends again and Ryan and I talked on the phone every night. Things were up in the air, but I liked Ryan and I wanted to see where our relationship took us.

"I can't believe we didn't kiss once," Declan said, staring at my reflection in the mirror over my shoulder.

"It's such a tragedy," I agreed with a solemn nod, knowing that he wasn't being serious.

If he had actually liked me, I would have wondered what had gotten into people lately. It was already a miracle to me that Joseph and Ryan both liked me. I mean, I wasn't Joann Hoozer. I was just "awkward June" who stressed way too much and tripped over her own feet all the time. Not much of a catch. Plus, I wasn't the girl boys were constantly falling all over. It just wasn't me.

"I guess technically the show isn't over until after tonight," he said raising his eyebrows at me. "Meet me in the stairwell in five minutes?"

"You're so romantic."

"Come on, you know I won't tarnish your reputation," he went on, holding up a printout of Ryan and me kissing.

"Where did you get that?" I asked, spinning around in my chair, my stage makeup only half taken off and my hair still in pincurls.

"It doesn't matter where I got it. What matters is that big-shot Hollywood didn't tell me she'd be getting some action from . . . which one is this? The non-boyfriend or the jerky ex-boyfriend?"

"It's not you, I can tell you that much," I said pointedly, pulling the paper from his hand and hiding it in my purse.

"Can't blame me for trying, right?" he asked in his

thick Irish accent, kissing me quickly on the cheek and exiting the makeup room as fast as his long legs would carry him.

"What was that about?" Joseph asked, leaving Jade's side for the first time that night and coming over to talk to me.

"Oh gosh, don't even ask," I told him in exasperation.

"I can't leave you alone for two seconds without someone hitting on you, can I?"

"All I want to do is act. Is that so wrong?" I asked, my voice taking on an overly dramatic ring as I draped an arm theatrically over my eyes.

"It is when you have so many gentleman callers waiting on you," he returned, sounding just like a character from an old movie.

I laughed as I pulled bobby pins from my springy hair and watched it fall around my face, as untamable as usual. You'd think being confined under a wig would have calmed it down a bit, but no; it was back and more rebellious than ever.

"Good job tonight," I said.

"You too," he replied with a big smile. "Hey, I want to take you somewhere tonight."

"By the time we're done with everything here, I think most places will be closed," I answered skeptically.

"The place we're going doesn't close."

As cryptic as his statement was, it made perfect

sense once we had pulled into our old spot at Bridal Veil Falls and sat in the back of his VW Bus looking out the open back doors at the stars up above. The ground was covered in snow and everything seemed blue in the night air. I could see my breath in little puffs, but we didn't mind the cold.

I cupped my chilly hands around a warm cup of hot chocolate and rested my head on Joseph's shoulder. Everything was just like it used to be, when we were friends and didn't have any problems between us.

Except for the fact that I liked Joseph. And he liked me. And I liked Ryan. And Joseph was leaving for two years.

But other than that, we didn't have any problems between us.

"I got my mission call," Joseph whispered.

The muffled world that was covered in snow somehow made you want to whisper so that the peace wouldn't be disturbed.

"Where are you going?" I asked, lifting my head from his shoulder so that I could get a better look at him.

"I don't know," he answered. "I wanted to open it with you."

"Really?" I asked, feeling honored that he wanted me to be the first to know. I was positive his mom would be mad, since he was their oldest son and the first to go on a mission, but my excitement won out and I took his hand in mine. "Let's open it."

Joseph let out a deep breath and pulled the thick

envelope out of his messenger bag.

"Here we go," he said, his face alive with excitement. After all, this would be his whole life for two years, and he had absolutely no idea where he'd be going.

"Thick envelope. That means it's not stateside," I guessed, wondering how far away he'd be. I could feel my heart pounding in my chest as he opened the envelope and his eyes darted across the page.

"It's stateside," he said, and I felt myself sigh audibly, glad that he wouldn't be too far away.

"Where?" I finally asked, practically shouting. The suspense was killing me.

"Anchorage, Alaska."

I stared at him for a minute and watched his face change as he took it all in.

"That's amazing," I told him. "Haven't you seen pictures of Alaska? It's supposed to be beautiful. And it's close enough that I don't feel like something bad will happen to you. You won't be kidnapped by a foreign government or something."

"I could get eaten by a polar bear," he pointed out.

"Or trampled by a dog sled," I added with a nod.

"Or swallowed by a whale."

"Okay, if that happens, promise me you'll start calling yourself Jonah," I said with a laugh.

"Deal," he agreed.

"How do you feel about the call?" I asked, wondering if he thought Alaska would be as amazing as I did.

"I feel really good about it," he answered. "I could never imagine where I'd go on my mission, but right when I read that I'd be going to Alaska, it felt right."

"I'm so proud of you," I told him, sitting up on my knees to give him a hug. "When do you leave?" I asked as I held onto him tightly.

"The end of January," he answered, his voice muffled by my mass of hair.

"That's so soon," I said as I pulled away from him, still keeping my hands locked behind his neck.

"That means I get back sooner, though," he said, smiling in a way that made his eyes get all squinty. It was my favorite smile of his.

"That's true. I'll still miss you either way."

"I still haven't decided what I want you to do if you get married while I'm gone."

"What?" I asked, completely taken aback by this quick change in topic.

"I think I just want you to send me a wedding invitation. No "Dear John" letter. Just the invitation and be done with it."

"I know you don't believe me, but I really won't be getting married in the next two years," I assured him as we began packing up the bus to drive back to Provo. It was almost three in the morning, and there was nothing I wanted more at that moment than my warm bed.

"I'll just have two years to figure out how to win you back from Mr. Wonderful," he shrugged, making me smile at his nickname for Ryan.

"Yeah, because that's what a mission is for," I

answered sarcastically before my phone buzzed. I had missed a few calls while my reception was out in the canyon. "Voicemail," I said by way of explanation as I held the phone up to my ear. "Two of them. I hope nothing bad happened."

"You always think something bad is happening if you get voicemails," Joseph pointed out.

"Last time I missed that many calls, something bad *had* happened," I pointed out, not sure why I thought it would be a good idea to remind Joseph of the time I'd ditched him for Lukas Leighton.

"Touché," he said.

"Bliss, you got it!" Gran suddenly said in my ear, her voicemail beginning to play. "I just got the call that they want to offer you the part in the movie with Ryan Hex! Now, I know you haven't made your final decision about school yet, but I may have already accepted the role on your behalf. That is my right as your agent."

Gran kept rambling, apparently unaware that I had already decided to put school on hold if I got the part. She went on trying to justify her accepting the role for me, and I wondered if Joseph could hear what she had said and was just being a good friend by waiting to react until I told him.

Once Gran was finally done justifying something I was completely fine with, the next message started playing, with Ryan's voice now coming through my phone rather than Gran's.

"June, I don't know if you already heard the news, but they want you for the part! How great is that?

We'll be in a movie together. I honestly can't think of a better way to spend my time. Okay, that was cheesy to say, wasn't it? I should probably just stop now. Also, I miss you. And that makes me sound like a clingy girlfriend. And I can't stop thinking about your beautiful eyes. No, really, I'm stopping now. Please accept the role! That's all I'm going to say. This is the most awkward message I've ever left. Oh, and I will resort to begging if you don't accept right away. The end."

I laughed at Ryan's spastic message before turning the phone off and putting it back into my purse. I'd have to call him as soon as I got home. Right now all I could think about was the fact that I had gotten the part. I, June Laurie, had walked into an audition for a big Hollywood feature film and had landed the role. I was sure it was some kind of fluke, but I wasn't about to suggest as much to the casting director. If I benefited from their poor judgment, that was fine by me.

Of course, now Joseph and I would be moving all of our stuff back to California together. I guess our big Utah adventure had been short-lived.

"Who was it?" Joseph asked. I had been so engulfed in my own happiness that I had completely forgotten to tell him the news.

"I got the role in that movie," I said with a little giggle of excitement. I wasn't really the giggling type, but when something this amazing happened, I couldn't be held accountable for my embarrassing impulses.

"That's amazing!" he exclaimed, now taking his turn to be excited for me. "June, that's such a big deal. I mean, I'll probably see you on a movie poster while I'm on my mission."

"Oh weird, you really might," I said, not realizing just how huge this opportunity was. "Sad that you won't see my movie until you get back, though."

"Who knows how many movies you'll be in by that time," he said with a waggle of his eyebrows. "We might need to have a June Laurie movie marathon."

"Yeah, by that time I'll probably have a personal assistant who writes missionary letters to you on my behalf."

"I kind of figured that's what would happen. Will you still dictate them, at least?"

"No, I don't think I'll have time for that. I'll just give her free reign over what goes into them," I said with a shrug.

"Fair enough," he agreed. "Hey June?" he said after a moment.

"Yeah?" I asked.

"Best night ever."

CHAPTER 18

Somehow it seemed like moving back to California was a lot easier than moving out to Utah. I already had labeled boxes, and Joseph and I were already experts on how to stuff everything into the back of his VW Bus in a way that still left a small window to see out the back. In no time, it was like we had never moved to Utah at all.

Whitney and Tiffany actually seemed genuinely sad to see me go, although the giant diamond ring on Tiffany's left hand made up for it a little. She and Scott had apparently wasted no time in declaring their love for each other, and as much as the girl drove me crazy, I was happy for her.

Of course, I did worry a little about Whitney being left to her own devices without Tiffany there to tell her what to do. However, I didn't have much doubt that Whitney would soon find another queen bee to worship and be perfectly happy again.

Umeko gave me an awkward hug when I told her

I was leaving and snapped a quick picture with her phone before going back to whatever conversation she was having before I had interrupted her. I would even miss her and our non-existent conversations. She didn't snore much, so she had been a good roommate in my book.

As I sat on the porch in front of my childhood home in California with Joseph, waiting for Candice to pick me up to go Christmas shopping, I couldn't believe how many changes were about to occur. I'd be without Joseph for two years when we had never spent more than a few days away from each other in our entire lives. I was about to film a major motion picture with my almost-boyfriend Ryan. I was living back in California and had no idea when or if I'd be returning to school.

Everything was unsettled, and for a person like me (who found any reason to stress), I was feeling more than anxious about the uncertainty of it all.

"I'll miss Utah," Joseph said after a long silence as we both stared at the hot pink sunset.

"I guess I will," I said stubbornly, not wanting to admit how much I had liked it there.

"You never gave it a chance. Besides, Annette had already poisoned you against it before you even got there."

"She just doesn't like Utah," I said. "It's not 'culturally enriching' enough for her, she says. I didn't think it was so bad."

"Then why did you always act like you hated it so much?" Joseph asked.

"Maybe because my best friend ignored me, my roommates ignored me, and there was way too much snow on the ground," I said with a grin, ticking off the reasons I wouldn't miss the place I'd called home for a few short months. Even if *maybe* I would miss it.

"Ouch, I guess I deserved that."

"You definitely did."

"Well, no matter what you say, I loved it, and I'm a little sad to be back," he said as Candice pulled into my driveway.

"I will miss the feeling of it," I offered. "It felt safe and happy."

"Too little too late," Joseph answered with a wink as he walked down the driveway back toward his own house. "Have fun," he said to Candice as he passed by her.

"I live to shop," she replied sarcastically from the driver's seat, obviously not very excited about our little outing.

I hopped into her car and pulled out my Christmas list. I had already shopped for everyone but Benjamin, which happened to be Candice's problem as well. Apparently the guy who had everything was really hard to shop for.

"Any ideas of what to get him?" I asked as Candice sped away from Simi Valley and toward Los Angeles.

"Benjamin is stupid because he already has everything. He doesn't actually need a gift . . . but he really *wants* people to get him gifts still," she said in her most monotone voice.

"So, maybe a gift card, then?" I asked, thinking that way he could get whatever he really wanted.

"He'd hate that," she answered.

Candice was nothing if not blunt.

"You, of all people, should know what to get him," I said pointedly as we got off the freeway and drove into the downtown area.

"What's that supposed to mean?"

"It wasn't supposed to mean anything, but that response tells me it *does* mean something," I said conspiratorially. "What's going on between you two?"

"You're right. We're having a torrid love affair. So this store should be perfect," she said sarcastically, stopping in front of the shadiest lingerie store I'd ever seen.

"Okay, fine, if you don't want to tell me, you don't have to," I said in surrender.

"Thank you," she answered. "You know, if you haven't gotten Ryan something yet, I think anything from that store would be the perfect Christmas present."

"Yeah, that's definitely not going to happen," I said with a little nervous laugh, wondering—not for the first time—if Ryan expected anything like that from me. I had been pretty straightforward with my beliefs, and I was sure he already knew where we stood on *that* subject.

But what if I were wrong?

"Relax June, I was joking," Candice explained,

putting the car into park. "But I actually do want to go into the shop next door."

I looked out the window to take in our surroundings. This definitely wasn't Rodeo Drive. I wasn't even sure which part of L.A. this was. It was getting dark, and the streets were starting to fill up with the kind of people who definitely made me miss Utah.

I got a sinking feeling in my stomach at the thought of getting out of the car, but Candice was halfway to the used bookstore and I definitely didn't want to be alone, so I followed quickly behind her.

"I'm pretty sure we're going to get murdered here," I whispered as we entered the dingy bookstore.

"I won't be long. Benjamin really likes old hardcover books . . . not that he reads them, but he likes the look of them."

"Okay, but be fast. This place is seriously not safe," I answered, feeling my head begin to pound.

I hadn't eaten much that day, and my recent "diet" (meaning I only ate when I was absolutely starving) was starting to take its toll with the daily headaches and dizzy spells. Still, I was looking a little thinner, so it was paying off, even if walking through aisles of dusty books was apparently too physically strenuous for me.

It turned out "a fast trip" for Candice meant slowly browsing through each overstuffed aisle. With every genre we passed through, my headache got worse and my balance grew weaker. Even though I had vowed to keep my calorie intake to the bare minimum, I was pretty sure I needed a cheeseburger right away or I'd pass out.

"This is the one," Candice said finally, holding up a dusty old leather-bound copy of *Twenty Thousand Leagues Under the Sea.*

"Perfect. Why don't you go buy it while I step outside? I'm feeling kind of lightheaded," I said, already moving toward the door and not waiting for a response from her.

Though I was positive my lack of eating was the cause of my sudden headache, the constantly flickering lights and stuffy air in the bookstore weren't helping one bit.

I could feel a light sweat break out on my forehead as I emerged into the cool night on the city street. Turning around the corner of the big brick building and leaning against the wall, I felt my phone begin to buzz in my purse. My stomach sank before I even looked at the phone and I wondered why I was feeling even worse now that I was out in the fresh air (or at least as fresh as the air got in L.A.).

"Hello?" I said, closing my eyes against my throbbing headache.

"June?" Joseph answered on the other line.

"Hey Joseph. What's up?"

"Are you okay? What are you guys doing right now?" he asked, not quite sounding like himself.

"Candice is buying a book and I'm outside getting some air. Why what's wrong?"

"I just . . . I got this feeling I should call and check

on you. I'm glad you're okay though. I just didn't want to ignore the feeling, you know?" he said, making me smile that he'd worry enough to call.

"That's sweet Joseph but I'm—"

I never did get to finish the sentence before a hand closed around my mouth and pushed me up against the wall.

"June?" I could hear Joseph's voice through the receiver I still held against my ear.

I made a little noise against the gloved hand, but I wasn't sure if he had heard me. The man was almost a foot taller than me and wore a black ski mask. I had no idea what he really looked like, but I did understand why I had felt so much worse when I left the bookstore.

Talk about the wrong time to ignore the Spirit.

"Hand over your phone," the man said in a gravelly voice. Had I not been completely terrified for my life, I would have laughed at how much this resembled an after school special on TV.

"June, are you there?" Joseph said again, right as I pulled the phone away from my ear and handed it to the man.

Both of my hands were free, the only thing being contained was my mouth, and I probably could have hit the man pretty effectively, but somehow I couldn't think straight and my body didn't seem to want to respond.

Honestly, somewhere inside of me, I was still convinced that nothing bad was actually happening. I almost felt like this whole situation was just a misunderstanding, and if I reacted hostilely the man would laugh and say, "I just needed to borrow your phone because my car broke down," and then we'd all have a laugh at how paranoid June Laurie was.

Ryan and Benjamin would make some joke at my expense, Candice would tell me to stop being a psychopath, and Joseph would say he couldn't believe I actually thought I was being robbed.

But no matter what my deeply ingrained social etiquette was telling me, the rest of my body seemed to understand that this wasn't a misunderstanding and that I wouldn't be laughing about it in an hour.

I always thought I would be one of those people who would spring into action when they're attacked, letting the adrenaline take over. Maybe it was because I hadn't been eating much lately, or maybe it was just the sheer panic, but I was paralyzed.

"Now give me your purse," he said.

I furrowed my brow, wondering how I could keep this man from taking my purse. My phone I could easily replace, but my purse had a letter from my dad, a picture of my mom, and a little picture Joseph had drawn for me one day at church. There were memories in there that I couldn't replace.

My free hand instinctively went to my purse and I clutched it against my chest, unwilling to part with it. The man, it turned out, was a bit more resourceful and prepared than me, because he didn't hesitate for a second to pull a small knife out of his coat and hold it against my neck.

That was all the persuasion I needed to hand my

purse over, memories and all. He dropped my phone inside, relieving my throat for just a moment before the knife was right back in place.

Once he had all of my belongings, I prepared for the pressure to leave my mouth and throat, and I braced myself for the shock of suddenly being alone in the dark alley after the man ran away.

But he didn't run away.

Instead, the man stared at me for a moment as if he knew who I was and was trying to put the pieces of the puzzle together.

"You're pretty, aren't you?" he said softly, still covering my mouth with his hand. I gave a small whimper and tried to look away from him, but the cold metal of the knife against my throat made any movement impossible.

"Look at those big eyes," he whispered, moving even closer to me.

I closed my eyes and said a silent prayer, asking for protection and wondering how I hadn't thought to pray before. In my defense, though, everything had happened so quickly that a coherent thought hadn't had time to form in my head yet.

"You're the girl from that TV show, aren't you?" he asked, obviously not getting the fact that I couldn't speak with his hand covering my mouth.

I could hear my phone buzzing in my purse and wondered if Joseph knew something was wrong—if he was calling back to make sure I was okay again. He had to have heard the guy demanding I give him my phone. I just kept praying that he'd have the good sense to call for help before things got worse.

"How about you come with me," the man said, smiling under his ski mask. "Put your hands behind your back," he ordered.

I knew that kidnapping 101 said you should never get into a vehicle with someone; the chances of coming out of something alive dropped dramatically when that happened, but I honestly had no clue what I should do.

I slowly brought my hands behind my back, tears spilling silently down my cheeks now.

"Hey, moron, get away from her," I heard Candice yell in the most terrifying voice I'd ever heard.

As relieved as I was that she had come to my rescue, I couldn't imagine little five-foot ninety pound Candice scaring this guy very much.

"Let her go," a deep male voice called out next.

Had I not been in complete shock, I would have wondered who the man was, but instead I just fell to my knees as the knife was pulled back from my throat and the man took off down the alleyway, accidentally dropping my purse in the process.

All of that, and he didn't even manage to hold onto my purse.

I put a hand over my neck to feel for blood, but there was none. There was only an indent on my skin where the knife had been pressed.

"June, are you okay?" Candice asked, her face truly scared for the first time since I'd known her. She got down on her knees beside me on the dirty ground and placed an arm over my shoulders.

Maybe she did have normal human instincts after all. She just tried *really* hard to hide them.

"Why don't you girls come back into the store until your friends get here," the big man said next to us. I followed them numbly into the bookstore and sat in the break room with Candice while the shop owner got us something to drink.

"What happened?" Candice asked, genuine concern on her normally blank face.

"I was feeling really dizzy so I went to get some air," I recalled, still shaking from the ordeal. "Joseph called me to see if I was okay, and while I was talking to him, that guy covered my mouth and took my phone and my purse."

"Joseph called you before the guy came?" Candice asked. I nodded in confirmation. "You Mormons must have superpowers or something."

I laughed at her statement, finding that even in my current state of shock, it felt good to laugh.

"How did you know to come outside?" I asked her just as the shop owner came back with two cups of coffee in little paper cups. I didn't have the heart to tell him I didn't drink coffee, so I just took the cup with a nod in his direction. "Thank you so much," I said. Without him, I didn't think the man in the alley would have run away. I loved Candice and I was terrified of her most of the time, but she just wasn't that intimidating to attackers.

"Any time honey," the man said with a kind smile. "You girls just stay back here and relax until your friends get here, all right?"

"Thank you," I said again, not sure what else I could say to the man who had saved me. He nodded at me as he left us alone once more. Even though I wasn't going to drink the coffee, it felt good to press my cold hands around the paper cup.

"Joseph called me," Candice said once the man left.

"What?"

"That's how I knew to go looking for you," she explained. "Joseph called me and told me to get outside right away because something bad was happening to you, so I grabbed the cashier and ran outside to find you. At first I thought maybe Joseph was playing a trick on me, so I wasn't too worried, but when I saw you—." Her words trailed off and she took a long drink from her coffee cup, making a face that indicated it apparently wasn't up to her normal standards.

"Thank you for saving me," I told her, placing my hand over hers and meeting her eyes. "Seriously."

"Don't get all emotional on me," she said with a shrug, pretending like she didn't care, even though I knew better.

"So, who are the 'friends' who are on their way?" I asked, thinking back to the shop owner's words.

"I told Joseph where we were right before I ran out to find you, so he's on his way," she answered. "I guess we don't really need him now that we're safe, but I think he's freaking out a little."

"Yeah, I would imagine so," I said, wondering

how I would react if the tables were turned.

"I'm glad you're not dead or kidnapped," Candice finally said after a moment of silence.

"Thanks Candice," I responded, knowing that for her to say something like that was basically a declaration of her friendship. Any semi-emotional statement was a pretty big deal coming from Candice.

"June!" Ryan called from the doorway, catching me by surprise.

He and Benjamin came into the room together, and Ryan quickly gathered me into a tight hug, pulling me up from my chair and folding me into his warm coat. I rested my head against his chest and closed my eyes, not knowing how he knew to come here, but not really caring at the moment. "Are you okay?" he asked, pulling me away from him so that he could get a good look at me.

"I'm fine now," I said, smiling up at him and feeling safe at last.

"How did you guys get here so fast?" Candice asked, standing an appropriate distance away from Benjamin, even though I could see that they wanted to be hugging . . . or whatever the equivalent of that was for Candice. Maybe making eye contact?

"Joseph called us," Ryan explained.

"And he said that you were going to go scare the attacker away?" Benjamin asked Candice, holding his phone is his hand as usual and looking impressed.

"I basically made him cry like a little girl," she said with a proud grin.

"That's my girl," he answered, ruffling her hair like she was a five year old boy at a baseball game.

"We told Joseph we'd bring you to Benjamin's apartment. He's going to meet us there," Ryan said, leading us out of the break room.

"He really doesn't need to drive all the way to L.A.," I said, feeling bad that he'd have to make the trip in his gas-sucking bus.

"I'm pretty sure he won't take no for an answer," Ryan pointed out.

"Good point," I agreed. "Thanks again," I said to the man behind the front desk as we made our way to Ryan's car.

"We'll meet you guys there," he called to Benjamin, who was hopping in to Candice's car.

I knew there was a lot going on right then and I was still partially traumatized from being attacked and everything, but as we pulled away from the bookstore in this sketchy part of downtown Los Angeles, I could have sworn I saw Benjamin lean over and kiss Candice in the car behind us.

"I wish I could meet that guy so I could punch him in the face," Joseph said as he sat with his shoulder pressed up against mine on Benjamin's couch.

He hadn't left my side for a second since he'd been there, and I think it was starting to get on Ryan's nerves just a little—not that he'd ever say anything.

Both of those boys were just *way* too nice for their own good.

"Really?" I asked skeptically. "*You* would punch him in the face?"

"I took a stage combat class. If nothing else, I would at least make it look very convincing."

"That sounds more like it," Benjamin said with a laugh, now holding a tablet instead of his phone.

Apparently that was his addiction of choice when he was in the comfort of his own home.

"That guy seriously asked you to come with him?" Ryan asked for the tenth time that night, still looking like he wanted to murder someone and pacing the floor like a madman.

"I don't think he was really asking," I said, shivering a little at the memory.

"*I* would have punched him in the face if he didn't run away like a little pansy first," Candice mumbled, looking over Benjamin's shoulder at his tablet.

"Are you feeling okay?" Ryan asked me.

"Yes, I'm fine," I said with an exasperated sigh, wishing people would stop using the term "okay." "I mean, it was scary, but now it just seems like a weird memory."

"No, I'm not talking about that whole thing. You said you were dizzy and that's why you went outside in the first place. Are you feeling sick?" he asked, concern lining his face as he stopped pacing and held his hand up to my forehead.

"I just haven't eaten enough today, I think," I said

quickly, feeling like we were treading on dangerous ground.

"If you like TV dinners or leftover takeout, you can knock yourself out in my kitchen," Benjamin said distractedly, still swiping his finger across the screen of his tablet.

"Like you would ever eat a TV dinner," Candice said with a scoff. "I bet the 'leftovers' in your fridge are from some disgustingly swanky restaurant."

"What have you eaten today?" Ryan asked.

It was an innocent question, and really, I wasn't doing anything wrong by cutting back a little on my normal self-induced sugar coma. So why did I have such a hard time answering that inquiry?

"I can't remember," I lied. It probably would have been much easier to just say that I wasn't feeling well, but apparently I wasn't that quick on my feet.

"If you can't even remember what you ate, you probably need to eat something," Ryan pointed out.

"Yeah, I'll have to grab something at home," I agreed, a little too quickly. I could feel both Joseph and Ryan staring at me, but I kept my eyes trained straight ahead. "What are you guys looking at?" I asked Benjamin and Candice, desperate for a subject change.

"A not-so-good Samaritan," Candice said dryly.

"What?"

I walked over to see what she was talking about, since her cryptic explanation offered no help at all, and there, on the screen, was a grainy photo of Candice and me sitting in the bookstore break room and another of Ryan and me hugging with Benjamin standing in the background, along with a headline that read *A Not-So-Warm Welcome Home for Former Forensic Faculty Star June Laurie?*

"Are you kidding me?" I exclaimed.

"I bet it was from his security camera," Candice said, as if she should have known better.

"This is ridiculous. What site is this on?" I asked.

"Just some sleazy celebrity news site," Benjamin answered.

"I just can't believe he'd send it in that fast."

"You can't be too offended," Candice said indignantly. "They called me an 'unnamed friend.' How rude is that?"

"You're right," Benjamin said. "They should have said 'unnamed Vanity Department worker'."

"Benjamin Hampton, if you call my makeup department the 'Vanities' one more time, I'll kill you with a makeup brush, and trust me, that's a slow death," Candice said darkly.

"Good thing we're about to hit the off-season, huh?" he returned smugly.

"Do you really want to test my creativity?" she asked him.

"Everything makes so much sense now," Ryan said from behind me. For a moment I thought he was on to my little weight-loss plan. "One day I made Candice really mad, and the next day she insisted on using a different kind of makeup. I bet she was planning on poisoning me."

"You're just lucky the director didn't approve the

change," she shot back with a playful glare in his direction, letting me relax once more.

"June, you should probably go home and tell Annette what happened," Joseph said from the couch.

I groaned at the thought of worrying Gran unnecessarily. It wasn't like I'd ever be stupid enough to wander around a dark alley in L.A. by myself again, so there wasn't really an issue. But I also knew that if Gran found out from someone else, she'd be furious with me for not telling her or Dad.

"You're right, sadly," I conceded, walking heavily over to Ryan to give him a quick hug before I left.

"Thanks for coming to my rescue Candice," I said over my shoulder, still keeping my arms wrapped around Ryan's neck. I wanted to kiss him . . . and the way he was looking at me, I was pretty sure he wanted to kiss me too, but we weren't exactly at the point in our relationship where we were kissing in front of our friends. Everything was still pretty new.

Plus, if we did kiss, Joseph would be super uncomfortable, Candice would gag, and Benjamin would find some reason to make fun of us for the rest of our lives. So I left it with a hug and gave Ryan one last smile over my shoulder.

CHAPTER 19

No matter how old we all got, it was universally known that Christmas Eve equaled no sleep in the Laurie household. It may have been because we were a house primarily dominated by actresses or a house primarily dominated by women, but whatever the cause, Christmas was always an excuse for me, Gran, and Dad to act like giddy children.

On Christmas Eve, my family and Joseph's family would get together and read the Christmas story from the Bible, which always proved to be difficult with Joseph's scores of siblings. But it was a tradition Joseph's mom and my mom had started before she died, and I was *not* going to be the one to break it.

After we came back home that night, Gran and I pretended we were going to sleep so Dad could think he was sneaky putting presents out. Then he went to bed while I pretended to be asleep and Gran would follow suit, probably being more dramatic with her "stage sneak" than she needed to be.

I will admit though—it just wouldn't feel like Christmas without Gran "sneaking" theatrically past my bedroom door in the dark.

Once Gran was really asleep, I'd go into bandit mode. Dad and Gran would swear every year that they were still awake while I set my presents out, but the snores coming from Dad's room and the lack of fake snoring coming from Gran's told me otherwise.

I wasn't quite sure when we had decided not to reveal Christmas presents until Christmas morning. I mean, it wasn't like we didn't know we were all getting each other gifts. I guess there was just something magical about waking up one morning and finding your living room suddenly filled with brightly wrapped packages.

As I lay in my bed on Christmas morning, reveling in the feeling of the sun on my face, I couldn't help but think that at this time next year, Joseph would be gone, my movie would have been out for a while, and some big decisions regarding my career and my future would have been made. That was a scary thought in and of itself.

But right at that moment, everything was fine. It was Christmas, Joseph was still here for another month, Ryan was the world's best boyfriend, and I had a movie to shoot.

"Bliss, I've got good news," Gran said when I entered the kitchen, a knowing smile on her face.

"It's Christmas?" I guessed, wondering how it could possibly get better than that.

"No, besides that," she answered with a long-suffering sigh. "They're going to shoot your film with Ryan on location in England."

"Wait . . . I'll be going to England to film the movie?" I asked, wanting to make sure those were the actual words Gran was speaking before I got too excited. "This can't be happening. England?"

"Told you it was good news," she answered.

"Are they going to take care of her over there? I don't know how I feel about my little girl in a different country without supervision," my dad said, glancing at me over his newspaper. "Merry Christmas, by the way, Button."

"Merry Christmas Dad," I answered quickly. "And don't worry about anything. Ryan will be there too."

"Is that supposed to make me feel better? That my teenage daughter and her older boyfriend will be abroad together with no adult supervision?"

"Oh gosh, Dad, nothing's going to happen. Have I ever given you a reason not to trust me?" I asked, knowing that he probably wasn't around enough for me to violate his trust. Even if he were, I was a good kid. I wasn't going to go crazy just because I'd be away from him.

"It's not you I have a hard time trusting."

"Ryan's such a good guy, though!" I protested.

"Yeah, *guy* is the key word in that sentence, Button. That's the only word I seem to have a problem with."

"Candice will be there too," I said, hoping that his

fatherly concern wasn't enough to keep me from taking the part. I highly doubted Gran would let it go that far. She was practically salivating over this role.

"Isn't she that angry Asian girl?" he asked, perfectly describing my best girl friend.

"Yeah Dad," I said with a laugh. "She's the angry Asian."

"I'm sure she could scare that boy away from your dressing room. I just might have to pay her to keep an eye on you two."

"You do that," I said with a roll of my eyes, knowing there was nothing to worry about.

"Where is your boyfriend today?" Dad asked, still not letting the Ryan conversation go. He was definitely persistent; I had to give him that.

"He's spending Christmas with his grandma in her nursing home because he's such a good guy," I answered pointedly, giving my dad a sweet smile.

"Now, isn't that adorable?" Gran asked, still obviously glowing from the compliments she had received from Ryan the last time he had come over for dinner.

"I still don't trust him," Dad responded grumpily. Even though I thought he was being a tad too overprotective, I was loving every second that he was home for the holidays.

It was kind of nice to have a dad who worried about you. The alternative was just no good.

"When are we shooting? Have they said anything yet?" I asked, changing the subject away from Ryan for the time being.

"You should be starting in early February," Gran answered. She checked her phone calendar for confirmation before nodding. "You leave for England on February third, check into your hotel on February fourth, and start filming on the tenth. They'll be briefing you guys and getting you ready between the fourth and the tenth."

"What about costumes and everything?" I asked. I had been on a set for the past two years for *Forensic Faculty*, but I hadn't ever shot a big movie. I still wasn't sure how everything worked out.

"I already gave them your sizes. I'd imagine they've started making your costumes," she said absentmindedly, opening the fridge and glaring at its contents. I was automatically scared for whatever she was going to do to the food in there to make it inedible. Suddenly I was thankful for my new self-prescribed diet.

"We should probably start opening presents before your grandmother tries to cook us something," Dad whispered to me as he walked to the sink with his cereal bowl.

"Way ahead of you, Dad," I told him, making my way to the family room.

The sun was already dipping behind the mountains when I began my run after dinner that night. I hadn't intended to eat much, but Dad had been pestering me for the past few days about how I wasn't eating enough and I was starting to look "too skinny," so I ate my weight in surprisingly good food for Christmas dinner, justifying it by saying I'd go running afterward.

Now as I ran in the chill evening air around the high school track right behind our neighborhood, I wondered how I could have gotten away with eating like I used to.

My mind lazily wandered back to the message boards and fan site posts with comments about my weight or my hair or my clothes, and I began to run faster. I wasn't unrealistic; I knew not everyone would like me and someone could always find something mean to say, but when the majority of comments about you are negative ones, that's when you need to take notice and think that maybe they're onto something.

I ran around the track until my feet hurt and the stitch in my side was so painful I thought I might collapse—and then I ran some more. I kept running until I couldn't take it anymore, and then I fell into the grass of the football field, watching the sun make its final decent behind the mountains as I gasped for breath.

"June?"

I emitted a sound that was something between a squeal and a scream when Joseph called my name, having failed to realize he was on the track, let alone standing right over me.

"When did you get here?" I asked between deep breaths.

"I went over to your house to give you your present and Annette said you had come out here to run," he explained. Now I could see a small package in his hand that I hadn't noticed before.

"Oh no, your present is still at the house," I told him with a frown. Not that it was really a big deal. We could walk to my house in literally two minutes.

"Not exactly," he said, pulling his own gift out of his coat pocket. "Annette wouldn't let me leave without it," he explained with a shrug.

"That's perfect, then," I exclaimed, pulling him down onto the wet grass with me. The sun had now disappeared and the heat that had coursed through my body during the run was quickly leaving.

"Why are you running on Christmas?" Joseph asked as he plopped down next to me.

"Just felt like a good run," I lied.

"You hate running," he pointed out, knowing me too well for my own good.

"Not always," I lied again.

"June, what's going on?" he finally asked.

"I'm just stressed about this movie. I don't want to mess it up." I would have felt bad about lying if I had completely lied. I truthfully *was* very worried about the movie and making a complete fool out of myself. I just didn't bother to add the part where people online were calling me fat and that I never wanted to eat again.

"All right," he said with a sigh, reluctantly accepting my story.

"Let's open presents." I was definitely anxious to

change the topic, which seemed to be an urge I had been having more and more often lately.

"You first," Joseph said, handing me a small black velvet box. I glanced over at him suspiciously for a moment.

"You know you can't propose before your mission, right?" I asked jokingly.

"Trust me, if I could have, I would have done it a long time ago," he answered with a laugh, though something told me he wasn't kidding. I tried to ignore the way my heart started beating at his statement.. Joseph and I were just friends now, and I definitely didn't want to do anything that would mess up my relationship with Ryan.

"And sorry in advance that it's not that green moped you wanted," he added. Apparently I had talked about that a lot more than I thought.

I shook my head at his joke and opened the present. Inside of the small box was a deep purple stone set inside of a Victorian gothic-style bronze heart. It was attached to a delicate bronze chain that looked as if it had been tarnished from age.

"I got it at an antique store," he said as I pulled it from the box so he could fix it around my neck. "That's why it doesn't look new."

"It's incredible," I breathed. I guess it shouldn't have surprised me that he would know exactly what I would want for Christmas, but somehow it always did. I looked down at my new necklace fondly. "Thank you Joseph."

"I hope it's not . . . you know," he trailed off.

"What?"

"Weird. I mean, since it's a heart. Do you think Ryan will be mad?"

I thought this over for a moment. It hadn't really crossed my mind that this gift might upset Ryan, mostly because Joseph and I had been close friends for so long and we had only been a couple for two years. Defaulting back to friends had been a little rough at first, but now that we were there again it felt natural . . . except when Joseph brought up marrying me, and then I felt completely guilty for the little flip my stomach did.

"You're my best friend," I said reasonably. "You love me and I love you just like we have for nineteen years. I'm sure he'll see it like that and won't be upset."

Joseph looked at me skeptically, obviously not having as much faith in Ryan's rationality as I did.

"I think he might flip out a little," he said.

"Then why did you get it, if you thought it might make him mad?"

"Because I knew it would be the perfect present for you the second I saw it."

"Well, then, why don't you just say that if he asks you?" I asked.

"Ah, blind him with the simplicity of the truth," Joseph said mischievously. "June Laurie, you are a devious one."

"Yeah, who would have thought of actually telling people the truth? He'll never see it coming," I joked. "Now stop stalling and open your present!"

I watched with a smile on my face as Joseph unwrapped the small package he held in his hands. As he pulled the little journal-sized book from the paper and began flipping through it, I scooted closer so I could look at it over his shoulder.

Each page held a picture with a quote underneath it from the day the picture was taken. There were a few of Joseph and me with his family, some with Candice, Ryan, and Benjamin, and one or two with Xani and our high school friends.

Most of the pictures, however, were of Joseph and me in various places. My favorite picture was one Joseph had snapped of me on the monkey bars at the jungle gym with a caption under it that read, "Acting is embarrassing. Now look angry, June!"

He didn't say anything about the present as he flipped through page after page of memories. He'd laugh every once in a while and glance over at me with the smile that made his eyes go all squinty, or he'd nod at a quote, remembering it well.

"Just so you don't forget everyone while you're gone," I finally said, when he closed the last page.

"This is the most perfect thing you could have given me," he said, leaning over to give me a tight hug. "I can't believe you actually remembered a quote from each of these days."

"I'm nothing if not a movie buff. Remembering quotes is what I do," I offered as a simple explanation.

"I love this one," he said, opening to a page with a picture of Joseph and me with his little brother

Sam in Solvang with two words written at the bottom: "Evil Skeevers."

"Your brother was so cute trying to say Aebleskiver," I said with a giggle.

"I think he just really wanted them to be evil pancakes," he responded.

"Evil pancakes would be pretty exciting," I agreed.

"June, thank you so much for this."

"It's nothing. I just wanted something you could take with you that wasn't another tie."

"Trust me," he said with a grin. "This is *way* better than a tie."

CHAPTER 20

Standing in Joseph's living room for the last time for two years invoked the most bizarre jumble of emotions I had ever felt. Being surrounded by his screaming siblings was one thing, but mixing that world with Candice, Benjamin, and Ryan was something totally different.

We had all gone to sacrament meeting together that morning to hear Joseph speak. For the most part, I had managed to keep it together pretty well, pretending that his talk was just a normal run-of-the-mill sacrament talk and not an, "I'm going away for two years and won't see my best friend June Laurie for way too long" talk. At one point that day I even laughed when Candice gave me a puzzled look at the bread and water being passed around for the sacrament.

"Do you have to pay for this?" she whispered to me as the tray passed her by.

I laughed softly, biting my lip to keep from

making too much noise, and shook my head. The best part about Candice, Benjamin, and Ryan coming to church with us, though, was Benjamin loudly exclaiming once we left the building that, "Mormons are actually pretty normal," and "where are we supposed to be hiding our horns?".

As well as I had kept it together that day, though, my tough exterior was starting to crack. I was so proud of Joseph for going on a mission and being willing to do something so dedicated for our faith, but I would also miss him. Like I said, it was a bizarre mix of emotions wanting him to go but not wanting him to go.

"So, how does this thing work exactly?" Candice asked as we snacked on sandwiches made from rolls and lunch meat as well as some cookies Gran and I had made (*without* any sort of healthy ingredient, might I add).

"He goes into the Missionary Training Center on Wednesday, but his family is driving him up early tomorrow to visit with some of their relatives up there," I explained, watching across the room as Joseph talked to Xani, our friend from high school who had always had quite the crush on him.

Even now she couldn't stop flipping her hair as she spoke to him.

"And then we can't talk to him for two years?" Benjamin asked, sounding quite disbelieving of the whole situation.

"Well, you can write to him," I answered. "He can call his family on special occasions, too."

"And *he* paid money to do this? This isn't like a summer sales job where you make money?" Ryan asked.

They were having a very hard time wrapping their heads around the concept.

"Yeah, he paid for it himself," I said, practically beaming with how proud I was of him. He had done the whole thing on his own, knowing that his parents weren't exactly in any financial situation to help him out at the moment.

"Why?" Candice asked after a brief moment of silence where the three of them were apparently trying to understand the logic behind something that you just can't explain in terms of what makes worldly sense.

"Because he would feel guilty if he didn't share the amazing things he knows with other people. It's a privilege he wants so badly that he's willing to pay for it," I answered, realizing for the first time that no matter how much I would miss him, this was one of the most important things Joseph would ever do.

If Joseph could be that unselfish, I could be unselfish enough to let him go for two years.

"He could do that here," Benjamin pointed out, looking down at his phone as he spoke.

"Not the way he could out there," I told him. "Out in the mission field he won't have any distractions. He can be completely dedicated."

"You guys are a little crazy; you know that, right?" Candice said flatly. "Although, I wouldn't mind having your superpowers of knowing when something bad is going to happen."

"Oh no," I said in exasperation. "First we have horns, and now we have superpowers?"

"Superpowers are *way* better than horns, you have to admit," she reasoned.

"I think it's cool," Ryan said, tossing his paper plate into a garbage bag hanging on a door handle. "Believing in something so much that you want to dedicate that kind of time to it? That's awesome."

"No, I agree that it's awesome, don't get me wrong," Candice began, "I just couldn't do it."

"I wouldn't shortchange yourself," Benjamin told her. "You put up with Lukas Leighton to do what you love."

"True," she agreed with a solemn nod. "That's definitely on the same scale as giving up movies and music and money for two years and going out to get doors slammed in your face."

"You guys wouldn't happen to be talking about me, would you?" Joseph asked. I hadn't even heard him walk up to our group.

"How was Xani?" I asked with a grin. "Did she confess her undying love and beg you to stay?"

"She asked for my address so she could write me," he admitted, crinkling his nose at me. "She's a sweet girl."

"So, you're off to become a man, huh?" Benjamin asked, putting his phone is his pocket for the first time since I'd met him over two years ago. "I always thought the age to become a man was eighteen, not nineteen."

"They actually announced not too long ago that you can go at eighteen now," Joseph said.

"I can't imagine doing something like that when I was eighteen," Ryan stated with a shake of his head. "You're a better man than me."

"They're all very impressed with you," I said with a laugh. "I know better, though. I know you just really wanted to see some dog sleds."

"You're not supposed to say that in front of them," he joked. "I want them to keep thinking I'm amazing!"

"Really, though," Candice said, "Are you nervous?"

"Of course I am! I don't think I'd be human if I wasn't at least a little scared. It's a pretty big responsibility."

"I don't know if Benjamin knows how to actually write if there's no keyboard involved, but I'll transcribe his letters and send them off to you," Candice said.

"Yeah, between your 15,000 siblings, your parents, my Dad and Gran, Xani, and us four, you're going to have way too many letter to respond to," I said, nudging him with my elbow.

"That's a good problem to have," he answered. "Thank you guys for coming today. Seriously, it means a lot to me."

"We wouldn't miss your farewell," Candice said.

"Technically we don't call it a farewell anymore. but since that's what June's been telling you for months. we'll just stick with it," he answered with a smile in my direction.

"I can't get out of the habit of calling it a farewell," I said with my hands drawn up in surrender.

"It was cool to hear you speak," Benjamin said. "I swear, you're more grown up than us sometimes."

"Sometimes?" Candice asked skeptically before turning to Joseph and saying, "We're very proud."

In Candice lingo, that translated to something like, "You're the best person ever. I can't believe how selfless you are. I'm going to miss you even if I would never in a million years admit to that by pain of death," or something closely resembling that.

"We definitely are," Ryan agreed with Benjamin nodding at his side.

"We'll be keeping a list of movies for you to watch when you get back," Benjamin said, looking like he was really going to miss Joseph.

"Including yours," Joseph said, looking at Ryan and me.

"Of course," I answered. "Assuming I don't ruin it, of course."

"Yeah, the director is pretty worried she's going to botch the whole thing and we'll just have to CGI some good acting in there over her parts," Ryan said sarcastically.

"You're such a jerk," I informed him with a smile.

"I'm past trying to reassure you that you'll do a good job. Now all I can do is tease you for not listening to me," he shrugged.

"Trust me, you'll never be able to convince her

that she's a good actress," Joseph said knowingly.

"But you can definitely keep the compliments coming," I said sweetly, leaning over and kissing Ryan on the cheek.

We continued to talk until the house slowly emptied out and even Candice, Benjamin, and Ryan went home. I helped Joseph's mom clean up the food and the dishes, and then ran out of excuses to be in the Cleveland household. I knew they were leaving at about four o'clock in the morning and needed to get some sleep, but I didn't want to leave. I didn't know how to say goodbye to my best friend.

When I couldn't delay any longer, I walked to his front door as slowly as I could before turning to give Joseph a tight hug.

"I think you're not supposed to hug me now that I'm set apart," he said as I released him.

"Not even at the MTC yet and you're already a bad missionary, breaking all the rules," I said jokingly.

We were both silent for a moment. There wasn't any protocol for how to say goodbye to your friend for such a long period of time.

"I'm proud of you," I said one last time. "This is amazing of you."

"Pretty much every Mormon boy does this, June. It's not that extraordinary."

"It doesn't make it any less amazing just because other people do it too. It still makes me really proud."

"We'll see how I get along without you for two

years, June Laurie," he said quietly, his chocolate brown eyes boring into my soul.

"I'll definitely miss you, Joseph Cleveland," I answered. "You have your book?" I asked, hoping he hadn't forgotten to pack my Christmas present.

He nodded silently, looking at the heart-shaped necklace he had given me for Christmas.

"And you have my heart."

I didn't sleep at all that night. No matter how proud I was of Joseph or how much I wanted him to do this, I still cried for a few hours. By the time four o'clock a.m. rolled around, I propped my head against the cold windowpane of my bedroom window on the second story and watched his family drive off into the early dawn, taking him away to do something he loved for two years.

CHAPTER 21

Dear Joseph (or is it Elder Cleveland now?),

I arrived in England a few days ago. The first thing I noticed is how green it is compared to California! I always thought Simi Valley was a pretty lush place, but after being here for only a few days, I'm seriously rethinking my assessment.

The second thing I noticed is the sun . . . or lack thereof. Talk about foggy! I think we should be filming a horror movie out, here not a Regency romance. Think, "The Hound of Baskervilles" style.

We're filming in a place called the Yorkshire Dales National Park. They've constructed a little set there, and the place is seriously like something out of a painting! I took a few pictures that I'll have to send to you once I figure out where to print them.

We're staying in a little town nearby called Settle. It's pretty much Harry Potter embodied in a town. They've told me the working title of the film is, Without Rain, *but who knows if that's what title the film ends up with. Let's see, am I rambling yet?*

I hope the MTC is treating you well. I've heard the food is supposed to be pretty good, though any excuse to get away from Gran's health food is a good one. Honestly, even if the food wasn't all that great, I'd still envy you for not having to eat anything with mysterious green goop in it. Besides the lunch catering on set, I've been eating at restaurants since we got here. It sounds like a good idea until you actually do it, then you miss anything cooked in a normal kitchen at home. Oh, and I also use the term "restaurants" loosely.

Let me know what you're learning, who you've met, and just about every other detail in your life! I'll let you know how filming goes in my next letter. We should be starting tomorrow. I'm not really supposed to give any details to people off set, but since you're not exactly going to go on Twitter and tell the whole world, I think I'm safe to tell you. Hope you're well!

Love,
June

"Wake up call for Miss Laurie," Ryan said outside of my hotel room door at 5:45 a.m. sharp.

I knew the vans would be arriving at the hotel at any minute to take us to set, and with our early call time, I was more grateful than ever that I wasn't responsible for my own hair or makeup. I just showed up and let everyone else deal with the monumental task of making me pretty.

Opening the door, I threw my arms around Ryan's neck and buried my face in the warm scarf he wore. On most film shoots the actors are put up in five-star hotels with huge suites that feel like a condo. Unfortunately, the selection was a bit limited in Settle, so we were in an old bed and breakfast with heating that only worked when it wanted to. This meant that I was always freezing and anxious to snuggle up to Ryan for warmth.

I gave Ryan one long, deep kiss, my eyes closed and the corners of my mouth turned up into a smile, and for a moment, I felt very grown up. My (now official) boyfriend and I were abroad together filming a movie, I was sort of out on my own, and for the first time I wasn't stressing about paparazzi or if people online were saying I was fat. We were far enough away from Hollywood that people weren't so obsessed with what we were doing.

People on Ryan's fan site were always speculating about his latest project, but so far no photos had turned up, so I was counting my blessings, since we weren't being secretive about our relationship anymore.

"You both make me want to gag," said a familiar monotone voice behind Ryan.

"Sorry Candice. I thought you'd already be asleep in the van," I said, lacing my fingers through Ryan's as we walked toward the waiting vans outside in the chilly morning air.

Ryan and I still weren't quite sure how she had done it, but somehow Candice had weaseled her way onto the makeup crew for the film. I suspected my Dad had pulled some government strings to get her here so she could keep an eye on us, but Ryan had a less pessimistic theory—something that had to do with her being an incredible makeup artist.

I guess I had to agree with that one.

The drive to set took about thirty minutes each morning, and somehow I always managed to fall asleep on Ryan's shoulder in that time. In my defense, it was way too early for anyone to be awake, and the movement of the van mixed with the beautiful scenery in the national park was enough to lull me into a state of complete sleepy happiness.

There were a lot of things I loved about acting, but one of the best perks was always knowing what you were supposed to be doing throughout the day. My schedule was perfectly planned out by someone else, and it didn't take long for me to fall into a routine on set.

We'd arrive on set by 6:30 a.m., eat a lovely catered breakfast at craft services (or in my case, watch everyone eat breakfast while I tried to remember how mean people online could be), get into hair and makeup, go to the costumes trailer, be in our places by 7:30 a.m., and then just listen to whatever the director told us to do.

It wasn't exactly hard pretending to be young and caught up in an unbelievable romance when I was in England with Ryan Hex as my love interest. In fact, most days I felt guilty that I was actually being paid to do something so amazing. I felt like I should be paying the director for the opportunity to finally be doing what I had wanted to do since I was little.

This film had given me the opportunity to build up the brand I wanted—to create an image for myself in Hollywood that said I was good for something more than immature, crude teen comedies or kids cartoons. I was grown up enough to be the romantic lead in a film, and I didn't have to give up what I believed in to do it.

So as Ryan and I stood on our marks while the crew rushed around making adjustments, I couldn't help but feel incredibly grateful for everything I had right at that moment.

"Are you ready for our steamy kissing scene?" Ryan asked jokingly.

"I still don't think Regency people would be kissing out in broad daylight like this," I told him, looking around and trying to remember if they kissed in the Jane Austen movies I'd seen before.

"Remember, this isn't historically accurate by any means," he said. "*Marie Antoinette* . . . or *A Knight's Tale*. You know, that kind of thing."

"I'm sorry, I just missed every word you said," I told him with a grin.

"Were you distracted by my clothes again?" he asked with mock sternness.

I had already told Ryan that every girl in the world had a thing for a man dressed in Regency period attire, but I hadn't realized until we'd started filming just how attractive the knee-high boots and breeches were. Ryan's blonde hair was shaggy for the movie, but he'd shaved his scruff away and now sported the smooth face I'd been so used to on *Forensic Faculty*.

"I just can't think straight when you're wearing boots. You know that," I said jokingly, though maybe it wasn't really that much of a joke.

"Good, you can use that for our scene," he replied with a laugh. "That'll make it less weird."

"It's not like I haven't kissed you before," I said.

"Oh, you don't need to remind me," he said with a grin in my direction. "But it's always different to do it in front of a camera."

I wasn't sure why he was warning me of this fact. I had been Lukas Leighton's love interest on *Forensic Faculty* for two years, and we'd had to kiss on camera a few times. Obviously it was awkward with him because he was a total jerk who was only after one thing that I definitely wouldn't give him, but I couldn't see how it would be awkward with Ryan. At least I didn't have to worry about Ryan's hands wandering during our scenes like Lukas's always did.

Gosh I disliked him.

"You're not going to do something to try to mess me up, are you?" I asked, having an unfortunate flashback to the time he and Benjamin had threatened to do something while I filmed my scenes on *Forensic Faculty*, which had resulted in the most skittish hour of my life. The scene actually turned out much better because of my nerves, though, so I guess they really did know what they were doing.

"No, nothing like that. It's just weird to kiss someone on film that you kiss in real life. It's not the same," he said, still trying to explain something that I just wasn't getting.

"Are you two ready?" the director, Lee, asked. We both nodded in agreement, instantly straightening up our posture. (Apparently we slouched a lot compared to how real Regency people would stand.) "All right, then we'll just take it from the kiss. Ryan, we'll cue up the rain, you'll say your last line, and then the two of you kiss," he explained. "June, I want you to be very aggressive with the kiss. Not reserved, by any means." I nodded like I knew what he was talking about, even though I wasn't sure how to kiss aggressively. I guess we'd find out.

"Cue the rain," the PA called, and we instantly found ourselves standing in a downpour on the side of the cottage they had constructed for the movie. My boots and the hem of my gauzy white empire waist dress were getting muddier by the second, but I ignored it and tried to focus on the task at hand.

"Action," Lee called over the sound of the pouring rain.

It was the weirdest occurrence, but any time a director called action, I instantly found myself very aware of the strangest things, like the fact that all this fake rain made me really need to blink a lot to keep it out of my eyes, or the fact that I suddenly couldn't remember if I had been standing with my arms crossed across my chest in the last shot or not. Acting was definitely all about remembering details and multi-tasking—both things I wasn't great at.

"It doesn't always have to matter," Ryan suddenly

said, catching me by surprise.

He was only saying the last half of his line, and it threw me off to go from joking around with Ryan Hex to suddenly being in a very dramatic situation with William Cutteridge. I knew that right after he said his line, I was supposed to kiss him in a very non-timid way, but I also didn't want to look like an idiot when I misinterpreted what that meant. Luckily, I didn't have to worry about Ryan thinking I was ridiculous. That was one of the big perks of acting opposite your boyfriend.

Deciding that I would just go for, it I moved toward Ryan, grabbed him by the back of his head and pulled him to me. I had planned to kiss him "aggressively," but instead our noses hit much more violently than I had intended and we both pulled away, slapping hands over our faces in pain.

"I'm so sorry!" I called to him through my hand.

He was laughing hysterically with water pouring down his handsome face when he turned to look at me. So much for him not thinking I was ridiculous.

"What in the world was that?" he asked between bouts of laughter.

"I was trying to kiss you aggressively," I shot back, just as the director called cut.

"That was definitely aggressive," he said with a smile now at least trying to hide his laughter.

His wet hair was sticking to his forehead in thick clumps and he shook his head to get the water out of his deep blue eyes. He had a little dimple in his cheek where he was trying to suppress another fit of laughter, and even though he was currently making fun of me, I had to admit that he was the most attractive man in the world.

"June, you don't need to pull on him so forcefully," Lee called from his position behind the camera. "I just meant that when he goes in for the kiss, don't be timid about kissing him back."

"Will do," I said with a forced smile.

All Lee had to do was tell me that in the first place, but I had a sneaking suspicion that directors really liked to make actors look like idiots at least once in every scene. That way they could keep the footage for blackmail. They must have written a book saying that the best way to embarrass an actor was to deliberately withhold important information from them.

It was working.

"Camera speeding. And action!"

"It doesn't always have to matter," Ryan said again, never ceasing to amaze me with how quickly he could turn his acting on.

This time he leaned forward to kiss me, and I held still, waiting for him. I didn't want to injure the poor boy again.

When he brought his lips to mine, I kissed him back with vigor, trying to seem like I wasn't being timid, and it didn't take me long to figure out what Ryan had meant about kissing on camera. I was so worried about cheating out to the camera, paying attention to the duration of the kiss, and monitoring whether my kiss seemed timid or intense, that I didn't enjoy it one bit. The whole thing was like reading from a kissing manual—way too mechanical.

Tilt head, raise chin, cheat to camera, make sure you don't have ugly hands, suck in your stomach. Not passionate at all.

It didn't even feel like a real kiss, and suddenly Ryan was just another actor who I was kissing because someone behind a camera had told me to. It was the oddest feeling.

"Cut," Lee called. "Good work guys," he said by way of praise, before turning to his assistant director to ask them something about the lighting.

"Thanks for not trying to knock me out again," Ryan said, rubbing his nose for effect.

"Yeah, that was pretty much the most embarrassing thing ever," I responded, pulling on the short cap sleeves of my dress. The rain had turned off, luckily, but now I was left to shiver in the freezing cold.

As if someone could read my mind, Ryan and I were instantly handed big puffy coats to put on over our wet clothes. It looked completely out of place against our period clothing, but I was not about to complain when they helped me finally start to regain feeling in my core.

"See what I mean about kissing on camera?" he asked after a moment of rubbing his cold hands together to warm them up before taking mine.

He rubbed my frozen hands between his and it didn't take long for them to warm up despite the chills the action was sending down my spine.

"It was such a weird feeling," I told him honestly. "I kind of hated it because it didn't feel like I was actually kissing you."

"It definitely takes some getting used to," he agreed.

"Okay, are you two ready for another take?" Lee asked. Even though I wasn't ready to relive the bizarre, emotionless kiss, and even less ready for them to take my warm coat away and turn on the rain again, I nodded, because that's what an actor did: whatever anyone else told them to.

CHAPTER 22

Dear June (because I'm definitely not calling you Sister Laurie),

I got to Anchorage yesterday. I'm pretty sure we don't spend enough time in the MTC before being sent out. I feel completely unprepared! But my trainer said that's normal and I should just count myself lucky that I'm not speaking a foreign language.

Xani has already written me about five letters before I've had a chance to respond to a single one of them. Something tells me she's taking our "breakup" well. Her letters are about as up-close-and-personal as she used to be in high school, so that's been fun to deal with.

I've learned a lot about how to approach people, but I think most of my training is going to come from actually getting out there and doing it. I think the best part has been becoming more familiar with the scriptures. I know that's like a textbook answer, but it's so true! I've never felt this connected before.

It sounds like you're having fun in England. I thought since I was going on a mission, I was supposed to be the one going to a new place with all sorts of amazing things to discover. Way to steal my thunder, Laurie.

Anyway, my hand is cramping up from the piles of letters I've written today. I hope you're not ruining the film (just kidding), and I hope you're taking a billion pictures. I haven't taken any yet, but judging by how beautiful this place is, you're going to get tired of me constantly sending you scenery pictures.

Take care of yourself, June.

Joseph

The long day of filming had left me feeling soggy and cold, and the lack of heat in my hotel room did nothing to help the feeling pass, no matter how many blankets Ryan piled on top of me. We both sat on the bed with a few boxes of takeout food between us. He ate, and I pushed food around my paper plate.

"Hey June?" Ryan said tentatively, sounding exactly like Joseph for a moment.

"Yeah?"

"I don't want you to get mad at me for this, okay?"

"That's a pretty awful way to start a conversation," I said with a nervous giggle, not sure what he could possibly need to say that would make me mad.

"I know, I just . . . I've noticed that you haven't been eating much lately, and I'm a little worried about you," he said after a long pause.

I felt my stomach drop, but tried to play it off like I had no idea what he was talking about. "I think my eating habits have changed or something," I lied, taking my first bite of food that day to prove my point. "I've been snacking a lot more and eating fewer actual meals, so it probably seems like I'm not eating as much."

"I've been paying attention, June," he said simply.

"Ryan, you're crazy," I answered, another nervous laugh sounding completely fake as it escaped my lips.

"I'm not the only one who's worried," he said.

"What?"

"Joseph told me to keep an eye on you before he left. He said you've been working out a lot, but not putting anything into your body to counter all the energy you're expending."

"And you're going to listen to Joseph?" I asked in disbelief, knowing that my argument made no sense. Why wouldn't he listen to Joseph?

"Remember how I said don't get mad?" he asked calmly, raising his eyebrows at me.

"I'm fine. Look at me—I'm as pudgy as ever," I said, getting more emotional than I meant to.

"What are you talking about? You're a stick," he replied in exasperation. "You don't have an ounce of fat on your body."

"That's not what your fans are saying," I blurted out before I could stop myself.

"What?"

I didn't want to tell him. I didn't want him or anyone else trying to stop me from dropping a few sizes, but it was too late for that. I had to open my big mouth, and I knew there was no way he'd let it go until I talked to him about it.

"When the paparazzi got that picture of us kissing on Thanksgiving, I went onto one of your fan sites to see what people were saying about it," I began.

"Yeah, that's never a good idea," he said instantly.

"I didn't think anything bad would come of it," I admitted, wondering how I could have been so stupid. "But so many people left comments about how I'd let myself go since I left *Forensic Faculty* and how I was getting fat, and it drove me crazy. I mean, if that many people are saying it, then it has to be true, right? They wouldn't all just happen to make up the same thing to focus on if there weren't some truth behind it."

Ryan studied my face for a moment before moving the takeout to the night stand and replacing it with my laptop. He scooted closer to me on the bed before opening the computer.

"What's something you love that you think is completely beyond anyone making fun of it?" he asked.

"What?"

"Just give me something."

"I don't know. I love silent films," I said.

"Okay, let me rephrase that. What's something *normal* people like too," he teased. "Something that's so universally good that no one can say something bad about it."

I thought this over for a moment, trying to think if there was something so generally accepted by everyone.

"The Beatles?" I ventured.

"Perfect," he agreed. "That's exactly what I was thinking."

Without an explanation, he pulled up a video of The Beatles performing somewhere. I'd seen the video before, and even now, in the middle of this little confession, it made me smile. They were definitely universally acknowledged as good.

"So The Beatles are pretty much above reproach; we can all agree, right?" he asked, and I nodded, although I still had no idea what this had to do with me. "Read some of the comments on this video."

I did as he said, scrolling through comment after comment. Most of them were good, talking about how people couldn't understand how we could go from The Beatles to today's music without feeling ashamed. But the more comments I read, the more I realized that there were a bunch of negative things being said as well.

"Seriously?" I wondered aloud. "They're The Beatles, people! How can you say anything bad about them?"

"That's my point, June," Ryan said, sounding like a teacher who had finally led his student to the correct answer as he snapped the laptop closed. "It doesn't matter how perfect something is. People online will find a reason to be mean. My own fans on my 'fan sites' say rude things about me all the time. I used to read through their comments and when they found out, some people thought it was conceited of me. Now that I don't read the comments anymore, they think I'm out of touch with my fans and they think I've got an ego. You can't make everyone happy. You just have to learn to ignore what's being said and know that it's not true."

"I know you probably don't think I'm fat now because I've lost all this weight," I began, now able to admit that maybe I was losing weight unhealthily. "But did you think I was fat before I started dieting? When I was up at college?"

"June, I think you're perfect," he told me, with so much sincerity that I almost wanted to cry.

Instead of crying, however, I leaned over to kiss him, thinking that it would be a better alternative. He tangled his fingers in my curly, out of control hair, and I put my arms around his neck. It was a slow, comfortable kiss that made me feel like I was home, and it felt like sheer perfection until he began to lean backward, pulling me with him. The movement was so slight that I had to wonder if I had imagined it, until it became obvious what was happening.

I was suddenly very aware of the fact that I was thousands of miles from home and from any supervision. I was sitting in a hotel room in England, on a bed, with my boyfriend, and I was kissing him.

I knew that Ryan knew what my values were, but

we'd never actually had any sort of talk about things like that, with my feeling like we already had a mutual understanding. But there was one fact that I couldn't ignore no matter how much I wanted to—Ryan wasn't Mormon and he wasn't held to the same standards as me. While I knew he wasn't the type to just sleep around, I also knew he didn't believe there was anything wrong with taking things to the next level with someone you were in a committed relationship with, even if you weren't married.

As he continued to lean back, our heads almost touching the pillow, I pulled away from him, sitting up straight and looking at the floor.

I didn't know what to do.

I had been in this situation before with Lukas Leighton, but in that instance it was completely obvious what I should do. Lukas was a womanizer, and he was a horrible person. Ryan, on the other hand, didn't think he was doing anything wrong. He was thinking that he really had feelings for me and it was only natural for him to express that. That's what made everything so difficult. How did I explain to him that this wasn't okay with me without making it sound like he was some sort of villain?

"What's wrong?" he asked, sitting up with me and kissing my neck gently. I desperately wished his kisses weren't so tempting, but I had to be the strong one here.

"I can't do this," I told him quietly.

"Do what?" he asked, his lips still moving gently over my skin and giving me chills. His voice sounded far away, and I could tell he was feeling that hazy comfort brought on by a good kiss.

"Ryan, you know I don't believe in sex before marriage, right?" I asked, realizing that maybe it had been naive of me to think he knew that without us ever having to discuss it.

This made him stop kissing me. Now he straightened up and looked at me with slight confusion lining his features.

"I know you don't just jump into bed with any guy you see," he began tentatively. He almost looked hurt for a moment. "But I thought that . . . you know . . . since we're together and our relationship is pretty serious, it was different."

This was exactly what I could have avoided with one simple talk a long time ago. Now Ryan was looking at me like I didn't want him, and I could tell his ego was hurt. This was definitely my fault.

"Ryan, I like you so much," I said, willing him to know it was true. "I'm so sorry I never talked about this with you. I guess I just kept thinking we were on the same page this whole time."

"I feel so stupid," he said finally, not meeting my eyes. "June, I didn't want you to feel pressured. I just really thought we were at that point."

"Don't feel stupid," I insisted. "It's my own fault for not laying out some ground rules when we first started dating." I paused for a moment, knowing I needed to be firm. "I don't *ever* believe in sex before marriage, no matter how committed to each other we are. It has absolutely nothing to do with you; it's just my own beliefs."

I waited for him to say something, but the silence was too much for me to handle. "I hope this doesn't change how you feel about me," I finally said, voicing my fears that he'd leave me because of this stance.

"Of course it doesn't," he reassured me. "I just feel really dumb for being on a completely different page."

"Don't worry—I feel just as dumb," I said. "How about we both agree not to worry about this now that we've talked about it, and on our next day off, we can do some sightseeing?"

"What does sightseeing have to do with this?" he asked in confusion.

"Nothing," I answered with a grin. "I just really wanted an excuse to work it into the conversation and couldn't think of an organic way to do that."

"Well, then, no more feeling dumb mixed with sightseeing it is," he said, giving me one last small kiss.

He sighed deeply, and even though I felt resolved on this issue, I knew our abrupt ending to this talk probably had more to do with my desire to avoid the awkward situation than with the issue actually being settled.

"Now eat something, you skeleton," Ryan emphasized, handing me my food and smiling sincerely, even though I could see the cogs still working in his brain.

I laughed at his statement and nodded. We had

definitely talked about a pretty big issue, but in the back of my mind, I wondered how far our relationship would go before I had to ask myself what I would do when I wanted to be married in the temple and Ryan couldn't give me that.

CHAPTER 23

Dear Elder Cleveland (is that better?),

Filming has been going really well. I'm sending some pictures with this letter so you can see how beautiful this place is. Now you won't need to feel bad about sending me all sorts of scenery pictures . . . We can call it even.

We had to shoot a few scenes in the rain for the movie. I guess with a title like Without Rain, *I should have expected that . . . or maybe I shouldn't have expected it . . . Either way, there's a lot of rain in a movie that's supposed to be without it.*

My mornings are early, my days are long, the heater in my hotel room barely works, but I'm having a blast. Nothing better than acting, right? You wouldn't like to be in this movie though. There's not much comedy in it, and I know how you love your funny roles.

I've had so many things I want to talk to someone about lately, but my best friend is away and I don't want to write those things in a letter. Wow . . . that wasn't meant to sound like a huge guilt trip, even though that's how it came out. Too bad there's no backspace on paper, huh?

Anyway, I'm really proud of you and it sounds like you're doing really well. I can't wait to see some pictures! Tell me more about the people you're meeting!

And most of all, know that what you're doing is important.

Love,
June

Sitting in front of the camera and waiting for the crew to make adjustments only a week later, I was still a little shaken by one important point that I should have considered ages ago. My talk with Ryan had ended well, and now that all of our expectations were out on the table, it took a lot of pressure off of our relationship. Apparently he had been wondering where we stood on that subject for a while, and *apparently* I was pretty terrible at realizing this.

Story of my life, I guess.

I was glad that we had worked that mess out, but the whole problem had brought on a nagging thought that I couldn't quite get rid of. What happened if Ryan and I got so serious that we wanted to get married? I knew it was too early to be thinking about something like that, but somehow I felt irresponsible for not thinking about it earlier.

It wasn't like there was something wrong with non-Mormon boys, by any means. Ryan had proved that he was a complete gentleman who respected my values and was willing to be patient with me. The problem was that ever since I was a little girl, I had wanted to get married in the temple, and I knew that Ryan couldn't give me that.

So what did I do?

Did I break up with him because he wasn't Mormon? Something told me that wasn't quite the right decision; it would be jumping the gun a little. Did I try to convert him so that we could get married in the temple? Somehow that didn't seem right either. I didn't want Ryan to join the church because I asked him to. I wanted him to join because he believed in its teachings. Did I wait to see if our relationship even got to that point, or would waiting just mean we'd end up in a situation like we had last week, where we're both on completely different pages but by the time we realize it, we're in so deep that someone's going to get their feelings hurt?

"Hey, are you all right?" Ryan asked. He had been standing behind the camera waiting to read lines to me for my close-up shot.

"Yeah, just thinking," I told him, deciding that I'd see if our relationship even went far enough to worry about this issue before bringing it up.

What can I say? I was a little bit of a chicken.

"Are you nervous about crying?" he asked.

"I wasn't until you said that," I answered with a laugh.

Here's the thing about acting: it's awkward. I've said it before, and I'll say it again. No matter how seamless and perfect movies turn out, there were a lot of awkward moments to get the film to that point.

At that moment, I was about to have a one-sided conversation with Ryan, who would be standing off screen, and then I'd have to suddenly start crying when I didn't feel sad at all. When the movie was all put together, Ryan and I would have just had a very emotional and intimate conversation, and anyone in the theatre would think it was easy to start crying. Heck, most of the people in the audience would probably be crying by that point if I did my job right.

But here and now, I didn't get the luxury of an emotional build-up to get the tears flowing. All I had were a few words from the end of Ryan's last sentence, and a crew of people all staring at me, wondering if I would be able to make myself cry on cue.

It was kind of awful.

"Okay, now I'm actually really nervous," I said desperately, looking up at him for help. "What do I do? What do you do to make yourself cry?"

"You need to stay in character between takes. Like, right now, I guess I shouldn't even be talking to you," he said with a slight wince, realizing his mistake. "It sucks, and it's the main reason I stick to comedy roles but you need to get yourself in a dark place and stay there even after they call cut. Getting out of character for a few minutes between takes totally ruins your momentum and makes it harder to build it back up again."

I nodded as I tried to take in everything he had said. I didn't really feel like thinking about things that would make me depressed, but acting meant doing anything you had to in order to get the right shot.

"Okay here I go," I said with a deep breath. "Don't talk to me." Ryan tried to hide a smile as he nodded and turned away, giving me some privacy to get myself good and depressed.

It wasn't as easy a job as it seemed. I was already self-conscious knowing that half of the crew was just staring at me while the director talked to the first AD. I knew I was probably making some pretty unattractive faces while I tried to think of something sad, but nothing really came to mind. All I could think of were things that were stressing me out, and those didn't really make me feel like crying.

I let my mind wander to Ryan and the questions I was having about our future. It didn't really make me sad. All it did was confuse me. Then I wondered what my mom would tell me to do.

That was all it took, really.

Coming to the understanding that I would never know what my mom would tell me to do because I had never known her was the only thought I needed to get myself to the place I needed to be right at that moment.

"June, are you ready?" Lee asked off camera. I could see Ryan watching me closely, his face holding concern. Had he been watching me pass into my dark place?

"I'm ready," I told him with more honesty than I wanted to possess at that moment.

"Do you want to talk about it?" Ryan asked, reading my mind the way Joseph used to. We were sitting in my hotel room once more after the emotional shoot that day.

"About what?" I asked, playing dumb and pretending to flip through a magazine.

"About whatever gave you such a perfect crying scene today," he clarified. "The acting was great, but I get the feeling it's because it wasn't acting."

"I did what I was supposed to—I got myself to a dark place."

"Yeah, but the other trick in acting is being able to get yourself back out again."

I thought this over for a moment, wondering how to come back from the part of my mind I had tried not to visit my whole life.

"Your mom?" Ryan guessed, and I nodded slowly. "I used to think about my parents when I needed to do an emotional scene."

"Used to?" I asked.

"I couldn't do it anymore. Any time I had a scene like that, I'd end up looking like you do right now for days. I couldn't pull myself back out very easily, so eventually I had to find something else."

"There's not a lot that makes me cry," I told him.

"Me neither, but putting yourself through this for every emotional movie isn't worth it. Trust me."

"Then what do you do?"

"If all else fails and I need to just get my eyes watery, I can teach you an easy trick for that," he said. "I think Candice even has this syringe full of menthol crystals so she can shoot the vapor into your eyes. The actual full-on crying is a little more difficult though. You need to find something sad to think about that isn't so close to home."

"Like what?"

"Sometimes I'll think of sad things that *could* happen. It's still just as awful to think about, but once you've finished your scene, it's easy to look around and see that everything is fine," he explained. "Or sometimes I'll just try to get really into character and put myself in the middle of whatever is making my character cry. That takes a little more work and it's harder to do, but it's not impossible and it sure beats being depressed for days."

"I think anything beats that," I agreed, glad to know that I wouldn't have to do this to myself every time I needed to cry on cue.

"Tell me about your mom," Ryan said, surprising me by not trying to change the subject or make me laugh like he normally would. He actually wanted to delve into this mess to help me sort through it.

"I never knew her," I said. "She had an aneurysm when I was nine months old."

"Then tell me what you know about her."

"She was really beautiful," I said with a little smile. I leaned over to pull her photo out of my purse—the photo the thief in L.A. had almost stolen from me.

Ryan scanned the picture, a smile in his eye as he examined it.

"You look a lot like her," he said, and it was true. My mom and I both had wildly curly dark hair and pale skin, but she had bright blue eyes where my eyes were a dark brown. "What was her name?"

"Vera," I said fondly, thinking it was the most beautiful name I had ever heard.

"Was she an actress too?" he asked.

"Not in film. She loved being in stage plays, though," I said, recounting the stories I'd heard from Gran. "That's actually how she and my dad met."

"Don't tell me your dad was in a play," Ryan laughed. I had to admit, the idea made me giggle too.

"Of course not! Gran was the director of the community theatre for a while, and my mom was in one of her plays. Gran, being the matchmaker she is, told my dad he had to come see her latest show."

"I bet he loved that," Ryan said.

"Oh yeah, Dad is all about the arts," I answered with a laugh. "So he comes to the play and ends up thinking my mom is the most beautiful girl he's ever seen—which she is—and he asks Gran about her."

"I'll bet Annette never gets tired of that story."

"She loves the fact that she was responsible for Mom and Dad meeting," I told him.

"Is your whole family Mormon or just you?" he asked suddenly, and it was odd for me to realize we'd never really talked about this.

"Dad is and Gran is, though she's not as active as she used to be."

"And your mom?"

"She wasn't until she met Dad. Then she started going to church with him and fell in love with the gospel, so she joined," I said, wondering if that story could run in the family.

"June?" Ryan asked, and I knew whatever he said next would be important.

"Yeah?"

"Do Mormons only marry other Mormons?"

The question was so simple and so easy to answer, but I knew that if I gave the one-word answer of "no," then I would be purposely ignoring an important issue that had been bugging me.

"No, Mormons can marry whomever they want," I began cautiously. "But if you want to get sealed together in the temple, you both have to be worthy."

"So you both have to be Mormon?" he asked, looking like he really was interested in my answer.

"Not all Mormons can go into the temple."

"Really?"

"Yeah, I think a lot of people who aren't Mormon don't know that, and it kind of catches them off guard when they first learn," I said with a smile in his direction. "Only Mormons who are living up to certain standards and covenants can go in."

"So, not only do you have to be Mormon, but you have to be like a super Mormon?" he asked, making me laugh at his term.

"Kind of," I answered.

"And do you want to get married in the temple?" he asked after a long silence.

This was it. I just had to buck up and tell him the truth.

"It's very important to me," I said carefully.

Ryan was silent for a while and I could see the thoughts flying through his mind. I wished more than anything that I could see what he was thinking.

"Remember how I told you I met with the missionaries but thought some of the stuff was a little hard to believe?" he asked, and I nodded. "I've met with them a few more times."

"Oh?" I asked neutrally, not wanting to lead the conversation at this point but desperately wanting to know what he was going to say next.

"I still have some reservations, but I started reading that book they gave me. I didn't want to tell you because . . . I don't know."

"You didn't want me to push you?" I asked, already knowing the answer.

"But being around you so much and seeing how you never push your beliefs onto me, I guess I didn't really have anything to worry about, did I?" he asked.

"Not at all," I told him, trying not to look too happy about the fact that Ryan had sought out the church on his own. "Just let me know if you have any questions."

"I will," he said with a nod.

"And Ryan?"

"Yeah?"

"I don't ever want you to feel like you have to join the church because of me. The only reason I want you joining is because you feel like it's the right thing to do," I told him, wanting to make absolutely certain that if he joined, he did it for the right reasons.

"I know," he answered, leaning over and giving me a quick kiss.

I pulled him into a hug and just held him like that for a long time. We were so good at helping each other. He had comforted me about my mom, I had put his worries to rest about any pressure to join the church, and now all I wanted to do was hold him forever. I rested my head on his shoulder, lightly kissing his neck with my eyes closed and playing with his hair.

"This is my favorite," I whispered to him as we sat like that for a while in the hotel room.

"June, I love you," he said so quietly that I almost couldn't be certain he'd said it at all.

My eyes snapped open and I debated on whether I should make sure he'd really said it or not. Pulling out of our embrace, I looked into his blue eyes.

"What?"

He didn't say anything for a moment, and I began to worry that I really had made up his words in my head.

"I love you," he finally said again, a bit timidly. My brain instantly flooded with hundreds of questions, but how I felt wasn't one of them.

"I love you too, Ryan," I said back.

CHAPTER 24

Dear June,

As promised, I'm sending you some pictures. Most of them are just beautiful places. You know . . . no big deal . . . I just happen to be in the most beautiful place on earth. Yeah, that's right. I went there. I just challenged you to a picture duel. Bring it on, Laurie.

I will—however reluctantly—admit that you are in a pretty beautiful place too. It's just not quite Alaska. But it was a valiant effort.

Oh, in case you're wondering, the guy in the picture by the fountain with me is my companion. His name is Elder Davies, and he's from New Zealand . . . like where Lord of the Rings *was filmed! How cool is that? I've nerded out with him a few too many times over that fact. And I've decided that when I get back, New Zealand is definitely in my future. I think if you and I ever decide to pick up accents, those would be the ones to get.*

I've taught a few families since my last letter. No baptisms yet, but there are a few people really interested. I'm going to go all serious missionary on you for a second, but there's honestly nothing better than sharing your beliefs with someone. It's something so personal and important to you that it creates an instant connection with the person you share it with. It feels amazing.

Okay, I promise I'll go back to being not serious again. I miss you, Laurie, and I can't wait to see you again. That book you gave me has been a lifesaver on difficult days.

Elder Cleveland

Walking through the streets of Settle with Ryan was my favorite thing to do on our days off. We invited Candice to come with us every time, but she'd just mutter about us being disgustingly happy and stalk off to her room to be moody. I'd make it up to her at night by forcing her to come to my hotel room and watch romantic comedies, which she barely tolerated on a good day. Still, I didn't want Benjamin mad at me for not entertaining his . . . whatever Candice was to him.

Being able to walk around a town without people jumping out with cameras was a nice change from back home. Ryan and I weren't exactly hugely famous, but that didn't stop paparazzi from being annoying when you wanted some alone time. Ryan had it worse than I did, and I suspected that the only reason paparazzi photographed me at all was because I was with him.

"I think we need to get these earrings to match your necklace," Ryan said as we passed by the window of a jewelry store.

We were bundled up in coats, scarves, and gloves, and all I really wanted at the moment was a hot chocolate, but I wouldn't turn down the opportunity to look at a pair of earrings. I was only human, after all.

"Those are gorgeous," I said, pressing my hands up against the glass like a little kid outside of a toy store.

The earrings in question were two small amethyst studs that would perfectly match the amethyst necklace Joseph had given me. Ryan had been secure enough in our relationship to know the necklace was an expression of Joseph's friendship, and I felt luckier and luckier every day that he was so level-headed and logical.

"Do you like them?" he asked, looking down at me with a smile, his nose red from the cold.

Could he get any more adorable?

"You can't get them for me," I said quickly, knowing they were probably expensive.

"Why not?"

"It's not my birthday or anything."

"It doesn't have to be your birthday," he answered with a laugh. "Can't it just be an I-love-my-girlfriend present?"

"Are you trying to buy my love?" I asked, leaning over and kissing him slowly in the freezing cold.

"Is it working?" he asked against my lips.

"Your money is the only reason we're dating, so it must be," I joked, pulling away and grinning at him with a quick raise of my eyebrows.

"Then we'd better hurry up and get in there," he said with mock urgency, pulling me behind him into the little shop.

Just as the man at the counter greeted us, my phone buzzed in my purse.

"One sec," I said to Ryan, who nodded and turned to talk to the man about the earrings.

"Hello?"

"Bliss, I am very disappointed at the lack of phone calls I've received from you," Gran said sternly.

"Gran, I called you last night," I countered in disbelief. I had called her and Dad almost every day since I'd been away, but they were both still convinced that I was up to no good out in England. The fact that I could never seem to get my head around the time change didn't help either.

"But then you had a day off today."

"And I was going to call you on my day off once I got back to the hotel," I said with a sigh. I couldn't be mad that they were worried about me, but there was a point where it became excessive.

"Well, if you had cared to speak to your grandmother a little more often, you would have already heard the exciting news," she said.

"What news?" I asked quickly.

"I don't know. Maybe I'll go tell someone who keeps in touch a little better," she said lazily, loving the fact that she had information I wanted.

"Gran!" I exclaimed, earning an odd look from the shop keeper.

"Ryan's agent and I are currently in negotiations with a network who wants to run a pilot for a new show with both of you in it," she finally said.

I looked over at Ryan, who was handing over some cash. Had he known about this? He glanced at me and winked before turning his attention back to the cashier.

"What?" was all I managed to say. "Why us?"

"You guys may be over there being all lovey-dovey and shooting your romantic movie, but people over here are eating it up."

"What do you mean?" I asked, wondering how people could know about us if we were so far away.

"Pictures, Bliss. They're worth a thousand words . . . or I guess in this case, they're worth a starring role in a TV show."

"There's a picture of us? I haven't seen a single paparazzi here," I said, my mind spinning from all of the news.

I wasn't sure which was more shocking—that there were apparently pictures of us floating around, or the fact that Ryan and I might be cast on another show together. This didn't happen in the real world. How was I constantly so blessed in my career?

"They can be sneaky. They're not as in-your-face over there, but that doesn't mean they don't exist," she said knowingly. "Honestly, though, this is the best thing that could have happened to you. You and

Ryan are all anyone wants to talk about, and networks are taking notice. They think this would be the perfect opportunity for them to cash in on your little off-screen romance."

I wasn't sure I liked the idea of people cashing in on our relationship like it was some cheap publicity stunt, but I definitely liked the idea of being in a TV show with Ryan.

"Where are you at on negotiations? What about *Forensic Faculty*?" I asked.

"I'm not sure what Ryan's agent is working out with that show, but he sounds very optimistic that the pilot will take off and your show will be successful enough for him to leave *Forensic Faculty*."

"Wow," I said slowly, not sure what else I could really say. Working on a TV show with Ryan again would be a dream come true, but I didn't want to get my hopes up until we had some solid news.

"When will you know for sure if they want us?" I asked.

"They'll have you both come in for an audition once you get back, as a technicality. They already know they want you. And then it's all just paperwork and planning."

"This is amazing," I said in awe. I had definitely been blessed in my acting career with getting good parts, but lately my luck was unbelievably good. "What's the show about?"

"They're still planning it out, but from what I gathered, you're supposed to be from the 1950s, and somehow you end up in modern times and Ryan is a modern man who takes care of you. It sounds sweet," she said fondly. "It'll be a lot of you adjusting to the new social norms and technology and all that."

"That sounds perfect," I exclaimed, wondering what cute fifties clothes I'd get to wear.

I was definitely a girl.

"They do like to bank on your old-fashioned look, don't they?" she asked.

"I'm glad they do," I said happily as I looked over to Ryan.

I wanted desperately to tell him the good news, but his phone had already begun ringing and I knew he was receiving the same information as me. I gave him a thumbs-up as he answered, and he just looked at me like I was crazy.

"Well Bliss, I'm proud of you," Gran said, just as she had every time we'd spoken.

"Thanks Gran! It's all because of the crazy acting classes you've given me. Keep me updated on the part," I said with a smile.

"I definitely will. Love you."

"Love you too," I responded as I hung up. Ryan was still on the phone with his agent getting the good news, so I left him alone for a moment.

My curiosity piqued by my conversation with Gran, I pulled up a search engine on my phone and typed in our names, wondering if there really were rumors going around about us. I was completely shocked when the results came back with page after page of articles, blog posts, and sightings on fan sites about us. I only had to click through a few to realize we were definitely not as alone over here in Settle as we thought we were.

There were endless pictures of Ryan and me walking through the streets, kissing and holding hands. There were even a few blurry photos of us in our costumes on set. It was amazing how many pictures people could take of you without your knowledge. I was taken aback as I scanned through all of the photos. Gran was right—people were going crazy about the fact that we were a couple, and all I could think was that it had to be a slow news day for people to really care about Ryan and me.

As I clicked on yet another page of photos, Ryan slipped his arms around my waist from behind and whispered into my ear, "Looks like you're stuck with me, huh?"

CHAPTER 25

Dear Elder Cleveland,

Looks like you're not the only one who can be a missionary.

Love,
June

Wrapping the movie was actually a lot sadder than I thought it would be. When you spend a few months completely isolated with a small group of people, you begin to get close to them. It's normal to see them every day and spend way too much time together until you wrap and suddenly never see them again. The change was always a little jarring.

Candice was ecstatic to be getting back to America, and as we walked through the airport, I linked my arm with hers.

"Are you excited to see Benjamin?" I asked conspiratorially, whispering so that Ryan wouldn't hear us. He was wearing a collared shirt, fitted jeans, and aviator glasses, and my heart skipped a beat every time I looked at him. How on earth had I landed Ryan Hex?

"No," she said flatly, shaking my arm away from her. She was about as cuddly as a steel bear trap.

"I'm going to find out what's going on between you two sooner or later," I warned.

"Great. Then you can add that to the list of completely useless things in this life, right next to Benjamin's strobe light app."

I shrugged and laced my fingers through Ryan's, knowing Candice was trying extra hard not to look excited about going back. I loved that I could see right through her.

It didn't take long for us to check our luggage and board the plane that would forever take us away from the few months of complete (minus paparazzi) seclusion we had experienced. It had been so wonderful to just be with Ryan and let our relationship develop without cameras (that we could see) or people harassing us about being a couple. We could just be ourselves and see where that led us.

I knew it wouldn't be the same once we got back to L.A., so I tried to enjoy our last few moments of peace on the plane.

"I'm really going to miss this place," Ryan said with a sigh as he looked out the small airplane window.

"Our place." I looked at Ryan and smiled, knowing exactly how he was feeling. We would never be at this point in life again. We had been able to start a brand new relationship in a remote and perfect setting. No matter what, things would never be as carefree and new as they had been in England.

"Time for a reality check?" he asked, sounding a bit weary.

"Not quite yet. We still have a long flight ahead of us," I reminded him, giving him a soft kiss and then laying my head on his shoulder and closing my eyes, letting myself be completely blissful in that moment.

The bliss didn't last very long. The second we stepped inside the airport, I could see people pulling out their phones to take pictures, and a few full-blown paparazzi unabashedly snapping shots of us.

"Vultures," Candice mumbled next to me, rolling her big brown eyes and putting on oversized sunglasses.

We tried to ignore the cameras as best we could as we picked up our luggage and headed outside to where Benjamin was waiting for us.

"Excuse me," a girl about my age said to our group, stopping us just before we got to the car. "Are you Ryan Hex?" she asked, although I was pretty sure the answer was obvious.

You know . . . paparazzi surrounding him and all.

If I'm being fair, I think I would have asked for positive identification too before just jumping in and asking for a picture. Still, it was bizarre to see Ryan's fandom in action.

"Yeah," he answered with a smile in her direction, definitely looking the part of the Hollywood heartthrob.

"Can I get a picture with you really fast?" she asked shyly, holding up her phone.

"Of course," he answered, dropping his bags to the ground.

"Can you take it?" she asked Candice.

"Not if my life depended on it," she answered immediately.

"I'll do it." I stepped in before Candice could scare the poor girl away and took the picture.

"Thank you so much. You're seriously amazing," she said to Ryan before walking back over to a group of girls who instantly bombarded her with questions.

"Welcome back to L.A.," I said with a shake of my head.

"So it looks like everyone in England had a party and forgot to invite me. Nice guys. Nice," Benjamin said after Ryan's fan had gone.

"We didn't think rolling hills and happiness were really your scene," I answered with a shrug.

"No, that's Candice," he said, sighing deeply. "I know you guys get us mixed up a lot, but *I'm* the fun-loving, awesomely handsome, charming one, and *she's* the . . . " his words trailed off as Candice shot him a look that could kill. "The other one," he finished quietly.

"I missed you too," she said, leaving her bag on

the curb beside him and hopping into the passenger's seat.

"I believe that means, 'take my bag and shut up'," Ryan translated, putting his sunglasses back on and tossing our bags into the trunk as we both got into the car.

Benjamin sped down the freeway away from LAX and I was quickly reminded why Ryan always drove. I gripped the armrest and Ryan's hand for dear life, trying to ignore the cars we were speeding past at an alarming rate.

"A little birdie told me that you guys might be on a show together," Benjamin said, turning around to look at us for a few too many seconds when his eyes definitely should have been on the road.

"Who told you that?" Ryan asked, sounding unconcerned by the fact that we were one car away from instant death.

"This is on the DL, but I may or may not have also been offered a supporting role in the show," he said in a way that told us he was definitely being offered a part.

"What are they doing? Headhunting *Forensic Faculty*?" Candice asked dryly. "I'll find some way to get into their makeup department. It's not like they let me work on anyone else on the show anyway. If you guys leave, it'll just be me and the corpses."

"And your life will finally be a quiet, happy place," Benjamin said sagely.

"Yeah, that's probably true," Candice agreed. "But I wouldn't want you two getting into trouble just because I'm not there to babysit you. No offense, June, but I don't think you could handle them on your own."

"None taken," I answered quickly. "When did you hear about this, Benjamin?"

"About a week ago," he answered noncommittally. "Apparently they like the chemistry between Ryan and me on *Forensic Faculty*, so they want us to be our funny selves on this new show."

"So if you guys decide to do this, you'll have to leave *Forensic Faculty*, won't you?" I asked, wondering if they could really just walk away from the show where they'd gotten their big break.

"I'd walk away in a heartbeat if it meant not having to deal with The Tall Ones ever again," Benjamin said with fervor.

Ryan didn't say anything for a moment, and I could tell he'd have a harder time leaving. He was the type to get attached to things.

"What about you?" I finally asked him.

I definitely didn't want to do the show without him, so my acting future was kind of in his hands at the moment . . . Not that I'd ever let him know that and make him feel guilty or pressured.

"I'd have to think about it. It's a pretty big commitment," he said carefully. "We definitely have job security on *Forensic Faculty*, since the show's been on for forever. I don't think it's going anywhere. A new show is always iffy. Most never make it past the pilot, and those that do rarely get a second season."

"And I thought I was the downer in this car,"

Candice remarked.

"It's not a decision I want to make lightly," he said.

"No one's going to rush you," I assured him, giving his hand a light squeeze.

"That's not true," Candice piped up. "The network will most definitely be rushing him for a decision. When is your audition?"

"I think it's the day before that TV award show," Ryan said distractedly, "So, like, a week from now?"

"That sounds about right," Benjamin answered, nodding in agreement. "Are you going with us to the award show, New Girl? You know, now that you and Ryan are publicly displaying affection and all that?"

I looked at Ryan for confirmation. I had only ever been to one award show before and that was during my second year on *Forensic Faculty* (the first year I'd been sick). They were definitely fun to go to, but I wasn't sure if it would be odd for me to be with the cast now that I wasn't on the show.

"I'd love it if you came," he said quickly. "Then I wouldn't have to deal with Joann Hoozer and Will Trofeos getting drunk and yelling at each other all by myself."

"Hey, I help you through those fights, don't I?" Benjamin asked, looking hurt.

"Yeah, but now you have—" I elbowed Ryan before he could finish his sentence, not wanting Candice to go all crazy on us just when I felt I was starting to maybe get some information out of her.

"Your phone," he lied quickly.

"Candice, are you going? I don't think I'd want to go without you," I said neutrally.

"They don't usually like to invite the Vanities to the shows," Benjamin joked, earning himself a punch in the arm from Candice.

"You'll be fine without me," she assured me.

"I definitely won't be," I countered.

"They won't invite me, so I can't go anyway."

"But Benjamin is allowed to bring someone, so you guys could just . . . "

"What?" she asked crossly.

"Go together," I finished.

"As a technicality," Ryan added hastily. We both grinned at each other behind Candice's back.

"I guess there are worse things I could participate in," Candice said slowly.

"Do it for me?" I asked sweetly. "So I'm not the only normal girl at the table?"

"Fine," she relented with a big sigh. "But if you, Ryan, and Benjamin get the parts on this new show, you'd better make them hire me as the head makeup artist. There's no way I'm going to stick around *Forensic Faculty* without you guys. It'd just be me and The Tall Ones eating lunch together. I might actually jump off a cliff."

"Deal," I said, giving Ryan a smug smile at my small victory over the hard, bitter exterior that was Candice.

CHAPTER 26

June,

This isn't a text message. You can't send me one cryptic sentence and expect me to know what the heck is going on.

So . . . what the heck is going on? It takes way too long between letters for you to pull a stunt like that.

So unprofessional. *Insert disapproving shake of the head here*

Elder Cleveland

The afternoon of the award show, I was in complete meltdown mode. I had done my audition for the TV show the day before, and they automatically offered me the part. To anyone else in the world that would sound great, but Ryan was still dragging his feet about making a decision, which meant *I* was dragging my feet as well.

I knew I could do the show without him, but I didn't really want to. TV shows weren't like movies. With movies you had the entire script right in front of you, and you knew what was going to happen for the most part, so it was easy to see if there was anything you weren't comfortable with doing. With TV shows, you had no idea what was going to happen in the next few episodes, and once you were already on the show, it made it a little harder to negotiate things.

Gran had assured me that she'd told the network what I was and was not willing to do, but I wouldn't be one bit surprised if they decided to ignore that once we got into the season and I was stuck in a contract. With Ryan there too, though, he could back me up. It wouldn't just be one weird girl who didn't want to take her clothes off on camera. I would have Ryan's support, and the network couldn't very well ignore both stars of the show.

As soon as I got to Benjamin's apartment to get ready for the award show with Candice, I voiced my concerns to her, wanting her take on the situation.

"You've got to convince Ryan to do the show," she said bluntly as she transformed my untamable mane into the big glossy curls that I loved but could barely manage on my own. "It'll be a better move for his career however the show turns out."

"What do you mean?" I asked, wondering how it would be good for his career if the pilot flopped.

"If the show does well, he'll be the star of a good

TV show, so that's never bad," she began, explaining the obvious. "And if it tanks, he won't be committed to *Forensic Faculty*, so he won't have to turn down movie roles anymore."

"He's been turning down movie roles for that stupid show?" I asked in disbelief. He hadn't ever mentioned that to me.

"He's loyal to a fault," she said with a shrug. "He feels like he owes something to them, even though they don't treat him nearly as well as they should. They're totally holding him back."

"Wow," I said, amazed that Ryan hadn't told me that he had been offered other parts.

"You're probably the only one he'll listen to, and honestly, I'm glad they cast you. I think he would leave *Forensic Faculty* if it meant doing a show with you," she told me as she finished pinning up my hair and started to pull her own long, dark, pin-straight hair into a low, messy side bun.

"He *has* to do this show," I said, as if Candice weren't well aware of that fact. "Think about it! All four of us would be on a show together again, except this time we'd be The Tall Ones."

"Hey," she said sharply. "Don't ever call us The Tall Ones."

"Sorry, I meant we'll be the ones in charge, so we won't have to deal with any stuck-up actors with overinflated egos."

"Except for Benjamin," Candice remarked with a bobby pin in her mouth.

"Yeah, except for Benjamin," I agreed with a

laugh as I slipped on my new dress.

I hadn't gone crazy with buying a dress since, in fact, I wasn't even on the show anymore. I was just Ryan's date. But I was still mildly in love with the dress I had found. It was made of deep purple lace that hugged my body all the way to the ground, flaring out slightly at my ankles. The neckline went clear up to my collarbone and the cap sleeves were un-backed purple lace.

I put on the necklace Joseph had gotten me and used the earrings from Ryan to pull it all together as I looked myself over in the mirror.

"You look good in purple," Candice said, giving me the first compliment I think I had ever heard from her.

"Thanks," I replied cautiously. "Am I in trouble or something?"

"You will be when Ryan sees you in that dress."

"It's like we're getting ready for prom," I laughed.

"Okay, one more word like that and I'm kicking you out of this bathroom. I'm serious," Candice threatened, apparently not wanting to think about something as beneath her as a prom.

"Yes ma'am," I responded with a salute. Candice quickly changed into her own dress—a strapless black cocktail dress that complimented her bright red lipstick nicely. "You look awesome," I told her.

"Shall we get this over with?" she deadpanned.

It was unfortunate that red carpet evenings were

always such a blur. All I could really remember about the red carpet with Ryan was the millions of flash bulbs, smiling until my face hurt, avoiding questions from the press, and Benjamin grabbing Candice around the waist at one point and pulling her close for a photo. Candice, of course, looked like she would kill him.

By the time we took our seats at the table reserved for the cast of *Forensic Faculty* and their dates, my head was spinning. I had been giving myself a pep talk all night to make sure I didn't mention anything about the new show to Ryan in front of the rest of the cast. I didn't want them finding out and making work hard on him.

I must admit though, that with every jerky comment that came from Joann Hoozer, I wanted to rub the new show in her face. It was hard being mature sometimes.

"Well, well, well," Lukas Leighton said, taking the empty seat next to me with his date. "June Laurie. I haven't seen you in ages."

"Good to see you, Lukas," I lied, biting my tongue as I smiled at him. Ryan was talking to Benjamin and apparently hadn't noticed the intrusion.

To say Lukas Leighton and I had a strained relationship would be the understatement of the century. What it came down to was everyone in Hollywood loved him, he could get any girl he wanted, and he was a total tool. Of course, if I were looking at things from his perspective, he thought I was a stuck-up virgin princess who wouldn't swallow her pride and give in to her more carnal feelings toward him.

Basically, we just didn't really see eye to eye.

The most frustrating thing about Lukas was that he still didn't get the fact that I didn't want anything to do with him after the stunt he pulled in his car more than two years ago. He really, honestly thought I wanted him. It was disgusting.

"You missed being on the show so much that you had to crash the party, huh?" he asked, leaning in way too close and placing his hand on my lower back. He smelled like alcohol, too, which I thought was odd, since they hadn't even served drinks yet.

"I think we're supposed to be quiet now," I whispered, thankful that the intro music had started playing, indicating that the award ceremony was about to begin. He slowly pulled his hand away from me and it took all of my willpower not to shudder at the creepy gesture.

"You having fun?" Ryan asked me, oblivious to the unfortunate conversation I'd just had with Lukas. "Ugh, look who's sitting next to you," he said a bit too late. "Hopefully he doesn't bug you too much."

Forensic Faculty only won one award that night, and unfortunately it went to the very drunk and very obnoxious Lukas Leighton. Some things in life just weren't fair.

Overall though, I had a good time sitting with Ryan, Benjamin, and Candice, and watching the real show, which happened after the ceremony ended. It involved Joann Hoozer "whispering" to Will Trofeos about treating her well and asking about some girl he was texting.

Benjamin slipped Candice some money, having placed a bet that before the night was out, Will and Joann would fight about something.

"This almost makes coming here worth my time," Candice told me with a smile as we stood from the table, getting ready to file out. "Don't forget to convince Ryan to do the pilot. As much as I love watching those two bicker, being stuck at the table with Lukas all night was enough to remind me why I hate that show."

"Will do," I answered with a laugh.

"So, where do you want to go?" Lukas said from beside me.

Silly me, I thought he was talking to his date, so I completely ignored him. Or, at least, I tried to ignore him until his hand reappeared on what should have been my lower back but definitely wasn't. I quickly took a step back, trying my best not to make a scene as I glared at him.

"Excuse me?" I asked looking around for Ryan who was, of course, talking to Benjamin.

"I said, where do you want to go, June? You know . . . to finish what we started," he said, his speech slightly slurred.

For a guy who drank as much as Lukas did, I was

surprised at how poorly he was holding his liquor. (Though I guess I couldn't really talk, having never tried alcohol before. I was pretty sure one sip of anything would put me on my butt.)

"Lukas, you're drunk. I think you should go home," I said evenly, finally catching Ryan's eye and motioning for him to join me.

"I like that you've been playing hard to get and everything, but by this point, it's just ridiculous," he answered, taking a step toward me and invading my personal space bubble. "It was nice at first, you know, to build up the suspense and all that. But why don't we just get on with it?"

"Right. Why don't you go find your date?" I asked, using the same voice I used with the little Sunbeams in church.

"Oh June," he began, placing his hand on my cheek and leaning in so close to me that I could easily smell the bitter alcohol on his breath. "Why do you always have to play games?" He gave me a smile that would have been charming had it not been lopsided and sloppy looking.

"Hey, Lukas, you need to go," Ryan said, coming to my aid and pulling me away from Lukas's sweaty, shaky grasp. So much for the perfect Hollywood heartthrob. Lukas had been reduced to a sleazy, wasted mess in a matter of hours. It wasn't exactly a charming look on him.

"Oh good, the extra is coming to her rescue," he shot back disdainfully.

"Gosh, I hate that guy," I heard Candice say

behind me, and I was quickly becoming aware of the crowd we were amassing.

"Seriously Lukas, just crawl back into your limo and drink yourself stupid somewhere else," Ryan said calmly. I had to give him credit—he was much more calm than I would have been. I was already shaking with how mad I was at Lukas.

"Oh, right, I forgot you guys were a *thing*," he said, motioning to Ryan and me. "Kind of a downgrade, June."

"Lukas, I don't want anything to do with you, all right?" I said slowly, wanting it to sink in while still being civil with way too many people watching. I wished I could think of some witty insult to hurl at him, but sadly my mind wasn't working fast enough.

"You'd really rather be with this guy?" he scoffed, pointing at Ryan and making it *so* obvious to me who I'd rather be with.

"Definitely," I answered with a smile in Ryan's direction.

"I don't need this," Lukas finally said. "I was trying to do you a favor, June, but Ryan, you can have her. She won't put out anyway."

If I hadn't seen it myself and if it hadn't been caught on about fifteen different cameras (which Ryan, Benjamin, Candice and I utilized to relive the moment later . . . and I may or may not have printed some pictures for Joseph) I wouldn't have believed it. But my wonderful, amazing boyfriend pulled back and punched Lukas Leighton in his million dollar face in front of everyone.

I brought my hand up to my mouth to try to hide my smile as Lukas reeled from the blow, stumbling back partly from the alcohol and partly from the awesome right hook Ryan had. (Who knew, right?).

"Okay, this made it worth it for me to come," Candice whispered to Benjamin from behind me as cameras flashed all around the room and other celebrities gasped at the scene that had just unfolded.

I was amazed at how quickly Benjamin and Candice had gotten their phones out to capture the moment.

"You do video. I'll do pictures," Benjamin whispered to her.

"I hope you don't think they'll let you back on set after a stunt like that," Lukas said in a muffled voice, his mouth hidden behind his bloody hands as he continued to stumble. I was actually glad he was drunk, because I was pretty sure he would have returned the punch if he had been in his right mind.

"Probably not," Ryan answered as he took my hand to escort me out of the building. We passed through the press—who luckily hadn't gotten wind of what had just happened inside—as quickly as possible. Candice and Benjamin hurried happily behind us as we hopped into a waiting car.

"Okay, you're officially my hero," Benjamin said, sounding giddy.

"Yeah, you've definitely just become the coolest person in our group," Candice agreed. I had never seen her smile so widely in my life. She was practically glowing. "Please pull that up on YouTube right now," she instructed Benjamin.

"Already on it," he said, his finger swiping madly across the screen of his phone.

"It can't be up already, can it?" I asked, holding Ryan's hand and feeling it starting to swell already.

"Never underestimate the speed of drama," Benjamin answered.

I rubbed Ryan's sore hand as the car drove us away from the award ceremony and hoped I hadn't just ruined his career.

"I'm so sorry Ryan," I said timidly. "Will they really kick you off of the show for that?" I knew that Lukas Leighton's makeup artist wouldn't be very happy when she had to cover up a giant bruise on his face when the show started up again in a week. At least if Ryan got booted, he could do the new show with me.

"They don't need to kick me off," he said with a proud smile. "I quit."

Dear Elder Cleveland,

I'm sorry about my last cryptic letter. I just wanted you to know that a certain friend/boyfriend of ours (your friend . . . my boyfriend . . . I just realized that wording was confusing and creepy) has been investigating the church. I guess you'd better talk to your missionary connections about him.

In other news, when you get back, Ryan, Benjamin and I will be starring in a new TV show. Yeah, you read that right, A TV SHOW! We didn't think it would get past the pilot, but a certain major network and their test group happened to love it, and we have the greenest light you've ever seen!

I can't wait until you come home and we get to talk about all of this in person. I miss you a ton and hope my best friend is doing well out there.

Love,
June

P.S. Ryan punched Lukas Leighton when he tried to hit on me. Punched him right in the face. It was the best moment of my life. I've included pictures from every angle and from every news site online to cheer you up. Try not to smile too much.

Chasing June

ACKNOWLEDGMENTS

This book, and this character are so special to me, but I don't think June's story would have come about if I didn't have the support of amazing family and friends who constantly encourage me when I feel like my writing isn't good enough. I'm hugely blessed with my remarkable family, and the incredible readers, writers, and book bloggers I've met ever since publishing *The Breakup Artist* a few years ago. I never thought the best part of writing a book would be the people I would meet because of it. So thank you to everyone who has offered so much support! I have to give a special thank you to Vanessa and Joseph Winter for always putting me in their movies and giving me so much writing material for these books! I love being on a film set, and that love of the trade is a big reason I write these books. Thank you to my family who I've forced to be my unofficial beta readers. Thank you to the entire writing community who I can't say enough about. The way you all support each other and me is incredible! And thank you to my Heavenly Father, for blessing me with this nagging in my head that won't let me give up on writing, no matter what.

Don't miss the next novel in the
June series:

Catching June

Turn the page for a sneak peek at
the first chapter!

CHAPTER 1

Ryan smirked at me from across the soundstage, the bright lights making me suddenly wish there weren't so many layers to a fifties dress. I was almost positive my red lipstick was probably melting down my face as I tried to look glamorous and perky all at the same time.

"You're so cute," Ryan mouthed from his position across the room and I tried to keep my face neutral, knowing that they could easily edit his little deviation out, but not mine.

The camera had to be pointing at someone, didn't it?

Ryan was constantly trying to mess me up on set. The second the cameras started rolling and the focus was on me, he'd make faces or mouth phrases at me, trying to make me slip up. I thought the game was pretty cute but the producers probably didn't, since they'd have to have it removed in post. In Ryan's words, he was trying to make up for all the times he was supposed to mess me up on *Forensic Faculty* but didn't. Now that we were on our own show he didn't feel too intimidated to be himself, which was good of course… unless you were trying to get through a scene without laughing.

"I don't think it's *that* old fashioned of me to suggest that Wyatt invite his new girlfriend over for dinner for us to meet her," I said stubbornly, playing with the short strand of pearls around my neck.

I had been playing with them in the previous shot, right?

Continuity was an awful burden.

"And I'm telling you that we can just go out to the bar and meet her so she doesn't feel so pressured," Ryan said seriously, now that he actually had to act.

The problem with being on a TV show where they used multiple cameras to shoot all the different angles at once, was that you never really knew which shot they'd be using. So really, Ryan shouldn't ever be making faces at me because they might want his reaction shot.

Not that this fact stopped him.

"Nick, she's a lady. She doesn't just hang out in bars," I insisted, still playing with the pearls.

I figured I might as well try to start being consistent now, even if I hadn't been in the previous scenes. I was just lucky our show wasn't filmed in front of a live audience like they had suggested originally. That would have been way too much stress to handle.

"Rosie this isn't 1950. Women hang out in bars now."

"That doesn't mean they should," I singsonged.

"Fine, we'll compromise," he promised.

"And how will we do that?"

"I don't know, I'll figure something out," he called as he walked through the door to his bedroom that, in fact, was actually just the end of the set.

"And cut," our director called.

It was amazing the magic that one word held. The second the director called cut everyone in the crew went from holding their breath, to suddenly bursting into action in a scene of complete chaos. In a split second the sound stage was filled with noise and commotion.

"You're such a monster," I called to Ryan.

He walked across the set and put his arms around my waist, still wearing the same smirk he often sported when trying to make me laugh during a scene.

"I have no idea what you're talking about," he replied, his voice dripping with innocence.

"You know that all I have to do is tell Candice and she'll make sure you look like a corpse in your next scene."

"Our Candice?" Ryan asked in disbelief. "She would never do that."

"I know it seems out of character for me, but I'll make you look bad in a split second," Candice droned as she walked out in front of the cameras to touch up my makeup. "June, you need to stop licking your lips during the scene. You're getting red lipstick everywhere."

"I can't help it! These lights make me so thirsty all the time," I said defensively.

Candice didn't say anything to my argument, she just let out a subtle, long-suffering sigh, and went back to her chair behind the cameras.

"You just have to get through one more scene and then no more hot lights," Ryan said almost sweetly. "Then you can stop being such a diva," he added with a grin, giving me a quick kiss on the cheek before running over to his mark so that I couldn't hit him for his comment.

I just loved that boy.

"Don't kiss her! You'll ruin the makeup," Candice shouted from somewhere off camera and all I could think was how lucky I was to be doing what I was doing.

ABOUT THE AUTHOR

Shannen Crane Camp was born and raised in Southern California, where she developed a love of reading, writing, and anything having to do with film. After high school, she moved to Utah to attend Brigham Young University, where she received a degree in Media Arts and found herself a husband in fellow California native Josh Camp. The two now live in either Utah or California. They can't ever seem to make up their minds.

Shannen loves to hear from her fellow readers, writers, and gamers, so feel free to contact her at Shannencbooks@hotmail.com or visit her website for more information: http://shannencbooks.blogspot.com